Jilted

Jilted

Niko Michelle

www.urbanbooks.net

Urban Books, LLC
300 Farmingdale Road, N.Y.-Route 109
Farmingdale, NY 11735

ISBN 13: 978-1-64556-333-4
ISBN 10: 1-64556-333-2

First Trade Paperback Printing June 2022
Printed in the United States of America

10 9 8 7 6 5 4 3 2 1

This is a work of fiction. Any references or similarities to actual events, real people, living or dead, or to real locales are intended to give the novel a sense of reality. Any similarity in other names, characters, places, and incidents is entirely coincidental.

Distributed by Kensington Publishing Corp.
Submit Orders to:
Customer Service
400 Hahn Road
Westminster, MD 21157-4627
Phone: 1-800-733-3000
Fax: 1-800-659-2436

Jilted

by

Niko Michelle

Chapter 1

Jilted bride. My new name for undoubtedly the rest of my life. At least, that would be my name every time someone told the heartbreaking, humiliating story of what happened on what was meant to be my picture-perfect wedding day, which I was sure would be shared in some fashion for the rest of my life.

Ugh, my life. I envisioned looking like a princess, taking some of the most beautiful professional photos once my floral, beaded wedding dress with metallic tulle donned my five-foot, two-inch caramel, curve-a-licious frame. The guests would gaze in admiration as I walked down the aisle and took the hand of my awaiting prince. We'd declare our love and commitment through our self-written vows, exchange rings, and seal the deal with a kiss. During the reception, I'd impatiently wait for the DJ to announce my new name over the microphone— the hyphenated Mrs. Avery Booker-Peterson.

Typical wedding. Mine just happened to go a lot differently than I expected.

Someone dared to object.

I heard the officiant when he said, "If anyone can show just cause why this couple cannot lawfully be joined together in matrimony, let them speak now or forever hold their peace."

And I heard the feminine but brittle voice say, "I object."

I whipped my head around and eyed the objector. She uttered something, but the gasps and commotion from the guests drowned out the rest of her words. I could've read her lips if it weren't for the distraction of her protruding belly draped in what looked like a white silk wedding dress. She stood with one hand on her hip while the other hand rolled over her stomach. She looked ready to deliver any minute.

I assumed the mystery woman was in labor and had stumbled into the church looking for help. I just knew one of the ushers would intervene. Escort her out. Get her the help she needed without any more major disruptions to the ceremony.

My naive thinking. Mystery woman called out to my fiancé—his full name at that.

"Lloyd Zachariah Peterson."

Her saying his name wouldn't have been a big deal. That just meant she knew him. No harm there. But it was what she said that sent shock waves throughout the church and an imaginary bullet through my heart. I'd never been shot before, but I would imagine the pain felt the same.

"Lloyd Zachariah Peterson, how can you marry another woman when you know I'm pregnant with your baby?"

Uproar filled the church like a street full of rioters.

Stay calm. There had to be a valid explanation. This had to be a joke. A sick one, but nonetheless a joke. I mean, who would object? The officiant could've skipped asking the objection question anyway. Everyone in attendance wanted this more than Lloyd and me, especially my father, Henry Booker. He loved him some Lloyd. The charismatic MBA HBCU graduate who now served as a financial manager of a Fortune 500 company and who happened to load my finger down with a huge rock. Not that I was materialistic or into designer things, but I was proud that my ring was packaged in the famous little blue box.

Lloyd would never hurt me. Not to this magnitude. He would never cheat on me or be so careless as to get anyone pregnant. I knew that for a fact. We had the same goals in life. One of which was no children before tying the knot. He and I talked at great lengths about when it would be the right time to start a family. At least get through the first year of marriage. We both wanted a son first. We planned to name him Lloyd Junior and call him LJ for short. He'd be like his father and play both football and basketball during high school. Then we'd try for a girl, not sure what we'd name her, but I'd dress her in various shades of pink, and she'd be like me, a cheerleader and a member of the dance team. And since neither of us had any previous marriages, we had no babies or possible babies, so this woman had to be delusional.

The ceremony was almost over. Ten minutes, maybe. Within that short time, I believed Lloyd or someone from the wedding party would yell, "Gotcha." The hired wedding crasher would then pull a pillow from underneath her dress, and we'd laugh it off. If not, we'd at least call an ambulance for the misguided woman to be transported to the psych ward, because clearly she had to be crazy to try to pin a baby on Lloyd.

I turned my back and pretended she wasn't there. I nodded for the officiant to continue. Instead, he clutched the Bible to his chest and mumbled. "Heavenly Father" was the only thing audible, but I assumed he was working his rebuking powers on this woman. I was all for it.

Too much detail had gone into our wedding, and I was determined to be Mrs. Avery Booker-Peterson before October 5 was over.

I smiled at Lloyd.

He didn't smile back. Sweat hung out in the creases of his worried, wrinkled forehead. "I'm so sorry, Avery. I love you."

That was sweet of him. And that gesture was why I loved him, too. It wasn't just about me. It wasn't just *my* day. It was Lloyd's day also, and he had apologized to me because some neurotic woman tried to sabotage our union.

There was a brief moment of silence, about as long as it would take to walk from a refrigerator to a stove, before that woman faced the crowd and yelled, "That's right, everybody, I am pregnant with his baby." She pointed back at Lloyd.

My right hand was joined to Lloyd's left hand. His hand slipped from my grasp. Did he pull away willingly, or was it from the perspiration that covered both of our hands? His eyes, which were usually a warm hazel brown, seemed . . . black.

Did Lloyd know that woman?

I looked from him to her. And back to him. He stared at that lady like he was familiar with her. Like the ridiculous words pouring from her mouth were . . . true.

Impossible. Call me naive, if you will, but she had to have stormed into the wrong wedding. I knew she had. I looked around Lloyd and over to the groomsmen. Maybe they'd set this up. I winked at them. "Nice try, guys." Their faces were stern, with no signs of this being a joke. My gown was big, but I shifted it while still holding my bouquet to look back at my bridesmaids. Their faces matched the groomsmen's.

"Why are you doing this, Oakley?" Lloyd asked.

Oakley? So, Lloyd knew her? "Lloyd, you know this woman?" I inquired.

"He knows me well." She pointed to her stomach. "Lloyd, we talked about this. You said you were going to tell her."

They had talked about this? Tell me what exactly?

I was frozen in one spot. Everyone was frozen, except Oakley. She waddled a little closer. "I object, and I'll say it again and again. This wedding is not happening today, or ever if I can help it." Oakley buckled over and let out a grunt. Through labored breaths, she said, "Lloyd." Breath. "I'm having." Breath. "Your." Breath. "Baby."

My hands fell to my waist. My bouquet hit the floor. Fear covered Lloyd's face as he rushed to her aid.

Oakley stammered over her words. "Llo . . . Llo . . . Lloyd," she yelped and bent over farther. She seemed to be in agony. Lloyd took off his tuxedo jacket and laid it in the middle of the aisle for her to lie on. The rose petals that were thrown on the ground for me to walk on surrounded Oakley's body as if they were meant for her and her bundle of joy. She panted and began Lamaze. So did Lloyd. How did he know Lamaze? He coached her through breathing techniques. Their breath was in sync as they held hands and stared into each other's eyes.

Instead of our wedding party and spectators witnessing Lloyd and me becoming one, they were about to witness Lloyd become a father for the first time, and it wasn't with me.

"Avery, help. This baby is coming." Lloyd's plea for help erased the shock in my body and gave me a boost of adrenaline. After all, I was an ob-gyn, and I was about to deliver my fiancé's baby with another woman I knew nothing about and on what was supposed to be our wedding day.

Chapter 2

A boy.

Lloyd and Oakley became parents to a son. She named him on the spot—Lloyd Zachariah Peterson, Jr.

Oakley tilted her head and familiar-looking down-turned eyes upward toward Lloyd, who was silent. "Our little LJ," she said through fatigue. Her long, dark, curly hair was wet and stuck to her bronze-colored face from the immense amount of sweat that her body had exuded from intense pushing.

I gasped and covered my mouth with my forearm to keep from screaming. So much for our dreams of calling our firstborn that. Oakley had stolen the name for my son, my rose petals, my moment, my attention, and my man.

Lloyd's eyes were wide and fixated on his baby boy, who I had wrapped in an ivory scarf belonging to one of the many onlookers and placed on Oakley's chest. Was he proud? Happy even? I couldn't quite gauge his feelings, but his mood seemed dark, like the small, dark blotches that had stained the front of my wedding dress. My mascara bled, and so did my heart.

The ambulance arrived a few minutes after I had done all the work. I watched Lloyd as he watched the EMTs rush in with a gurney and load up their two patients. His six-foot, three-inch stature sprouted as he stood on the tips of his toes, craned his neck, shifted his weight from one foot to the other, and repositioned his solid

200-pound body to get a better view over the backs of the medical professionals.

Instead of us celebrating this date as our wedding anniversary every year, he'd be celebrating this date by singing "Happy Birthday" to his child.

How did this happen? And right under my nose. Lloyd and I had spent too much time together for this to be true. If he wanted to be with someone else, he wouldn't have popped the question last Christmas in front of my family. It was cute how he did it.

"Avery," Lloyd said, "did you look in your stocking?"

I gave him a mean side-eye. It was a tradition for us to sleep over at my parents' and empty our stockings on Christmas Eve, which we had already done. "We did that last night, remember?" I reminded him. "Lay off the eggnog, silly." I leaned over and planted a kiss on his nose.

Lloyd slid my bangs from my eyes. "I think I saw Santa put something in there last night. Go check."

I laughed. "Santa? Really? How old are we?"

"Just check, Avery."

Another mean side-eye.

The candy-cane-decorated stocking with my first name embroidered on the top swayed from side to side when I thumped it. My finger met with something hard. I looked back at Lloyd. He was still sitting on the floor with his back against the sofa.

"Lloyd, I swear if this is some kind of rodent or bug to scare me, I am going to kill you." Lloyd was a prankster during the moments when he wasn't bogged down with work, so there was no telling what he had slipped into my stocking. I palmed it, trying to make out what it was. A box.

"It will be next Christmas by the time we see what it is." That remark came from my snooty yet surly mother,

Florence Booker. My two brothers and I sometimes referred to her as the devil behind her back. She was evil for no reason. Her genetic makeup had to be half human, half devil. In her case, a lower percentage of human because the actual devil was probably a lot nicer.

After three attempts of sticking my hand halfway in the stocking and snatching it out, I finally retrieved the box that held my engagement ring. The box bounced within my trembling hands. Tears of joy escaped my eyes and splashed on the porcelain marble tile in front of the fireplace. When I turned around, Lloyd was on one knee. There was no speech attached to his proposal. He was straight to the point. "Avery, will you marry me?"

When I answered yes, Dad let out a feminine squeal. My mother was nonchalant. Not that she expressed anything other than judgment anyway, but I didn't think she cared for Lloyd much. Maybe she picked up on something that I didn't. A clue that she didn't see a need to share.

Clues? Let me think back. Did I see any flags waving in my direction, trying to get my attention, cautioning me to turn around and head in the opposite direction?

Embarrassment swallowed my ability to think and only allowed me to hang my head. When I finally got the courage to look around, nothing but fog emitted throughout the sanctuary from the throng of lingering, nosy-ass, polluting-ass people who circled me like we were about to play a reversed version of Duck, Duck, Goose. Why didn't these people disappear when Lloyd and his family left with the ambulance? What more did they want? To hang back and witness my breakdown?

I knew why my immediate family stayed behind. Well, everyone except for the devil. If she stayed, she probably hid to save herself the embarrassment of being inundated with questions of how her "oh so perfect" family just got hit with the biggest scandal this town had seen since probably . . . *never.* Or she was somewhere crying, playing the victim, soaking up all the sympathy. I always said that if Florence Booker ever decided to become an actress, she'd make a damned good one, because she stayed in character while around her church family.

It made sense for the officiant to remain. He was the pastor of the church. However, I didn't understand why he maintained his position at the altar, even with the Bible still close to his heart. I wondered if he thought another couple would spring forward, confess their love, and request permission to marry. That only happened in fake life. This was real life. *My* real life. The ceremony was over. It concluded with a bang. Well, a birth. There'd be no completion of unity for me, nor would I have approved of another couple using the ideas I spent months and countless hours planning. And they damn sure weren't going to marry using the thousands of dollars my dad spent to make it the wedding of my dreams. His only daughter at that.

I crouched on the floor, devastated. I guessed everyone else thought it was okay to crowd around me as if I were a quarterback in the NFL calling out a game-winning play to my team. But I was determined to break up the huddle like I was one of the highest-paid in the league.

"You all are smothering me. Can I please get some space?" I asked nicely. Given the circumstances, everyone should have respected my request. I didn't look up to see who had touched my shoulder. I jerked away. "I don't want to be consoled. I just want space to think."

Everyone slowly backed away, but I could still feel their eyes burning through my skin like a laser.

I took a couple of deep breaths and tried for a quick, broad recap. Nine months ago, what was I doing?

Planning the wedding and working crazy hours. Work was life for me, especially working as a doctor in the small town of Augusta, Georgia, about two and a half hours from Atlanta. Not only did delivering babies bring much satisfaction, but so did being able to look out of my office window at the green glass building across the parking lot, knowing that my man was in there working just as hard.

Lloyd and I made it a point to spend our lunch hour together unless he had a meeting or I had a baby to deliver. Speaking of delivering babies, I delivered my fiancé's firstborn during our wedding. Who does that? Me apparently, but what kind of coldhearted, trifling person places who they claimed to love in that kind of position? How did Lloyd even know this woman?

Her eyes, though. I'd seen them somewhere before. Did Oakley work at the hospital? No, Augusta Regional Medical Center wasn't that big. I would've recognized her face.

Her face. It was permanently etched. I would never forget the face of the woman who boldly humiliated me and took part in ruining my life. I'd always remember the way my soon-to-be husband ran alongside the stretcher when the ambulance arrived and loaded them up. Nor would I forget how the three of them looked—like a family.

I was supposed to give Lloyd that child. Now, I wasn't sure if I would ever have children of my own. We were supposed to have been a family, and now he had one, which left no place for me.

The only thing left was a bleak outlook on love and marriage, nowhere near what I pictured for myself.

I was supposed to make love to Lloyd for the first time as my husband. Since becoming engaged, we agreed to a sabbatical to make our wedding night special. Maybe he couldn't handle it, and if that was the case, he should've told me. I would've much rather caved than to have my life altered in such a drastic manner.

Or could it have been the name change thing? We rarely argued, but we had many tense discussions over what last name I'd carry. Lloyd wasn't pleased with the idea of me keeping my maiden name, but because of my profession, it was easier. We compromised on hyphenating, which he still wasn't happy about, but that wasn't a reason to drive a person into the arms of another.

I knew there had to be a calendar somewhere. I needed to see the prior nine months.

We were engaged for a little over ten months, so that meant Lloyd got Oakley pregnant right after he proposed to me. I had to *see* it.

I was still propped up on my knees when I asked, "Does anyone have a calendar?"

For the first time since the bombshell announcement, the church silenced.

"Oh, I see what this is." I wagged my finger around and rolled my neck. "There has been nothing but chatter and whispers, and now y'all wanna be quiet?" I was going to *see* nine months and figure this out, and every nosy person who littered the church would help me whether they wanted to or not. "Can someone get my phone?" I asked. No one moved. I remembered it was still in the room I used to get dressed. "I'll get it myself." The extra material from the cathedral train of my wedding dress made it difficult for me to stand with ease.

My dad grabbed my arm to help me up. "Sweetheart"— his hand swept across my shoulder and then rested there—"let me take you home."

"No! Not until I get a calendar. Not until I figure this out." This was the beginning of the mental breakdown that everyone had stayed behind to witness.

The embarrassment. They should've thrown me in a casket and pushed me back to the front of the church, because I was going to die. The sanctuary was already decorated in white, khaki, and my favorite shade of blush pink. The pastor still hadn't moved, so at least he could have the satisfaction of completing something, even if it was my eulogy.

"Avery, please. Just let me take you home, and we can figure it out from there." Hurt lay behind my father's eyes. He barely looked at me, and when he did, it seemed as if his gentle soul had escaped and was replaced with a VACANT sign to a rundown motel. I knew how much this day meant to him.

"I'm not leaving." I peeled off the gloves that someone handed me before the delivery and staggered over to my oldest brother, Anthony.

My feet tingled from the amount of time I'd spent on bended knee delivering Lloyd's baby and staring at the purple carpet of the church in disbelief. I never realized how much that carpet clashed with my wedding colors. Still, I allowed my mother to convince me of an indoor church wedding instead of an outside wedding like I wanted. I was sure her desire was intended to keep up the facade of having the perfect Christian family image. She said, "God will only bless the unions of those who marry under His house." I went along with it, hoping it would bring us closer, but it didn't.

By the time I made it over to my brother, the feeling in my limbs had returned. "Anthony, give me your phone."

He circled the pews, randomly yelling out philosophical quotes and what he would do to Lloyd when he caught up to him.

My dad was hot on my heels, still trying to talk me into leaving. This time he draped his suit jacket over my bare, shivering shoulders, thanks to the strapless wedding dress that turned out to be a waste. The shivering wasn't from being cold. It was from being profoundly scared. I shimmied the jacket off and ran over to my other brother, Amil. Adhesive had to be attached to either his phone or hand because the two rarely parted. But the element of surprise worked. I snatched it and made a mad dash to the bathroom without anyone catching me. And in the gown that I struggled to walk in before.

With a click of the bathroom lock, I was free to sort through the mess. I went into the last stall with the baby changing station, but I couldn't handle it. Too soon. I slowly backed away.

A baby. Lloyd just had a baby.

I moved into the middle stall, locked the door, and sat on the toilet. Sanitary concerns were the furthest thing from my mind.

I hung up on whoever Amil was talking to. I swiped through his phone. He had way too many apps. I swiped until I found the calendar. The white box that displayed Saturday in all red letters and the number five in one sizeable black number was about to change my life even more. My thumb trembled as it hovered over the calendar.

Banging ensued outside of the bathroom door. "Avery, open this door." My mother's voice startled me, causing me almost to drop the phone. *Look who decided to join the after-party.* Usually when she demanded something we did it, but not today.

"I'm sorry, Mother." My hoarse voice struggled to make sure she heard my refusals through the thick wood door. "I can't right now."

More banging. Different voices. I ignored them all.

"We are going to call the cops if you don't open this door," she threatened.

I cleared my throat. "Go ahead. What I'm doing is not an arrestable offense." What were the cops going to do? If anything, they should have arrested Lloyd and Oakley for attempted murder, sabotage, or whatever the appropriate jargon was for what they did to me. It's not a crime to lock yourself in the bathroom for privacy. It's a bathroom. They're made for privacy.

My thumb made contact with the calendar. All twelve months stared back at me. Three columns, four rows, and one of the twelve months held the answers I desperately needed.

Not only did the banging continue, but so did the phone calls to Amil's phone. I sent each one to voicemail before putting the phone on airplane mode. I wasn't going to answer, and I wasn't going to unlock the door and come out. Not yet.

The lock jiggled. Attempted forced entry, invasion of privacy. I should have been the one to call the cops because my family was disturbing my concentration.

"Avery, can you let me in? I'll be glad to help you figure this out and get that fool, that girl, and if you want, the baby too." That mention of violence came from my best friend and maid of honor, Tracy. She was the most supportive friend and had been since kindergarten, which was why I couldn't let her in the bathroom. I knew her too well. I knew her motives were to get in here, find out some information, steal a car from the parking lot since we all came in a limo, and make good on those threats. That was Tracy for you. A protector. No one was safe. I thought about giving her the okay to rough them up, but I was better than that. *I think. I want to be. I have to be. I already have "jilted." I don't want "scorned" too.*

"I'll be out in one second, Tracy."

I focused my attention on the months staring back at me. October, so nine months made conception to have been at the beginning of the year. January. We were newly engaged. Not even a month.

I thought back to January. What changed? Anything in our routine? Did we have a fight that caused Lloyd to lose sight of our relationship and love? Nothing jumped out. What was I missing? I rocked back and forth. The longer I stared at the calendar, the more likely I was to see something. Something was going to click soon. I didn't know what that something was, but something was going to jump from these dates like a jack-in-the-box. Then I'd know the reason why the man I devoted so much time to betrayed me. So many thoughts went through my head. Blackmail? But who was Oakley to blackmail Lloyd? Was she powerful? That had to be it. Lloyd had no choice but to engage this woman, or she would destroy him. I didn't know what she had on him. His image was clean. He volunteered in back-to-school drives for the low-income population. He gave free haircuts—his other passion since high school. He and I also set up random tables and fed the homeless. His heart was too pure to hurt me like this purposely.

The banging and yelling grew louder. I unlocked the stall door and paced the floor, hoping that would allow my thoughts to flow. "Think, think, think." When I turned around, I was met by my parents.

They'd found a key.

My dad rushed over and embraced me. That wasn't what I wanted. I slithered from his arms. "Dad, I don't want to be held. I want answers."

"They're not in this bathroom. I can tell you that," the devil said.

Leave it to my mother. She always had something smart to say. Who asked her anyway? She never had the right words to say. If things weren't to her liking, she'd definitely judge. Lloyd was not to her liking, and I was waiting on the "I told you so" to roll from her lips. Now that I thought of it, she never liked anyone her children brought home. She demeaned Anthony's ex-wife because she couldn't cook, and she shaded Amil's ex-girlfriend because she came into the relationship with a kid.

"All right, just give me five minutes," I said.

"We have already been humiliated enough. Don't add more to it by acting weak in a dingy bathroom."

"Have some compassion for your daughter, Florence. She's in pain."

While my dad stood up for me, I turned my back, slid the phone from airplane mode, and dialed Lloyd's number. Straight to voicemail.

"I'm ready to go." I walked over to Amil, who stood at the bathroom door, and handed him back his phone.

"Thank God," my mother said. "Since we've been trying to coax you out of the bathroom, most everyone has left the church. Apologies have been issued, although I'm sure you'll be one of those me-me things on the internet." She paused a moment and pinched the bridge of her nose before continuing. "I must prepare myself for that and when dealing with the ladies of the church and my book club. Gosh, my life." She wet a napkin and dabbed her face.

"The term is 'meme,' and this situation is not about you. How about a little sympathy for my sister?" While it never did any good, I appreciated Amil for trying to defend me.

"Whatever. Had she chosen Scottsdale, as I suggested, we would have a completely different ending. A happy one."

"Ma, you do know Scottsdale is gay, right? Besides, what kind of name is that for a black person anyway?"

The devil rolled her eyes. "I've told you several times not to call me that, and just because he dresses nice and speaks eloquently, unlike you, it doesn't make him gay. Plus, he's a man of God and would have never pulled a stunt like this." She waved her hand to dismiss my brother and the "stunt." "I'll be in the car. Don't keep me waiting."

And in so many words, there was that "I told you so." I could always count on my brother to get under our mother's skin. Amil called her Ma when he wanted to make her squirm. She believed that addressing her by anything other than Mother was disrespectful and ghetto. That specific title matched her bougie attitude.

On another note, Scottsdale was totally gay. He told me so himself when my mother first tried to hook us up at the church Christmas party. As a matter of fact, his exact words had been, "It's great what your mom is trying to do, but you do know she has it all wrong, right?"

I'd nodded and raised my glass of water. "Duly noted."

He and I had laughed, which she mistook for chemistry, and I let her believe that until I brought Lloyd home. Had I known what I knew now, I may have had a better chance with Scottsdale.

I massaged my throbbing temples. I just needed answers. "Dad, can we make a stop on the way home?"

"Of course we can. Let me guess, ice cream?"

Love will make a person do bizarre things, even when knowing better. "No," I said. "The hospital. I need to talk to Lloyd and Oakley."

Chapter 3

My dad took the scenic route to avoid driving anywhere near the hospital. I didn't expect him to take me,
but it was worth a shot. Even the devil encouraged the
field trip every time I pleaded.

"I say take her, Henry." My mother turned her gaze
from the window over to my dad. "You have always cod-
dled this girl anyway and turned her weak." She adjusted
her seat belt and wiggled in the front seat until she faced
me. "Even if you have the guts to confront Lloyd, which I
doubt, you're facing even more humiliation and the risk
of losing your license for such unprofessional behavior."
She looked at her watch. "Now that my day has freed up,
by all means, bring more humiliation to this family."

I never understood why this woman was so evil. My
paternal grandma once told me that my mother was
jealous of me for bumping her out of the number one
spot in my dad's life. It had to be more than jealousy.
Wouldn't a mother want the man she had children with
to be an active part of their life and for daughters to be
daddy's girls? At least, that was what I would want for my
children.

*Children. I hate that word, along with father, son,
baby, birth, labor, and anything else associated with
babies. Babies, mothers, pregnancies, deliveries.*
Everything I loved, and now I couldn't even stomach my
own livelihood.

I didn't want to go back to my parents' home, but what choice did I have? Lloyd and I had just bought a three-story townhome, and there was no way I was moving in with him after what he had done. Was I supposed to let his kid and baby momma move in too?

When the car came to an abrupt stop in the driveway, my dad hopped out and power walked inside. I didn't know if it was the insults my mother hurled my way, her nagging him about babying me, or just the sound of her voice alone that caused him to react that way. Usually, he'd open the door for my mother and help her out of the car. He'd always done the same for me. The only door he opened was his own and the big red door to the house. He didn't even look back, and I couldn't say I blamed him. She used the car ride home as a bashing session, and neither of us wanted to hear it.

My poor dad. Lloyd's secret life devastated him too. He always said how he trusted Lloyd to take care of me when he was no longer on earth to fill that role. He even included Lloyd in the monthly father-son fishing trips with my brothers. Something he held dear to his heart. If Henry Booker invited a person on his sacred fishing trips, they had stolen that organ responsible for pumping blood through the body.

My mother followed him, sashaying like she didn't have a care in the world. I needed to go inside too. At least scrub my hands. My hands. I held them up and stared at them. There was a feeling of grossness loitering throughout my fingertips and palms. I remembered holding Oakley's placenta in these hands. I remembered holding Lloyd's baby with these hands. I stared at the lines that ran through my palms. If I could read them, would they have warned me? I stared at my hands like they were foreign. Like a baby discovering its extremities for the first time.

A baby.

One day Lloyd's baby would discover his extremities for the first time.

Lloyd had a kid. With another woman. Those same hands that I examined and needed to scrub were what hid my face while I sat in the back of my dad's Lincoln and sobbed. The back door opened, but I was too ashamed to uncover my face to see who it was. I didn't have to. Even through my clogged nose from excessive crying, I could still identify Tracy and Amil by their overpowering fragrances. Tracy climbed in on one side and Amil on the other. Neither of them said anything. Tracy started humming. She had a beautiful voice, and I loved hearing her sing, but this made me uncomfortable—another trigger. Tracy sang and hummed like this to the babies around the office, where she worked as my nurse.

"I can't take this," I screamed and pulled my knees into my chest. "Stupid-ass, bulky-ass dress." I tried to rip the gown off. It wasn't worthy of touching my skin. "I hate him. Why would he do this to me?" I punched the back of the passenger seat, pretending it was Lloyd's face. It would've been a knockout if I were a boxer and the seat were a human opponent. Knuckle prints in the black leather interior held my gaze until the devil approached the car.

She lightly tapped the window. "Hey, take that noise somewhere else. I can hear you all the way inside, and now the neighbors are coming out. You don't have to live in this neighborhood, but I do, and I refuse to be made fun of around here too."

I fell over onto Tracy's lap.

"I am so sorry, Avery. You did not deserve this." She hummed some more as her fingertips caressed my scalp. This time it was "Jesus Loves Me." I didn't care to hear that either.

Keys jingled. Then I heard my dad's voice. "Amil, drive her around and let her get it out."

"I don't know, Pop. I think you'd have better luck calming her down than I would."

"Go on. I need to have a conversation with your momma."

Good. I didn't know what my own mother had against me or why she wouldn't be supportive of me in my time of need, but I hoped my dad would put a stop to her behavior. I wanted to sit up, but I didn't want the neighbors to see me.

Amil wildly reversed and spun wheels down the street. His aggression behind the wheel told me everything I needed to know about how he felt. Frustrated. I didn't know if it was more toward Lloyd or our mother.

Other than passing cars and the hum from the engine, we rode in silence. "Is this a dream?" I finally spoke.

After some hesitation, Tracy said, "I wish it were. You don't deserve this."

"What do I deserve?" I sat up and looked at her for the answer. My contacts were blurry. I was surprised I hadn't lost one from wiping and rubbing my eyes.

A single tear fell from Tracy's eye. "You deserve a man who can be honest. And one who can avoid temptation. Don't ever think you are less than because of some egotistical idiot."

I scooted over and leaned against the door. I looked to the heavens and watched the clouds as if I would find the answer written across the sky in bright colors or spelled out using the stars.

I was so deep in thought that I didn't realize we had stopped. "I'll be right back." The car rocked when Amil slammed the door.

I groaned and gently massaged my throbbing temples, further exacerbated by my brother's use of force. "What are we doing at Walgreens?"

Tracy shrugged. Neither one of us had the energy to fill the car with pleasantries.

While we waited in silence, I turned my attention back to the world outside of the car. Two homeless men sat on the curb in front of the pharmacy with a piece of cardboard that said HUNGRY, WILL WORK FOR FOOD. For a moment, I wanted to trade places with them. That kind of discomfort couldn't have been worse than the discomfort that I felt. My attention shifted to the bug crawling across the window. Crazy thing, I began to envy the bug. I'd never heard of a bug feeling the emotions associated with being cheated on. Lucky them.

I jumped when Amil swung the car door open. "Here. Take these." He handed me two capsules, a bottle of water, and a bottle of pharmacy wine.

"What is this?" I asked, looking at the purple pills.

"Something to help you sleep."

I didn't need anything to help me sleep. What I needed was the black eraser wand thingy from *Men in Black*. I just needed this day to be wiped from my memory.

My palm blanketed the pills. "You know I'm not taking this." I pushed my fist out to Amil, but he refused.

"Take it," Amil said with extra bass in his voice. "It's not addictive. You've had a long day. You need to get some sleep."

"What difference will sleep make? It will all be here when I wake up. I will still be the town clown. And homeless." I was renting a condo overlooking the Savannah River, but since my lease ended two months before the wedding, there was no point in renewing it. Lloyd and I had agreed that neither of us would live in the townhome we bought to serve as our marital home until we were official. I reluctantly moved back in with my parents, and he continued living with his brother.

"Don't say that, Avery. I am going to be here to help you with whatever you need. And you know you can stay at my place until you figure things out." Tracy was such a good friend, and I hoped she'd still want to be friends once she found out my plan, which would impact her life.

"I'm here too," Amil added. "My place is available if needed. Just sleep on it, and tomorrow we figure out your next move."

Although I appreciated Amil's gesture, he lived in a tiny one-bedroom apartment that barely had enough room for him. The apartment complex he lived in offered him a heavy rent discount in exchange for being the on-call nighttime officer. I'd stay there too if my rent were practically nothing.

"I already know my next move," I casually tossed out.

Maybe my tone caused Amil to stare at me through the rearview mirror. "What move is that?" His tone was off, just like mine. My brother knew me well. He knew I was up to something before I could say it. When I didn't answer, he added, "I'm not taking you to the hospital to start no shit. You'd get fired and lose your license for sure. Let me and Anthony take care of Lloyd."

"I'm not worried about getting fired because I'm not going back to work anyway. I can't deliver another baby, not after this. I quit."

Chapter 4

"You quit your job over some man?" my mother asked and then laughed, causing a little coffee to spill from the unfitting mug she drank from. It was a stocking stuffer from my brothers and me, and it read #1 MOM. *Wonder what we thought when we gave her that?* Maybe we hoped she would take the message to heart and become what the mug said.

My parents made me sit on one of the backless counter stools on one side of the kitchen island, while they stood on the other side, going back and forth, expressing their disappointment in my decision to leave my job. I felt like a college student being reprimanded by their parents for dropping out. I only told them because after riding around all night with Tracy and Amil, my parents were awake when we stumbled into their house at seven in the morning, and of course, they had a ton of questions. During my interrogation, it slipped out.

"I don't expect you guys to understand, but it was a decision that I had to make for myself."

"Shameful." My mother lifted the mug to her lips and blew her coffee. She stared at me awhile before she spat more negativity. "You cannot be my child. You had to have been switched at birth."

That stung. Her venom was more harmful than a wasp to a person with an allergy. I hoped my dad would've talked to her about her behavior and comments when he sent Amil to drive me around. Not saying he didn't. The devil never really listened to critiques when it involved her being on the receiving end.

"Sweetheart, don't allow that man to have that much power over you. You didn't go to school all those years just to stop practicing." It hadn't been twenty-four hours since I had last laid eyes on my dad, but he looked like he had aged overnight for some reason. The whites of his eyes were red. Both carried bags. Gray peeked more than black in what little hair he had on top of his head. He looked more wounded than he did after the delivery.

Not changing my mind.

Naturally, the devil had to add more of her two cents that weren't worth anything. "Not to mention the money your father and I spent to fund all of that schooling."

I stopped breathing for a few seconds over her words. My mother never worked, so if anyone spent money outside of my scholarships, it was my dad. All she did was sit back and cash in on the salary he made as a cardiologist.

"I didn't say it was forever, but I need time to heal," I added. "How can I do that when I deliver babies for a living? I don't want those constant reminders."

"Well, for starters, if you weren't so weak and in need of a man's validation, then you wouldn't have this problem. Secondly, your career choice wouldn't have impacted anything if you had gone to law school as I wanted instead of following your father to become a doctor. Now, would it?"

I groaned at my mother's words. I was tired of her insults. I was tired in general. Although I swallowed an over-the-counter sleep aid, sleep never came. "Do you have any sympathy for me at all? I mean, I'm supposed to be leaving for my honeymoon, and instead I am stuck here being persecuted."

"Yeah, a honeymoon your father and I paid for along with an entire fairy-tale wedding that didn't happen.

You don't need my sympathy. You need my strength. I'd never." She frowned as if she was disgusted by me. And she wasn't finished expressing that disgust. "Don't think you are going to stay in this house and mope around like a sick mutt. I'm not having it."

I looked to my dad for help.

"Don't look at your father. He can't help you this time. He's the reason you're in this mess." My mother looked at my dad and grunted, then looked back at me with a smirk. "I knew that boy was trouble from day one. If your father did more fathering than babying you and kissing up to Lloyd, he would've seen it too. All he cared about was you and Lloyd. Nothing else mattered. He just went along with whatever his little princess wanted, especially this sham of a wedding." She paused to sip her second cup of coffee. "That's all your father talked about. Lloyd probably never wanted to marry you. This is something you're going to have to figure out for yourself."

"Dad," I sobbed. "What do I do?"

My dad rushed over to hold me. I accepted his embrace this time. I needed it.

"Henry," my mom said, interrupting our moment, "if you dare cave, you'll be sleeping on the sofa until you die." She folded her arms across her chest to say she meant business.

"Dammit, Florence. I am not about to sit here and allow my daughter to hurt just so you can feel good about whatever issues you have going on. To hell with your ultimatum."

My dad's reaction surprised us all. He had never disagreed with my mother in front of us before. Plus, we'd never heard the man curse.

Amil and Tracy came running into the kitchen like they were bodyguards.

My mother swept her bangs from her eyes and cocked her head to the side. "Excuse me." She held her mug out to the side like she was about to lunge it at my dad.

What have I started? "Guys, please. I never meant for any of this to happen."

Thunderous laughter erupted from my mother's tiny frame. Fire rested in her downturned eyes when she looked at me and scoffed, "Oh, Avery, shut up. You meant for all of this to happen. You'd do anything to have your father at your mercy as always."

"I swear I didn't—"

"As a matter of fact, when you leave, take your father with you."

"Now wait a minute, Florence. If you want to be technical, this is my damn house. You leave."

"Yours? I'm sure a judge will see it differently."

"That's fine if he does. I hope you and the judge enjoy paying all the bills that come with it."

I'd never seen my parents like this. My dad had never entertained the devil's insults. I felt terrible that they were at each other's throats because of me, but I was glad my dad attempted to handle her. I always wondered what made him fall in love with her and why he stayed. I only loved my mother because I was supposed to based on her title.

There was no point in my dad trading words with the devil. One would never win against her. She always had to have the final say.

I waved my hand in front of my dad's face to get his attention. I talked over the devil directly to my father. "I don't want you guys fighting because of me. I will be okay. Thank you for always supporting me." I leaned over and kissed his cheek. He softened like a stick of butter.

The look my mom gave me told me that she would make me pay for this day even though I did nothing wrong. What she felt toward me, or the lack thereof, had to be more than maternal jealousy. Why couldn't she set aside whatever her issues were and love me as a mother should love a daughter? Or how a woman should love another woman? I wanted my mother to help me pick up the pieces the way Tracy tried. I shook her world last night when I told her that I was taking a hiatus from work. Because she worked as my nurse, she'd be taking an involuntary hiatus too. Meanwhile, she stayed right by my side. For the inconvenience, I offered Tracy the money in my savings account to keep her afloat until I resumed business or until she found another job. I gave her false hope. I knew I had no plans of practicing as a doctor again. I'd have rather worked retail by myself during Black Friday than deliver another baby.

"The two of you are pathetic," my mother spat, exiting the kitchen, thinking she had the last word as usual.

Before she could completely disappear, my dad fired back, "And you aren't as perfect as you want everyone to think."

My mother pivoted. The way her chest rose and fell said a high-intensity storm brewed within her. "Henry Booker, I swear to God—"

My dad was unbothered. "That's one of your problems right there," he said and wiggled his finger at her. "You prance around like you're this perfect Christian woman, and here you are swearing to God. What would the church think of how you talk to everybody outside of them? Why is that, Florence? You are the most critical woman, and it seems to be worse lately."

Amen on that assessment. Joy filled me upon hearing my dad put her in her place. I'd never seen my mother sweat, but her forehead dripped.

The argument between my parents continued with pleas from Amil and Tracy to stop. The commotion drowned out the doorbell. I heard it, though. It rang, and then a knock immediately followed. Lloyd always did that.

I slid out of the stool undetected. Even when I tripped over my dress, no one noticed.

Whoever was at the door was impatient. They had knocked and rung the doorbell again.

I flung it open, prepared to give them a piece of my emotionally drained mind. Instead, my breath was taken from me. "Lloyd."

"Avery, can we talk for a minute?"

Chapter 5

Can we talk for a minute? Did Lloyd think he was Tevin Campbell or something? Was he about to apologize or make a plea to me using R&B lyrics?

"Avery, baby." Lloyd moved toward me. He touched me, and I let him, knowing that his hands had been over another woman and a baby. My skin tingled from his touch. Not in a good way. It was the tingle you'd get from an unwanted bug crawling on your skin.

I had the chance to ask Lloyd all the questions that had been running through my mind for the past seventeen hours. However, my brain wouldn't signal to my mouth for audio. What was wrong with me? So many why's. Why couldn't I react? Why couldn't I reject him touching me? Why couldn't I slam the door in his face? Why couldn't I speak to ask him the questions swirling in my head? Did he change the baby's first diaper? Did he feed the baby? Most importantly, who was Oakley, and where did she come from?

Lloyd stood inches from my face. The smell of liquor on his breath swayed past my nose. I couldn't express the disgust I felt inside when his lips touched my forehead. At first, I thought it was an accident. Multiple pecks later, I realized it was intentional. *He can't be this crazy.* But then again, he showed up at my parents' house knowing that my brothers were loco. Lloyd kissed me again, and I let him.

Repulsiveness existed within me. I wanted Lloyd to stop, but I couldn't make him stop. Where was my action? Where were my words? It was like I suffered from paralysis.

"Can we go somewhere and talk?" Lloyd asked.

I said nothing, nor did I resist when he grabbed my hand and tried to lead me to his car. I was glad my feet wouldn't move, or I would have gone with him. Knowing what I knew now, Lloyd probably would have driven me to the hospital to meet that kid of his. Another question I wanted to ask: was he even sure the kid was his?

"Avery, please, can we go somewhere and talk?" he asked again.

I had a lot to say. *No. Go to hell. I hope you die a slow, painful death.* Still no audio.

"Please hear me out," he said.

Lloyd looked unkempt. Like shit. He still had his tux on, minus the tie, but who was I to talk about appearances? I still had on my gown.

"You look like shit." Finally. Audio. Not pleasant audio, but still audio. I kept it low because I didn't want to tip off anyone inside. Tracy and Amil would both come out swinging and walk away with used silver bracelets, an unflattering portrait for the world to see and poke fun of, and a murder charge. Dad was so chill he'd probably cry and then pleasantly disown Lloyd. My mother, I never knew what would come from her. At this point, she'd probably clap and tell Lloyd, "Job well done."

"I feel like shit, so that's a fair evaluation," Lloyd responded.

"Baby already keeping you up at night?"

He didn't react. Too soon for baby jokes, I guessed. Curious about the answer, I repeated the question. "Did the baby keep you up all night?"

He dropped his head. "Look, I know this—"

I yanked my hand from his. "Don't touch me." The anger started swirling like debris in a tornado.

Lloyd held his hands up in surrender. "Avery, I know you're upset, but please hear me out and let me try to fix this."

"Fix it? Like it's a broken arm or a broken toe? How do you fix this, Lloyd? How do you fix a shattered heart? How do you begin to repair a life or lives that have been turned upside down because you couldn't keep it in your pants?" I leaned forward and thumped his private area. "Explain that to me."

He winced and cupped his junk. "I don't know, but I'm willing to do whatever it takes."

"Whatever it takes" was the most basic answer a person could give, and it did nothing to soothe me. "You should have done whatever it took to keep us from being in this position." I didn't condone violence, but I hauled off and slapped Lloyd.

He rubbed his face. "I deserve that."

"Where did she come from, Lloyd?"

"I will explain it all to you, but not here." His voice softened. "Not here."

"Why not? Does the story change based on where you tell it?"

"No. I took a chance showing up, hoping you'd answer the door. I'm sure your parents don't want me on their property. And once they realize I'm here, they will make me leave. I'd rather do it in private anyway. No interruptions or influences."

"What difference does it make? Becoming a father was explained to me at the church in front of my family and friends, so hearing details shouldn't be a big deal. They are going to find out anyway because I'm going to tell them." I leaned against the frame of the front door, trying with everything within me not to knock Lloyd upside his head. The sight of him disgusted me.

"It's not like I wanted that to happen."

"I'm sure you didn't. You were just going to have a whole baby and keep it a secret."

"I was planning to tell you."

I inched closer toward him with my fists balled. "Really? When was that going to be?"

"I don't know, Avery, but I knew I had to tell you. I wanted to get a DNA test first, and then I was going to tell you."

"Wait a minute." I held up my index finger. "So you need a DNA test, which means you aren't sure if this is your baby?"

"I'm not sure, no."

"So, you're just out here having unprotected sex with whomever?"

"It's not like that."

"Explain how I'm going to look among my colleagues when I walk into a doctor's office to request an STD screening because I was too foolish to think that the man I loved was faithful to me?" I didn't give him a chance to respond. "I'll tell you how I'll look. Like a damn fool. Same as yesterday."

"You don't have to get checked. I've already been tested."

I never knew my neck could roll like it did. Secret woman, secret babies, and secret screenings. "And?" I asked with much attitude.

"I'm fine. It was only that one time after our engagement. I swear."

Lloyd must have thought I was a damn fool. "There is no telling who else you've been with outside of her."

"I'm not a cheater, Avery." He dropped his head and shook it in defeat. Even he knew how ridiculous that sounded. "I know it looks bad, but—"

"But what? What can you possibly say to me? Look at me." I stretched out my arms to give him a full view of how disheveled I looked. "I'm a jilted bride, and I don't deserve this."

"I know you don't."

"So why did you do it?" This time my voice was elevated, and I didn't care if my parents or the neighbors heard.

"Avery, please, keep your voice down. Can we go somewhere else and talk about this? You can yell and hit me all you want."

"I can do that from anywhere. I have no face left to save."

"It's not too late to catch our flight."

Was he talking about what I thought he was talking about? "Flight? What flight?" I asked.

"Our honeymoon. Even though we didn't marry, we can use the trip to talk and see where things go."

A psychotic evil laugh escaped me. It kind of sounded like the Joker. Lloyd thought I would take advantage of our honeymoon when we weren't even honeys. I didn't want to share a porch with him, let alone a flight or a vacation. A vacation that I happened to be looking forward to. My goal was to get white-girl wasted at one of the floating bars, snorkel, and bask on the beach, sneaking in some nasty time with my new husband. His loss.

"What do you say, Avery? Do you think you'd still want to go?"

Think. Fiji. Exotic. Warm. Beautiful. Dreamy. All the things that Lloyd and I were not. "I would love to go." A glimmer of hope appeared in Lloyd's eyes. Little did he know I was about to stab him and twist the knife. "But not with you," I added with much pleasure.

He nodded his understanding. "I knew that was a farfetched idea."

I rolled my eyes, and my neck rolled with them. "You think?"

"Can we at least go somewhere and talk? I would feel more comfortable than standing on your parents' porch. I'm sure they hate me."

"Hell yeah we do." Amil lightly pushed me out of the way and lunged toward Lloyd. While I grabbed hold of Amil's left arm, thinking I was stopping him from advancing on Lloyd, he hit him with a right. Lloyd staggered backward and took a tumble down the four stairs that connected the porch to the walkway.

Amil roared something inaudible as he headed down the stairs to serve Lloyd some more.

There was blood.

"Oh, my God. Amil, stop it, please," I begged.

Revenge was in my brother's eyes.

My dad rushed down the stairs and blocked Amil from getting to Lloyd, who was sprawled on his back.

Tracy yelled out, "Hit him again."

I crouched beside Lloyd. "Are you okay? Do you need a medic?"

Lloyd didn't answer. He just spit out blood.

"Look how pathetic she is. Running over to him," the devil added.

My mother was right. I was pathetic for still caring about Lloyd. But my love for him wouldn't disappear overnight. Neither would the knot on his forehead. It grew at a rapid pace and was satisfying to see. And while I wanted his face covered in a few more of them, I didn't want my brother to get into any trouble for trying to protect me. Definitely not in his profession. Amil was a police officer, and punching Lloyd would end his career. Plus, the devil would discard my brother altogether. Amil wouldn't care, but our father still held on to hope that we would magically become a happy family. The four of us were happy when she was not around to change the energy in the room.

Our mother probably sat back and waited for the perfect moment to throw each of us away. Especially Amil. She had been ashamed of him since he made the news during his senior year of high school. He was a typical teen. The same day the drug-sniffing dogs showed up on campus, Amil got busted for having marijuana in his car. Because he was a student, my mother thought she could hide his arrest, but because he was 18, they plastered his face all over the news and in *The Augusta Chronicle*. The charges were expunged from his record after he completed community service and an outpatient drug program, but my mother reminded him of it any chance she got. Amil was kicked out of school, and instead of going to an alternative school, he took the GED and passed with flying colors. From there, he earned a two-year degree in criminal justice and entered the police force, where he'd received promotion after promotion. I would have hated for him to lose everything he had worked so hard for because of me.

More blood poured from Lloyd's mouth and stained the concrete and his tuxedo shirt that he was supposed to marry me in. It kind of reminded me of my stained wedding dress. The only difference was that his was blood and mine was mascara. Both results of pain over Oakley's pregnancy.

There was too much blood to be from just a busted lip. I tried to move Lloyd's hand from his mouth, but he snatched away.

Lloyd held his hand in front of his mouth and told Amil, "You knocked out my tooth. You're done as a cop. I'm pressing charges." He reached for his phone, which was clipped to his belt. "Fuck," he yelled, causing blood from his mouth to splatter onto my arms.

My heart and Lloyd's screen matched. Shattered. He couldn't make that call to the police.

He looked at me. "Your brother is done."

Amil tried to break away from my dad, but he didn't stand a chance. Old Henry Booker was strong for a man in his early sixties. Plus, my mother stood in the middle of the stairs with her arms outstretched like she was Jesus on the cross, thinking that would stop Amil if he broke free.

"Wait until I catch you," Amil yelled. "I care more for my sister than I do any job."

I tuned out Amil's insults and the struggle between him and my dad. "Lloyd, I'm sorry Amil hit you," I said. "Please don't get him in trouble with work." I pleaded for my brother. He loved his job. He couldn't lose it. I pulled my hand back from Lloyd's arm when I realized I was caressing him.

"Why the fuck are you apologizing to him? He shouldn't have brought his ass over here. He's lucky that's all he got."

"What can I do, Lloyd? Amil was just trying to protect me."

Blood covered his lips and dripped down his chin. "Give me a moment of your time, and I won't press charges."

"Fuck you," Amil roared to Lloyd and then addressed me. "He's trying to blackmail you, Avery. Even if he does report me, I was protecting you. His word against mine."

I looked back at my family. This was all my fault. The nosy neighbors hadn't called the police yet, or they would have shown up already. I had time to fix it. "That's it?" I asked Lloyd. "Just a conversation, and you won't press charges?"

"I promise I won't. Just hear me out. That's all I want."

"Fine. I'll go. Just don't call the police on Amil."

Against my family's wishes and protests, I hopped in the car with Lloyd.

Chapter 6

We rode in silence. Every street name, pothole, turn, and stoplight was familiar. I knew exactly where Lloyd was taking me. He knew I loved the water, and my favorite places to visit to clear my head were Clark Hills Lake or the Savannah River within the Hammond's Ferry area.

He pulled into an empty spot, put the car in park, and sighed. "How was your night?"

It took everything within me not to uppercut him. "What the hell kind of question is that? You fought for my time, and this is how you lead?"

Lloyd buried his face in his hands, and for the first time, I witnessed him cry. It was an ugly cry, too. About 80 percent of me wanted to laugh at how his dumb-ass cry sounded, but the remaining 20 wanted to console him. I did neither. A couple walked by and caught my attention. They laughed as the man pushed a stroller.

A baby.

Lloyd, Oakley, and LJ.

I was surprised I didn't ugly cry myself or shed at least one tear. As much as I cried yesterday, maybe my ducts hadn't had a chance to replenish. "Why did you do it, Lloyd? What was wrong with me? Why wasn't I enough?" I asked over his sobs.

Once Lloyd settled his emotions, he replied, "There is nothing wrong with you. You were . . . are perfect."

"Bullshit answer. If something is perfect, why destroy it?"

Lloyd shook his head and stammered over basic kindergarten words.

"It shouldn't be that hard to answer, Lloyd. You know why you did it, so just spit it out."

His face and hands met again. The need to console him decreased to 0 percent. Irritation brewed. I kept balling and unballing my fists. I would recreate that *Waiting to Exhale* moment if he didn't start saying something worth my time and pain. Trees surrounded us. I'd gone camping plenty of times. I knew how to start a fire.

"Say something, goddammit!" My screams slowed down two joggers who started circling, looking for the source. Lloyd was startled enough that his ass stopped crying and started babbling.

"I'm sorry, Avery. I didn't mean for any of this to happen."

"Heard that already. Now I want to hear an explanation." That came out calm, but the longer he tried pulling answers from a rabbit's ass, the more the calmness faded. "There is nothing you can say that will make me feel any better or worse. But saying nothing will only increase the desire to kill you right here in broad daylight in front of all these witnesses." After my threat, the couple with the baby stroller walked past us again. I pointed in their direction. "And that doesn't help."

Lloyd's eyes were red and puffy, and his voice cracked. "I had one too many drinks and . . ." He rubbed his wet eyes and runny nose with the inside of his shirt.

"And what?" I said, my tone full of attitude. "Where did this woman come from, Lloyd?"

He cleared his throat, let the driver's side window down, and stepped out. I frowned as he leaned into the window and started explaining. "I was headed to my car after work, and she was parked near me, looking under her hood. I asked if help was on the way, and she said she hadn't had a chance to call anyone because her phone was dead. It was getting dark, and I didn't want to leave her by herself. I let her use my phone to call a tow truck, and because the ETA was an hour, I waited with her." He stopped as if he had covered every detail.

My scowl silently forced him to reveal more. He seemed to have a harder time confessing than I had hearing it. Numbness, perhaps.

Lloyd let out a deep sigh and continued. "I allowed her to give my number to the insurance company for roadside assistance. Apparently, she memorized it and called me the next day."

"And there was no family member she could've called to pick her up?" I asked.

"She doesn't have any family in this area, is what she told me."

"Well, why is she here, Lloyd?"

"She said she was recently divorced, her ex-husband is military, but she stayed in the area." His stutter had returned.

"Did you have this same speech problem with that woman?" I asked, not necessarily looking for an answer. "Please, get your shit together before I lose it on you."

"These questions are making me uncomfortable. I don't want to hurt you any more, Avery."

"You can't hurt me any more than what you already have, so just say it. Specifically, why?"

My dumb-ass ex-fiancé leaned into the car and retrieved a bottle of water. He guzzled it like it would be the last thing he ever drank and then backed away from the window. "It was refreshing to feel visible and to talk to someone about something other than the wedding."

All because of the wedding? That was supposed to be a reason to celebrate with the homies, smoke some cigars, and have a few drinks, not wiggle around inside of another woman. Guessed I was wrong. Lloyd could hurt me more than he had already done. The side of my fist slammed into the armrest of his Mercedes. It left a dent. Good.

"Avery, please," Lloyd pleaded, still feet away from the car. "This is the worst thing I could have done."

I had one more question, and I was done. I didn't want to hear any more. My heart couldn't handle it. "When did y'all meet?"

"January."

"Take me home, please."

"I will, but can we hash this out first?"

I shook my head. "I can't handle any more of you and your bullshit right now."

"Just hear me out. Let me try to win your forgiveness," Lloyd said and babbled on for hours. I tuned most of everything out and never spoke another word. After hours of ignoring him, he finally drove me home.

The sun began to set when we pulled up to my parents' house. Lloyd had been with me for hours. Oakley must've been worried sick. I couldn't blame her if she was. She probably thought he abandoned them, and for all I knew, he could have. Lloyd could've told her he was going out for a pack of diapers with no intention of returning. That was unlike him. Or was it? I questioned how much I knew about the man I planned to spend eternity with.

The growl in my stomach was in sync with the discomfort that penetrated my heart. I realized I hadn't eaten anything in over twenty-four hours. More than twenty-four hours. That was how long it had been since the devastation. That thought. My stomach, my heart, my head—they all hurt simultaneously. The combo of feelings reminded me of when my brothers would spin me on the merry-go-round until I'd puke. If there were any contents in my stomach, they would have made an appearance. I didn't have an appetite, but my stomach growled for nourishment the same way my heart yearned for the nourishment of uncomplicated love. With my heart in a million shattered pieces, I wasn't sure how it continued to beat.

I looked at my parents' house and realized I had only two choices: stay in the car with Lloyd or go inside. I glanced at Lloyd. The sight of him made me nauseated. I looked at the house and moaned. Tracy and Amil were waiting on the porch. I'd had enough of everyone for one day.

"Let me get your door." Lloyd unhooked his seat belt and grabbed the door handle.

I tugged at his sleeve to stop him. "It's best you don't get out." I unfastened my seat belt, cracked the car door, and stuck my leg out.

This time Lloyd grabbed my hand, but I pulled from his clutch. "Say what you need to say without touching me."

Lloyd talked over the warning chime for the ajar door. "I just wanted to know if I can see you again."

I shrugged. There was an iota of a moment where I felt like I wanted to see Lloyd again. Only to say things to make him hurt like I was. But there were substantial moments when I felt the next and last time I wanted to see him was when he was casket sharp. Either bitterness would invade my consciousness and I would put him there, or maybe Oakley would show another side of crazy and do it. Possibly my brothers would. Amil had gotten up from the porch and started toward us.

"I gotta go, Lloyd. I don't want a repeat of earlier."

"Consider it and let me know. I love you, Avery, and I hope you have a good night."

Have a good night. That tacky statement pissed me off. "How does one in my current situation have a good night, Lloyd?" I rolled my eyes and kicked my other foot out of the car. I twisted my body at the waist to look back at him. "I hope the opposite for you. I hope your night is filled with a crying baby and a nagging baby momma."

My wedding dress seemed heavier, like it carried some of my emotional load. I fumbled with it until I was able to stand.

Amil was inches away from the car. With panic in my eyes and alarm in my voice, I yelled, "I'm okay. Go back, Amil." I pointed toward the porch, but he didn't listen. Tracy, who had been an advocate for the beatdown earlier, must've had a change of heart, because she ran in front of him to keep him at bay. Weightlifting sessions with her personal trainer paid off, because it bought me a little time.

Before I could shut the door, Lloyd called my name. I didn't turn around, so he said what he wanted to say to my back. "I am going to get my phone fixed tomorrow. Is it okay if I call you?"

"You should worry about calling the mother of your kid. I'm sure she's wondering where you are." I added a ton of force when I shut his door. I had hoped to shatter the window like Tina Turner did Ike's window, but it didn't happen.

Tracy ran to me, and after she shot a middle finger at Lloyd, she asked, "Are you okay? We have been worried. We tried calling you only to find out you left your phone here."

I hugged Tracy. "I'm okay. I promise."

"Serial killer" still rested on Amil's face. "What did that fool say?"

My stomach growled over the beginning of my words, which helped transition the conversation to something else.

"Your dad made steaks. I put you a plate up. Let me get it for you," Tracy said and started inside.

"No, that's okay. I'm not hungry."

Tracy's eyes cut to my stomach. "What I heard says otherwise. Just eat a little bit."

I trudged up the stairs but didn't go in. I allowed myself and the weight of my world to collapse into one of the rocking chairs. I wished it could've rocked hard enough to shake the last twenty-four hours from my system.

Rocking chair. Oakley will probably rock that kid in a rocking chair. Somehow, I was able to associate everything with a baby.

The landscape lights lining the walkway won my attention. They were bright enough to illuminate bloodstains on the concrete from the punch Amil delivered to Lloyd.

"Here," Tracy said and shoved a plate of food in my face.

I pushed it away. The smell made me queasy.

"You need to put something on your stomach," she demanded.

"I need a shower first. I've had this stupid dress on since . . ." I stopped talking when I realized what Tracy and Amil had on.

Amil threw up his hands. "*We* still have the same clothes on."

We were all emotional and dirty.

"I'm still waiting to hear what that fool had to say." Amil's feet stopped just before the bloodstains.

The scuffle replayed behind my eyes as if it were in real time.

"Yeah, I'm dying to know too," Tracy said.

"After I shower. Can y'all stay with me tonight?" Since Tracy and Amil loved animals, I gave them my best puppy-dog face. "We can pile up in the den for old times' sake?" The good ol' days. Tracy would come over, and we'd hang out in the den using hairbrushes as microphones while attempting to learn the dance moves to every video. Back then, Amil had a crush on Tracy and would always make his way to the den, talking about how every video had a sexy man in it, so we needed him.

Tracy draped her musty arm around me. "You know I got you, girl. I don't have any clothes, though."

I pinched my nose. "You definitely need more than clothes. That should be the furthest thing from your mind."

"Shut the hell up, Avery," Tracy said and gently pushed my shoulder.

"I can give you a shirt and some shorts," Amil volunteered.

"Or I can just give her some of my clothes, duh." Tracy and I were about the same size. She was more muscle. She was just a few inches taller, five five, and I came in at five two. We both wore a size nine in clothes and shoes.

"Whatever," Amil said and pushed my head.

"Thank you. Y'all know the drill: pick a bathroom, and no more than ten minutes." That was tradition. We had to be showered, dressed in our pajamas, and in the den within ten minutes, or we'd risk getting punched five times by each person. Dumb kid games.

"Are the parents asleep?" I asked so I'd know what I was up against before I stepped inside.

"Yeah. Pops paced the floor for hours," Amil said. "I'll be surprised if he has skin left on the bottom of his feet."

Tracy and Amil laughed.

This was no laughing matter. I felt terrible leaving my dad in that position. "I'm sorry."

"Stop apologizing for something that isn't your fault. You keep listening to your crazy momma if you want to," Amil said.

"She's your momma too," I reminded him.

"I'll believe it when I see the proof."

"Well, that's one way to look at it. Anyway, I don't want to make too much noise and wake them, because I don't want to hear it. Forget the sleepover."

"Nah, I want the sleepover." Amil looked at Tracy.

"I'm cool with it too," Tracy said.

"Oh, Amil, can you give me two more of those pills from last night? I hope to get some sleep tonight. Hopefully, they will work since I'm not as emotional."

"Pops called you in a prescription for something stronger."

My forehead wrinkled with curiosity.

"Ambien," Amil said, answering my nonverbal question.

"I'm not taking that."

"It's temporary."

"It's habit-forming."

"It's not that bad, Avery. Remember I took it? It helped."

Of course I remembered my brother taking that medicine. That was the main reason why I didn't want to take it. Amil suffered from depression when he was kicked out of school. Between my mother and her insults and his pending court date, Amil barely slept a wink until he started on that medicine.

"Yeah, but you were a zombie, always staggering to the fridge after taking it, eating random combinations of junk," I reminded him.

"But it still helped. Sometimes you have to rely on things temporarily until you're strong enough to do without them. It's just for a little while." He pointed between him and Tracy and added, "We will make sure you don't become dependent on it or do anything crazy."

Tracy tapped my leg to get my attention. "Listen to your brother, Avery."

I'd have rather listened to the rain that had started to fall. Perfect weather for cuddling, only it would be with one of the pillows that lined the oversized sectional in the den. I looked at the bloodstains. The rain had already started to wash away remnants of Lloyd clean from the concrete. I wished my mind operated the same.

Amil broke through my thoughts. "Pops left the pills on the breakfast table whenever you're ready to take them."

Thunder roared, and a bolt of lightning flashed, which finally scared us inside.

"Let's hurry up and get these timed showers so I can find out what that fool had to say."

"Ten minutes as usual?" Tracy asked.

"Ten? No, that won't work. We've been in these same clothes since yesterday afternoon. Let's make it twenty," I said as I headed upstairs.

After my thirty-minute shower, I met Tracy and Amil in the den. First, I had to sit through their grievances about my extra shower time. I didn't mean it. I just lost track of time replaying my time with Lloyd. They could punch me all they wanted. I doubted I'd feel it.

Tracy warmed up my food *again* and had it waiting for me—*again*.

"Thank you, but I told you I'm not hungry," I said and slid the plate to the other side of the glass coffee table.

"Dr. Booker told us to make sure you ate something before you took this medicine." Tracy pushed the plate and a bottle of water in my direction. Then she held her hand out with one pill. I didn't want any of what she offered, but I took it from her anyway.

I swallowed as much food as I could stomach and then that dreaded pill—ten milligrams of Ambien. The time that I took the pill was strategic, though. From studies on the sleep aid, I knew that I'd be passed out within thirty minutes. Enough time to tell Tracy and Amil what Lloyd said before they could press me with too many questions. That was why I started the conversation with, "Two rules. Don't flood me with a barrage of questions, and this is not up for discussion after tonight. Deal?"

Through groans and a couple of F-bombs, they both said, "Deal."

Then Tracy suggested the most ridiculous thing ever. "And because you are moving on after tonight, I am going to set you up with the dating agency I'm using."

Amil frowned.

I rejected Tracy's offer. "Too soon. I was about to get married yesterday, remember? And I doubt that I will ever be open to love and dating again."

"It's not too soon, and you will. You know what they say?"

"No, I don't know."

"The fastest way to get over one man is to get under another," she gushed through chuckles.

Amil smacked his teeth. For whatever reason, he was not amused.

I should've just pretended to know so she wouldn't say it.

"I'm going to set you up with a profile, and we can go together."

"Doesn't seem to be working out for you," Amil uttered.

"That's because I'm not looking for anything serious right now."

"Neither am I, so I will pass." I adjusted the pillows on the couch and wrapped a throw blanket around myself.

"What's the point of going then, Tracy?" Amil asked what I had been thinking.

"Just for fun. Keeping myself entertained until the right one comes along. And that's all you need to do too, Avery. Help take your mind from Lloyd."

"Yeah, okay," Amil said to Tracy with a bit of attitude and then turned to me and asked, "So what did that fool say?"

"Give me time." I rolled my eyes and lay against the sofa like I was lying on a therapist's sofa about to divulge my innermost secrets.

"You had plenty of time. We even waited an extra ten minutes," Amil said, referencing my extended shower time.

"Shut up, Amil, before she decides not to tell us anything," Tracy cautioned.

I winked at her. She hit it on the head—in my time. I wasn't sure if I had the energy to tell it.

We all turned in the direction of the door when we heard the alarm lady announce, "Front door open."

"What in the hell?" Amil jumped from the sofa in defense mode.

We all sighed in relief at Anthony coming around the corner.

I sat up. "Boy, you scared the shit out of us. What are you doing over here at this time of night? And why didn't you call and tell somebody you were coming in?"

"I'm asking the questions," Anthony responded. "Why in the hell would you leave with Lloyd? Not only that, but you ran off and left your phone." He never took his eyes off of me, even as he sat in the recliner. When he started quoting statistics on how many black women were murdered by their significant others, I tuned him out.

I shrugged, not caring for the lesson.

Amil shook his head and whispered, "Here we go."

Anthony was more overprotective than Amil. When I was going through school, I looked at my teachers as professional saints. I'd never seen a thug teacher until Anthony became one. A weird thug described him best. He leaned forward and tapped the side of my knee. "Yo. Don't do that shrugging shit with me. Use your words."

"Don't be talking to me like that," I hissed. "I am not one of your students."

"I took a break from grading papers to come over. Grades are due tomorrow, so I need to know what's going on."

Amil snickered at our brother's sternness toward me. I rolled my eyes and shot him double middle fingers.

"We all here. What did he say?" Amil asked for the umpteenth time.

"Typical man stuff," I said through a yawn.

"What is typical man stuff?" Anthony asked.

"You know, he cheated with Oakley because I became so obsessed with the wedding that I wasn't giving him enough attention."

"I can't believe he turned it around on you," Tracy said.

"First off, that's not typical man shit. That's immature little boy shit. If he were a real man, he would have understood that every girl dreams of a chance to plan a wedding, and he would've respected your time to make sure you had everything you wanted."

I was sure that was how Anthony would've handled the situation. He was always so delicate with his ex-wife. She'd finally had enough of my mother and moved on with someone else.

"Amen." Tracy waved her hand like she had just heard a good Word in church. "They don't make men like that anymore. They are all selfish."

Amil gave Tracy a hard stare.

"And furthermore," Anthony added, "if he were that bothered by the lack of attention, he should've come to you and had that conversation with you. That's a cop-out."

"I agree with Anthony," Amil said. "What else did that fool say? Start from the beginning, when you left with him."

"You and I will discuss it in more detail later, but I have a huge problem with you leaving with him." Anthony was older than me by ten years, and he swore he was my daddy. He was harder on me than our dad was.

"I know leaving with him wasn't ideal, but I was trying to protect Amil. Plus, I *needed* to hear what Lloyd had to say."

"Was it worth it?" Anthony asked.

"What do you mean?"

"Did he say anything that magically made you feel better?"

"No, probably worse."

"Exactly my point. You didn't *need* to hear anything he had to say because he showed you in his actions. That was a want. And not only will you replay the wedding in your head, but his weak explanation, too."

"I disagree, Anthony. I would have been wondering why."

Anthony challenged my statement. "And you still don't know why. You just know what he told you. And from what I can tell, he's blaming you. Sometimes the unknown is better than the known. At least then you can write your own version."

"Oh, that's deep, bro," Amil said and swiped away a fake tear.

I would've hit him, but Tracy did because she was closer.

"Amil, shut up." I gave him a glare that substituted for physical contact. I couldn't stand his ass sometimes.

My speech started to slur as I gave them more details of how things went with Lloyd. "I asked him how they met."

"And what did that fool say?" Amil sat up on the edge of the sofa and rocked back and forth like he was a gossip head craving the latest. I could expect this behavior from Tracy, but she was calm and patient, which was good for my soul.

I rolled my eyes at him again and repeated what Lloyd told me.

"How convenient," Tracy said. "A damsel in distress. The easiest game for a man to fall for."

"So, how does that translate to him getting her pregnant?" Anthony asked.

"Honestly, I didn't have the courage to ask those particular details."

"I call BS," Tracy said. "Oakley is a unique name for a black girl. I took the liberty of trying to look her up, and nothing. Nothing on Google, no social media, nothing. It's like she's a ghost."

I shook my head at Tracy. She was a master when it came to prying into people's business.

"I wonder how he got her pregnant." Amil insisted on discussing something I had already said I didn't have the answer to.

"They had sex, duh." That came from Tracy, and when she said it, my mind did something it hadn't done because it was so focused on that baby. I visualized Lloyd and Oakley together in *that* way.

Sorrow stung my eyes, but no tears. My yawns were more frequent, and my speech slurred, but I was determined to finish this interrogation and be done with it. "He said the tow truck driver looked a little sketchy, so he drove her home."

"And is that when they had sex?" Amil just wouldn't let it go.

"Amil, shut up. And please stop asking about sex. I don't know any of that. For the last time, with my fragile state of mind, I couldn't bring myself to ask details about their encounter. I guess they hit it off, and it happened."

"Hit it off as if he weren't engaged to be married?" Tracy asked. "When did they meet?"

I lay back on the sectional. "January."

"January? Wow. And she already had his kid." Tracy shook her head.

"Lloyd's right. I was way too consumed with the wedding."

Tracy rubbed my leg. "Don't let him convince you that you were the cause of this."

I yawned. Maybe the effects of the medicine made me say what I said next. "I was . . ." I yawned again. "I was all about the wedding and not him. Lack of attention caused this. He deserves my forgiveness and a chance to win me back."

Chapter 7

"About time you woke up. All that damn snoring." Amil folded the blanket he had slept under and tossed it on the couch.

I sat up and stretched. "Good morning to you too." I wondered if that "good morning" was as dry as my throat.

Amil walked past me and pushed my head. I fell over trying to hit him back. I grazed his calf. "Where's Tracy?"

"Making my breakfast," Amil said and winked.

I followed the aroma of bacon into the kitchen. Sure enough, Tracy was standing behind the stove, making breakfast, but it was for everyone, not just Amil.

"Good morning, people," I greeted them. Noticeably absent was my mother, and I was not about to question her whereabouts.

Dad looked over his newspaper. "Good morning. How'd you sleep?"

Amil rounded the corner, "Yeah, how *did* you sleep?" He hovered over me like he was a helicopter looking for a landing pad.

"Like a ba . . ." I paused when I realized what I was about to say. I couldn't say that word. Ever. "Like a queen," I corrected myself and popped a grape into my mouth. Although Lloyd and the wedding were on my mind when I woke up, I managed to enjoy seven hours without thinking of him or it, not even in my dreams, and I loved it.

I joined my dad at the breakfast table and waited for
him to open with questions about me leaving with Lloyd,
but he didn't. I appreciated that. He continued reading
his newspaper as he sipped coffee from his mug that read
THE BEST FATHER IN THE WORLD in cursive. The writing on his
cup explained our true feelings.

"Tracy, how did you get stuck cooking?" I asked.

"Your pesky brother was all in my face this morning,
begging me for some French toast."

"You could've said no," I told her.

"I did. Multiple times. He said you kept him up all night
with your snoring, and since we are besties, I had to
make it up to him."

"You don't owe him nothing. But was I snoring that
bad?"

Tracy's eyes got big as she turned to the stove. Amil
stared at me with a blank expression.

Guess that means yes. "I usually don't snore."

"Well, you killed it last night," Amil said. "Kept us up."

Amil walked past me and pushed my head again. I
hated when he did that.

"Sorry. Probably because I was drained in every aspect."
When I said that, a flashback of the wedding hit me. I
squeezed my eyes as tight as I could, trying to rid myself
of the visual.

"Yeah, that tiredness had you delusional and *talkative*."

I opened my eyes to Amil's voice. Something about the
way he emphasized "talkative" plagued me with curiosity.
Dare I ask with my dad around? I'd wait and ask Tracy
later.

I pretended to brush it off. "It was probably that
medicine. I didn't want to take it to begin with." I looked
over at my dad to see if my explanation was enough to
divert his eyes back to the paper. He still inquisitively
stared at me.

"Yeah, let's hope it was the medicine and not reality. You had some pretty disturbing things to say." Amil sipped his juice but kept his eyes on me the whole time.

The subtlety. I couldn't take it anymore. "What are you talking about?"

"Leave her alone, Amil, or you won't get this food you asked for."

My dad's eyes were also asking Amil what he was talking about.

"Do you want to eat or not?" Tracy asked my brother through clenched teeth.

She tried to help me out, but I wanted to know. "He obviously wants me to know, so let him say it."

"I'm not going to put your business out there like that, but just know those pills are like truth serum."

My dad was fully engaged. He folded the newspaper and stared from me to Amil.

I shifted in my chair and cleared my throat, wondering what I could've said.

Tracy peeped my uncomfortable posture. "Don't pay your brother any attention. He's just being an annoying big brother." She dropped Amil's plate in front of him, which caused some of the food to fall on the old-fashioned floral placemats my mother insisted on using.

Those floral placemats were another trigger. The rose petals reminded me of what Oakley had lain on while pushing out that kid.

Tracy placed the skillet in the sink, removed my dad's barbecuing apron, and asked, "Avery, can I talk to you for a moment please?" Her face showed concern.

So, was there some truth to the truth serum after all? I couldn't make it back into the den fast enough.

Tracy wrung her fingers and started the conversation very delicately. "Memory loss is a side effect of Ambien, so you may not remember any of what I am about to say."

I waved my hand, encouraging her to spit it out. "Okay, go on."

"After you took that medicine last night, you were fighting your sleep a bit." Tracy's words eased from her tongue like she was about to deliver some life-altering news to a patient. "You received a phone call from Lloyd that you took in private, and what you two talked about is concerning to us."

I shook my head. "A phone call? I would've remembered talking to Lloyd."

"I'm sure you would have had you been unmedicated."

I'd never known Tracy to lie to me, but I didn't believe what she said. I would have remembered talking on the phone. "Where's my phone?" Tracy kept talking while I searched. I used my hip to move the sectional and tossed every pillow onto the floor. In the creases, I managed to find some loose change that I planned to keep.

Calmness laced Tracy's voice. "Trust me, Avery, you told us the rest of what happened when you left with Lloyd." She paused and whispered, "Among some other things."

"Found it." These wide hips of mine were good for something. I clicked on recent calls, and sure enough, Hubby's Work appeared. The day Lloyd proposed to me, I immediately reprogrammed both of his numbers. His personal cell changed from Lloyd to Hubby, and his work cell changed from Lloyd's Work to Hubby's Work. According to my call log, Hubby's Work and I talked for over twenty minutes, and I had no idea about what. Lloyd never used his work cell on the weekends, but I guessed he made an exception since his phone was damaged.

"Okay, what did I say?" The words tarnished my taste buds before hoarsely rolling out of my mouth and echoing throughout the den.

Tracy looked uncomfortable. She lowered her head and fidgeted with her squared white acrylic nails. "It seems Lloyd sweet-talked you into agreeing to some things that I know you would not have agreed to had you been fully aware."

I felt the deep crease in the middle of my forehead. "Like what? Just tell me. No need to sugarcoat it."

"That you had plans to work things out with him, and how we all needed to mind our own business and let you live your life."

I covered my face in shame. Was that true? Did I feel like that? I needed her to coat this news with sugar after all. "Do you believe I'm going to do that?"

Tracy shrugged. "I don't really know. I hope not, but . . ." Her sentence abruptly ended as if her throat reached up and snatched the remaining words.

"But what? You don't believe that I can move past this, do you?"

"I'm sure with time you will. I've had my heart broken before, but never like this. Everyone can say how they'll act in a certain situation until they are in it. But I hope after you take the necessary time to heal, Lloyd is no longer an option for you."

"What if I want him to be an option? How would you feel about that?"

Tracy inched closer to me. "Please tell me that's not what you're thinking."

"I don't know what I'm thinking." I plopped down on the couch, feeling even more confused. Why in the hell would I tell Lloyd something like that if I didn't mean it? I couldn't comfortably blame it on the medicine.

Tracy shook her head. "You can do so much better, Avery."

"But what if, Tracy? What if after all is said and done, I decide I want to work it out and move forward with him?"

Tracy's jaws clenched a couple of times before she spoke. "So, you're okay with being stepmomma to his surprise firstborn and dealing with baby-momma drama?"

"I don't know what I'm okay with. I'm still shocked. One minute I'm sad, the next minute angry, another minute passes and I feel violent. My emotions are all over the place."

"Don't let shock impair your judgment. You'd be crazy to give him another chance." Tracy sat beside me on the pillow-less sofa.

"But you just said you don't know how you'd react if something like this would've happened to you."

"And that's true in most situations. However, this situation . . . this is a dealbreaker. No one should have to put up with this, and I am not about to let you."

"Let me?" I moved away from Tracy and started pacing. I was tired of everyone's opinions and judgment. "No one has the power to let me do anything. Not you, my dad, nor my brothers. Let's be clear on that."

"Clear. I didn't mean it that way, Avery."

"As my friend, you are supposed to support me with whatever decision I make."

"I have always supported you, and I always will, unless you get back with Lloyd. I cannot and will not support that. It's not right."

I stopped and stood in front of Tracy with my hands on my hips. "How do you know if it's right? I don't remember reading your name in the Bible as a substitution for God or Him granting you permission to judge me."

Tracy closed her eyes and inhaled deeply. Once she exhaled, she gently explained, "I don't feel like I'm judging you more than trying to get you to open your eyes. If this were right, you wouldn't be here. We wouldn't be here." She waved her hand from me to herself. "Your ceremony would have been complete, and you would be on a plane headed to celebrate. Maybe real love is out there for you, and Lloyd wasn't it. God had to get your attention somehow."

This was the first time I felt a need to question Tracy's friendship. "Call me crazy, but it sounds like you're happy my wedding failed. What, are you jealous or something?"

Since the pillows were still strewn across the floor, Tracy struggled to find solid ground when she aggressively jumped up from the couch. When she stabled herself, she kicked a pillow out of the way and laughed. "Jealous? What am I jealous of? And why would I be jealous of someone who's practically my sister?"

"Because I found someone to marry me, and you haven't found anyone who wants to date you, let alone marry you."

Tracy took a step back. The hurt was visible in her eyes.

"You know, Avery, there are a lot of things that I can say right now that will hurt you just as much as that comment hurt me, but I don't want to hurt you any more than you are hurting now."

"Say whatever you want to say. Don't use our friendship as the reason. Let the ghetto come out. Because we all know that's what you are and where you're from."

Tracy and I had attended the same private school, but we lived in two different worlds. Her world was riddled with graffiti, gangs, and bullet holes, while mine consisted of an expensive two-story home, manicured lawn, and friendly neighbors who waved in passing. My dad paid for my tuition, which was around the cost of a college tuition. Tracy attended on a scholarship.

"Avery, I may be from the ghetto, but I'm nothing like my circumstances, so how dare you?" she fumed as she gathered up her belongings. Her chocolate skin was no match for the patches of angry red that decorated her face. "I am and have been a real friend to you. I understand you are in pain, and you're lashing out at the closest person to you, but let's get one thing clear. I have never been, nor will I ever be jealous of you or anyone. I am content with myself."

"Bullshit. You have always been jealous of me. Lloyd tried to tell me, but I brushed it off. Now I see he was right." Lloyd planted that jealousy seed in my head a while ago. He believed Tracy wanted my life because she always called, and when he and I would have date night, sometimes she'd ask to tag along to get out of the house.

Tracy chuckled. "Lloyd? The same Lloyd who betrayed you? That Lloyd?"

"He made a mistake, Tracy. He said so in these messages." I wiggled my phone. "He said so in the car last night."

"And what reasons does Lloyd give as to why I'm jealous of you?"

I held up my index finger. "Number one, you can't get or keep a man." I raised my middle finger to give the other finger some company. "And number two, because I am a doctor, and you had to settle for being *just* a nurse because you didn't have the money to pursue anything more."

Tracy twisted her lips and nodded her head. "Just a nurse, huh? You rely so much on me as your nurse when we are at the office, and now you want to minimize my position."

"I call it like I see it," I retorted.

"Well, apparently, your vision is blurred in more ways than one. You're holding on to the words of a man who disrespected you and humiliated you in front of hundreds of people. I have always been a true friend to you, which means I am proud of every one of your accomplishments, and because I am a genuine friend, I hurt when you hurt. It's a shame I have to explain the concept of friendship to you."

"Bullshit again."

"Okay, well, congratulations, Avery, I guess you have it all figured out." Tracy picked up her bridesmaid dress and draped it over her arm.

"You're leaving?" I asked as if I were stunned. Truthfully, I was. Tracy and I had had disagreements before, but never to the point where one of us had stormed off.

"Yeah. What's the point of staying somewhere where false accusations are being made against me and my friendship is being called into question?"

My phone buzzed. It was Lloyd. Tracy saw the name on my screen.

"How long are you going to allow him access to you or leave his name programmed in your phone like that?" she questioned.

"I don't know, but it's my business, and I need to take this call."

Through clenched teeth, Tracy growled, "If you answer that phone . . . Avery—"

I scoffed. "What are you going to do? Stop talking to me? You may be able to control other people like that, but it won't work on me."

"You need to block his number. This is a delicate time, and you are too vulnerable to have an open line of communication with him."

"I'm not blocking his number. There is no harm in hearing from Lloyd until I decide what to do. His ass needs to apologize every day."

"Do you know how this sounds?" Tracy condescendingly asked.

"Yes, like I'm a woman who doesn't run at the first sign of a problem."

Tracy frowned and cocked her head to the side like she was trying to figure out who I was. "That is the most ridiculous thing I have ever heard."

"And this, my dear, is why you are better off not married. You'd never make a good wife with that mentality."

"Avery, I'm sparing you because I love you, but if you keep talking to me like that, I don't know how much longer it will last."

I waved off her threat. "Whatever, Tracy. You don't know the value of a relationship. That's why you run through men like a jogger runs through a park."

Tracy's head rolled around like a ball, and her dress fell to the floor. "Excuse me," she yelled like she was trying to get the attention of someone across a parking lot.

"Why are you offended? No one in your family has ever been married or had a lasting relationship, but you expect me to listen to you for relationship advice. I don't think so."

"I'm glad to know how you really feel. Don't call me when he messes up again, because he will. And if you were someone else, I would have knocked your ass out by now. You better be glad, Avery." She shook her finger near my face. "You better be glad." Tracy took a few steps back. "And just so we are clear, that offer for you to stay at my house is off the table."

"That's fine," I hissed. "Why do I need your two-bedroom shack that was built in the sixties when I have a newly built three-story townhome?"

Tracy leaned forward and held her stomach while she hysterically laughed. "Yeah, and I can see you, Lloyd, that baby, and the baby momma living there together."

"And it will still be better than what you have," I teased.

Tracy balled her fists and stepped into my personal space. "Keep talking like you're the Big Bad Wolf. It's only a matter of time before you realize how stupid you are being."

"Woah. What is going on in here?" my dad asked. He appeared in the archway with Amil.

"Nothing's going on, Dad. Please leave us so we can talk."

My dad crossed his arms over his chest, his way of silently demanding an answer. "Sounds like a lot more than nothing. What is going on?"

Tracy turned to my dad. "I'm sorry, Dr. Booker. I'm not trying to be disrespectful in your home. I was just leaving." Tracy turned to me. "Do whatever you please, but don't call me looking for support when Lloyd breaks your heart again."

"Good, leave, and don't worry. You will be the last person I call," I blurted out to her.

"Avery, if you want to be mad, then be mad, but don't lash out at the people who have been by your side throughout this ordeal. You need to direct your anger to the right person. Tracy is not that person," my dad scolded me as he picked the pillows up off the floor and placed them back on the sofa.

"I'm not lashing out at anyone. I'm speaking the truth." I pointed toward the bay window that overlooked the driveway. "She's trying to manipulate me into being single like her. Every marriage has challenges. We just have to work through them."

"You'd have to be married first, dummy." Amil's top lip curled. He looked disgusted with me. "I'll be back," he added. "I'm taking Tracy home."

"You see?" I pointed. "She's manipulating Amil. He's running behind her like a dog in heat. He's my brother. He's supposed to stand with me."

"If I weren't in here talking to you, then I would have followed Tracy outside too. You had no reason speaking to her like that. Tracy has been a wonderful friend to you, and she is just trying to protect you."

"Protect me from what?" I wondered, where was all this protection when it mattered?

I could see my dad's chest rise and fall through his multicolored sweater. He closed his eyes and rubbed the nape of his neck. I could hear the frustration in his voice as he eased out, "Anything that can hurt you."

"Lloyd made a mistake, Dad. He said so himself. Look." I tried to show my dad the messages, but he wouldn't look. "You and Mother have had y'all fair share of problems that had to be worked through."

"Every marriage does and will. However, you have to have boundaries. If you take Lloyd back prematurely, he's going to think he can do whatever he wants without consequences. You're showing him he only needs to beg for your forgiveness and all is well."

"Some may question your boundaries and why you have stayed married to the devil all these years."

A loud thud filled the room when my dad slapped the wall. "Watch yourself."

I'd only ever gotten one spanking from him, and it did enough damage to scar me for life.

"Yes, sir." I retreated.

After Dad put the last cushion on the sofa, he sat down and patted the seat next to him. He draped his arm over my shoulder and pulled me in so that my head rested on his shoulder. "This is still fresh. It's like a death, and with that, there are multiple stages of grief. Each day will bring a new challenge. Take the necessary time and let things fall how they may. I am with Tracy. You don't want to make a rash decision and risk getting hurt again."

"You don't know that he will hurt me, Dad."

"And you don't know that he won't, Avery."

"I love him," I sobbed.

"True love doesn't go away overnight, so I understand there are still feelings. True friendship doesn't fade immediately either. You owe Tracy a huge apology. The things you said, Avery, I am disappointed in you. I have never seen you act like that, and it's all directed toward the wrong person."

"Yes, sir."

"Promise me one thing."

"What's that, Dad?"

"Give it thirty days, no contact with Lloyd, and if you still feel a need to communicate with him and work things out, then that's your choice."

"Why thirty days?"

"Absence will either make the heart grow fonder, or it will be just that—an absence that won't be missed."

"Just thirty days?" I asked.

My dad nodded. "Just thirty."

"Deal."

Chapter 8

I'd read enough about prison to understand that I was pretty much a prisoner in my parents' home. Although elective, solitary confinement was a better term to describe the past twenty-one days of my life. The only difference was that I had access to what would be considered contraband: a laptop that I was sure was dead because I never bothered to get the charger from the townhouse, and a cell phone that I barely used because Tracy and I still weren't speaking, Lloyd was blocked, and I took a hiatus from all social media platforms.

In this prison, my mother served as the warden who always tried to micromanage instead of lovingly parent. Anytime my bedroom door creaked and I emerged from my room, she'd always somehow appear. Day twenty-two was no exception.

"I hope you at least plan to comb your hair today," she said as I shuffled my way into the kitchen for a couple of bottles of water. "It looks matted."

I was sure it was matted. I hadn't taken a comb through it since the wedding, and I didn't have a plan to anytime soon. As a matter of fact, the same bobby pins that held my side bun and curls were still clinging to my hair. What was the point in combing it? I was going back in my room to swallow the other half of the Ambien anyway.

"And you can stand to shower," my mother said, sneaking in another jab.

I was already headed upstairs and didn't bother responding, nor did I turn around to greet Amil when he came through the front door.

As I was about to take the other half of the pill and snuggle back under the comforter, Amil barged into my room. "You saw me come in, and when a king enters, he requires everyone's attention," he joked and clicked on the light. He made a gesture with his hand. "Now, bow down to me."

I pulled the comforter over my head. "Not today, Amil. Turn my light off and get out." Light hadn't entered this room in I didn't know how long. The darkness matched my mood.

Typical Amil. Everything I said went in one ear and out the other. "Avery, this room is disgusting, and it stinks in here. It smells like feet and dirty mop water."

"Well, if you leave, there won't be a problem," I huffed, my face still hidden.

"I've seen some disturbing crime scenes, but this is far worse," he said and yanked the comforter off me. "This ain't you. You are so much better than this."

I ignored him.

Amil tugged at the feet of my onesie. "You need to get up and do something with yourself."

"You are so annoying," I said and kicked at his hands.

"Oh, well."

"I'm not in the mood for company. Turn my light off and close my door."

Before leaving my room, Amil turned on the bedside lamp too.

"Asshole." I got up to close the door, which he left wide open. I switched off every light. I wished I had the thought to lock the door, because no sooner than I plopped back down, Amil was back with cleaning supplies.

"Get yo' ass up," he said and brightened the room once again. "I have sat back and allowed you time to shake this off, and you haven't, so now I'm making you, and I won't stop until I see progress."

I groaned. "I'll do it tomorrow."

"The rate you're going, tomorrow may not come."

"Good." I didn't mean to say that out loud.

"Good? You're suicidal over a dude? I'm telling Pops and calling the mobile mental health people out here."

For the first time since Amil had entered my room, I turned over to face him. "No one is suicidal. Shit. Get out." I jammed my index finger toward the door.

"What does that comment mean?"

"Not suicidal, I can tell you that."

"Tell me more than that. Dumb-ass, wack-ass Lloyd has had you sequestered in this bedroom for three weeks, and it ends today." Amil completed a circle. "Look at this room. You don't live like this. This is some crazy, depressed witch shit, and I'm not going for it anymore."

This fool called me a witch.

Amil was right about one thing—my room was disgusting. I hadn't noticed until I watched him step over water bottles, old fast food bags, and clothes that littered the floor. Damn, this was embarrassing. My nightstand was worse. It was junky. More water bottles, crumbs, and used tissue decorated it.

My brother's mouth never ran low on smart-ass remarks. He had a skill set that would make a grown man cry, and I was relieved he hadn't panned me too badly over the condition of my room.

I shifted to the top of my bed and rested my back against the headboard. "Thank you, Amil."

"Thank me by getting yourself together." He opened a black garbage bag and picked up trash off the floor.

I didn't know what to say back, so I just watched him clean my room. If I told him I was trying, he'd call me out on that lie. The only thing I had done was sleep, hoping to sleep away the hurt, hoping that one day I'd wake up and it would all be gone. So far, nothing. Still the same thoughts, still the same pain.

Amil took a break from sprucing up my litter-filled nightstand. He pulled the white bench from underneath my vanity mirror close to my bed. "Can I ask you something, Avery?"

Uh-oh. I couldn't remember when my brother and I had ever had a serious conversation. The way his brows furrowed when he pulled up the seat told me this was about to be deep. "Ask away," I said and picked at the fibers of my onesie.

"Do you plan on patching things up with Tracy?"

An awkward silence filled the room. Amil was in search of answers that I didn't have myself. I didn't even have the guts to tell him that I didn't have the guts to call Tracy. My idiotic blabber mouth messed up our friendship, and I didn't want to risk saying the wrong thing again.

Amil thumped the bottom of my foot. "Well?"

I gave a half shrug.

"The two of you have too much history to throw away."

"I know."

"Tracy feels the same way the rest of us do. No one wants to see you back with Lloyd, except Lloyd himself. We all know you deserve better than him, so why settle?"

"I don't think it's settling, Amil. I am in love with him, even still." That was the first time those words were mentioned anywhere other than inside my brain. "I am ashamed to admit that. I know that if I choose to take him back, I'll lose the people I love behind that decision."

"You can love a person from a distance and not tolerate their bullshit. It does take time, but each day, you have to make an effort. Something more than staying locked away in this room." Amil looked around and shook his head. "Busy yourself to help pass the time. You can start by doing a deep clean in here."

"Shut the hell up, Amil. No matter what I do, I don't think this pain will ever stop. I can't believe I still have feelings for him after what he did."

"I get it. It takes time, though. And there is no guarantee it will fully dissolve. All I'm saying is make an effort to move forward. Look at my ex and me. It took a while to get over her, but I did, and I still have love for her. I'm not in love with her. There's a difference. I still check on her from time to time, as she does me. We have history, and while we aren't a couple, if there is anything she needs from me, depending on what it is, I help her out. That's as far as it goes. Nothing romantic."

"I just wished I hated Lloyd by now. I at least thought he wouldn't be on my mind as much, but every time I wake up, he's there. It's depressing."

"I wish you hated him too. But it's still fresh. I get that. It's easy for us to hate him because we weren't invested in him like you were. He committed the ultimate sin, and he shouldn't have access to you, period. A relationship with him doesn't need a second look. You're grown, so it's your decision either way." Amil shrugged and started sorting through my clean laundry, which had overflowed three baskets. He folded and talked some more. "I blame you, Avery, for the argument with Tracy. You got beside yourself as you do at times, and hopefully, this space has given you a chance to reevaluate some things. I think Tracy meant well in what she was trying to say." He stopped folding and, uninvited, sat on the edge of my bed. "How are you doing with the Ambien?"

There was no way I could tell him that I had become dependent on it. "Dependent" sounded better than "ad-

dicted." I didn't want to lie to my brother, nor did I want
to divulge the whole truth, so I said, "It's going."

"Going" as in "going into my body more than it should."
"Going" as in "going to cause me some serious health
problems if I don't slow down."

The bottle said I was supposed to take one ten milli-
gram pill at bedtime. Instead, I'd break one in half and
take five milligrams at night and the other five the following morning. Sometimes, I'd take even more. Ordinarily,
I fought through adversity, but what Lloyd did broke me.
I just wanted to sleep so I didn't have to feel.

"What does that mean exactly?" Amil asked.

I wouldn't dare tell him, my dad, or anyone about the
sleepwalking. I had awakened on the bathroom floor on
more than one occasion and picked myself up off the
staircase a few times. Once when my parents were out
of town, I woke up at the kitchen table with food stuck
to the side of my face. Apparently, I cooked Hamburger
Helper. Dangerous, I knew, but I refused to say anything
for fear of losing the medication. Again, it was not an
addiction, but a dependency issue that I could fix when
the time was right.

I shrugged. "The medicine is okay, I guess. I'm getting
plenty of rest."

Amil nodded. "I know. Every time I peek my head in
here, you're asleep. You should be getting ready to wean
off soon."

The dependency devil inside me called Amil all kinds
of names for insinuating we should break up. But I had
to play along. "Yeah, I can't wait to return to the norm."
Wordplay so I didn't actually lie to him. I did want to
return to normal, whatever that was. Goose bumps
covered my arms anytime I pondered how my life would
be. Lloyd was my norm. Would he be there too?

Amil's voice reminded me that he was still present. "Back to Tracy. I think it's time you reach out to her."

I shook my head. "Tracy has probably moved on with her life. We've never gone this long without speaking. I'm sure she wants nothing to do with me, and I don't blame her."

"All you women have issues." Amil rose from my bed, shaking his head. "Dudes can get into an argument and squash it immediately after. Women—y'all stay mad, die, get reincarnated, and still be mad about shit that won't even come up in your new life." He chuckled, leaned a shoulder up against the doorframe, and crossed his arms over his chest.

"Tracy has every right to stay mad. I said some harsh things. And even attacked her upbringing." I sighed and mumbled, "The one thing she wanted to distance herself from."

Meals were scarce for Tracy. The utilities were shut off and turned on like a kid playing with a light switch. Somehow, her mother faithfully paid the drug man and the liquor store across the street from their house like it was Georgia Power. And yet, Tracy championed on. After graduating from nursing school, she qualified for a first-time buyer loan and purchased a place. For the first time, and outside of college dorm beds, she had her own bed to sleep in. No more worrying about going to the neighbors to fill up jugs of water just to flush the toilet, brush her teeth, or wash up. I was proud of her accomplishments and disappointed in myself for throwing the negative shit in her face.

Amil nodded in agreement. "Indeed, you did. However, I think all it will take is a conversation, and the two of you will be right back where you started as if it never happened."

"Easier said than done. If I were Tracy, I wouldn't want to restore our friendship."

"The only way to find out is to reach out to her and lay it all out there. Be honest. She shouldn't have to assume that you are sorry. She needs to hear it." Amil dropped his hands and stepped closer to me. "As long as I've known Tracy, she's always had your best interest at heart, and just because the two of you aren't speaking doesn't mean love is lost. That girl cares about you and the decisions you make, and that's all she was trying to convey to you. You got offended."

I inhaled deeply. "Thank you, Amil."

He leaned over my bed and tapped my foot. "Thank me by doing me a favor."

"I should've known," I said and rolled my eyes. "What?"

Amil moved the vanity bench back and waved me in that direction. "Come over here."

I felt a little lightheaded, but I managed to follow him to the other side of the room. He grabbed my shoulders, repositioned me, and forced me down on the bench. "Look at yourself. In all the thirty years that we have been a part of each other's lives, I have never seen you look like this. I'm a man, and I know we do some stupid shit when it comes to women. Your situation has made me look at my actions. It's tough watching you transform from the happiest person I know to this unidentifiable person." Amil shook his head. "It's all fun and games until it hits close to home."

Tears fell from my eyes as I stared at my brother through the mirror. I had never seen myself this unkempt, nor had I witnessed Amil this transparent. He had matured because of my hurt.

"Something else," Amil said. "On behalf of the men who haven't done their part, I apologize." He leaned over and kissed my cheek. "Don't be scared to move on. Don't be scared to find out how strong you are. Don't be scared to win Tracy back. Reach out before it's too late."

I didn't get a chance to respond. A call came over the radio about a burglary in progress, and Amil shot out of the house, but not before pushing my head.

A response would've taken away from this pivotal moment anyway. I hadn't looked in a mirror since my wedding day. Not even a glimpse in the bathroom mirror. Hell, I didn't even recognize the person looking back at me through the vanity. My hair was matted, as my mother said. It looked like an old, abandoned bird's nest, and I wouldn't be surprised if there were some sort of creature living inside. My armpits reeked as if I grew and picked onions on a farm for a living.

The more I stared at myself, the more I started to realize that changes were needed and needed fast.

Chapter 9

As soon as the water from the shower touched my body, I felt better. It took a while, but I successfully washed and detangled my hair and shaved my armpits, legs, and unmentionables. They were much happier being bare than having the same amount of hair as a bear.

In the spirit of change and freshness, I took a *bold* leap. I approached my dad with the craziest idea, which he agreed would be a way to remove some bricks from my mother's wall. At least enough to get a glimpse inside.

I'd heard her complain that the house they were using to hold their book club meeting only served cheese and crackers, and she'd usually be starving afterward. I decided, along with help from my dad, to surprise my mother by having dinner ready when she returned. I even went a step further and purchased the book they read to open up a line of positive dialogue with her. I had never been much of a Christian fiction reader, but *Faith Alone* by Terri Ann Johnson had me drawn in from the first sentence.

I imagined the smile that would spread across my mother's face when she walked in and saw the barely used formal dining room table adorned with her favorite flowers—lilies and an orchid. Her smile would grow as she inhaled the scent of her favorite meal—baked chicken and brown rice (she always watched her figure). Then her eyes would drift over to the book that lay on the table beside my plate.

I should've known that my imagined version and reality would be different.

My mother's routine was predictable. It was nearly eight at night, so she was due home any minute. We had set the table and waited.

In the meantime, my dad thought it was the perfect time to ask me a question that I didn't want to answer. "How's the thirty days' no contact with Lloyd coming along?"

Why, Dad? Why? I didn't know whether to tell him the truth. Not a day had passed when I hadn't thought of Lloyd, wondered if he'd thought of me or if he had been trying to contact me. I didn't know whether to shrug it off like it was a piece of cake. The mention of cake was another trigger. Cake reminded me of the wedding cake I never tasted outside of the tasting. I couldn't wait for Lloyd and me to smash it in each other's faces. We both had fallen in love with the exquisite look of the cake. Six tiers shaped like a horse and carriage made of red velvet, German chocolate, and lemon. That rare combination was mouthwatering.

The garage door was raised, which helped me change the subject. "Your wife is home," I said instead of answering my dad's question.

"Garage door open." The alarm lady's alertness usually annoyed me, but I welcomed her creepy voice on this occasion.

"What's going on in here?" my mother asked. She set her oversized purse down and continued. "It smells wonderful."

Dad got up to greet her. "A little something special." He pecked her on the cheek.

It was my turn in line to see what kind of welcome or thanks I would get. "Hey, Mother, how was the book club meeting?"

She shrugged and then turned her attention back to my dad. "I am starving. Thank you for cooking for me. It smells and looks good."

"It was Avery's idea. She cooked it."

One of her brows lifted at the mention of my name. That was an indication that dinner would go as I expected it to and not as I hoped it would. "Oh," she responded. The suspense that covered her face grew more profound when she caught a glimpse of the book sitting next to my plate. I hoped she would acknowledge it, but instead she said, "Let me change out of these clothes, and I'll be right back down."

At least her tone was enthusiastic. Maybe there was hope after all.

My dad and I sat in silence, waiting. "This was a good start," he whispered to me, breaking the awkward quietness.

"We will see," I said. I eyed my food, anxious to dig in.

"Well, I'm proud of you for trying."

"Trying what?" my mother asked when she returned. I looked her up and down, noticing she had the same clothes on that she claimed she was going to change out of. I was convinced she hid behind a wall and eavesdropped.

"Avery's dinner," my dad answered.

Instead of addressing me, she addressed my dad. "Did you cook anything, Henry?"

"I only seasoned the chicken with that seasoning you like."

"And I did the rest," I added. "I wasn't sure of the flavoring you wanted on the chicken."

"Oh." That was it. Nothing more came from my mother's mouth. Not even a thank-you.

The scrapes of our forks against our plates were the only noise that filled the room for a while. I watched as my mother picked over her food.

"I heard you talking about this book"—I tapped it—"and I decided to buy a copy. Excellent read. What did you think about it, Mother?"

She let her fork crash to her plate like she was annoyed that I was talking to her. An expressionless look stained her face before she said, "It's a great book that teaches faith and strength when moving on from tragedy. I hope that's what you took away from it."

I attempted to ask another question, but she gathered her plate full of food and took it into the kitchen.

"Everything okay, Florence?" my dad asked.

"Yeah. I'm not so hungry after all. I am turning in early. Good night."

I sat confounded. And no matter how hard I tried to blink away the tears, they came rushing out like a floodgate had given way.

"I'm sorry, sweetheart. You may be excused. I'll take care of the dishes."

My dad didn't have to tell me twice.

I sat on the edge of my bed, reflecting on and re-thinking the possibility of moving into the townhouse. I needed to get the hell on. I knew I wasn't wanted.

Loneliness overpowered me like a robber with a gun. I needed someone to talk to. I would have called Anthony, but I was sure he'd lecture me like I was one of his students. Plus, it was late, and he had school in the morning. Or did he? What day of the week was this? Unless I looked at a calendar, I had no clue.

I could've called Tracy, and she would've been right there for me. I missed her a lot, and I wished I had a better explanation for my behavior. Love hurts. The one I loved hurt me, and I, in turn, hurt one of the ones I loved. Not that that was the excuse I'd go with, but it was accurate. I planned to contact Tracy and own up to my non direct aggression.

Tracy wasn't the only one I missed. Shame still roared through me at the thought of missing Lloyd. Usually, when my mother hurt my feelings, he was there for me. Her actions over dinner made me yearn for Lloyd.

Black slash marks on the calendar that hung on the wall near the light switch counted down the days until I could unblock him. So many questions surrounded where I stood with him. Mainly, had he forgotten about me? Had I not blocked him, where would we be? I'd considered unblocking him, but I didn't want to break my promise to my dad.

Sometimes I wondered what Lloyd was thinking. Were his thoughts about me? Did he feel like he'd lost me for good because he couldn't get through to me? Would he still want me if I decided to take him back after thirty days? Had he given up on me and moved on with Oakley? Were they a family now? Did the three of them go to doctor appointments together? Did the three of them sleep in the same bed, that kid in the middle? I had so many questions that I didn't need answers to. Answers were unhealthy. This was a sick obsession that I didn't know how to combat.

Amil's words penetrated my ears, as did the promise I made to my dad.

I grabbed my cell phone, wondering if I should text or call Tracy. Texting was so informal when apologizing, but I was afraid she wouldn't answer. What if she rejected me? After all, she told me not to call her. Instead of calling, I clicked on her Facebook page. She didn't unfriend me. I scrolled through her page, and there was nothing out of the ordinary. The usual health-tip posts. Then I saw where she had started a new job. A pediatric clinic of all places. I wondered if it was the clinic for Oakley and Lloyd's kid. Tracy would have at least told me that. *I think.*

I scrolled through my contacts until I got to the T's. Tracy's name stared at me, and all I had to do was tap to make the call. My hand rattled. The things I said to her were unforgivable, and I wouldn't blame her if she snubbed me. *She seems to have moved on with her life, so I may as well leave it alone.* I tossed my phone across the bed and returned to staring at the ceiling. I wished the spinning blades could spin away my thoughts.

Maybe I'll have enough courage to call tomorrow.

It was like Amil could read my thoughts from afar because when I looked at my vibrating phone, The Annoying Brother appeared on the screen. "Have you made that call yet?" he asked as soon as I answered.

"I was, but I chickened out. I will try again tomorrow."

"Call Tracy tonight. With my profession, tomorrow isn't promised. I see it all the time."

I nodded and accepted that tidbit of information as confirmation from God. All would be well if I called her.

I planned to call Tracy, but somehow I scrolled to Lloyd's name. It was still listed as Hubby. "Might as well go ahead and change that." I tapped on it. "Delete the number, Avery." Pointless. It was etched in my brain. I could unblock him just to see. Or I could text him. What would I say? "Hey, bighead." Nope. I'd appear healed. "How's that kid?" Nope. I couldn't care less.

Forget Lloyd. I had to do something else or I would break the promise to my dad or go crazy, if not both.

"Forget Lloyd" didn't last long. His entire existence invaded my soft spot again.

Tracy or Lloyd? I'd rather be rejected by Lloyd than Tracy.

My phone rocked back and forth within my shaking hands. It felt like the temperature in my room rose by twenty degrees. I stared at the name, trying to build up enough courage to send a text. I waited for a sign telling me not to go through with it. I couldn't take it anymore.

Deep breath.

What the hell.

I typed: I miss you.

Send.

Chapter 10

My heart fluttered while I waited for a response. I paced, and when my bedroom became too small, I ventured into the hallway. If it worked in my favor, with some effort our lives could return to the way they were before the wedding fiasco.

My phone vibrated loudly against my nightstand. Every organ pounded in my body. I crossed my fingers and hoped it wasn't rejection. I opened the text.

I miss you too. I'm so glad to hear from you. Call me when you can so we can talk.

I breathed a sigh of relief and immediately called.

"Hey, girl. I'm glad you reached out," Tracy said the minute she answered.

What a relief. Because had she not been accepting, I probably would've been foolish enough to call Lloyd.

"Tracy," I said and paused. A heavy sigh exited my parted lips before they formed to speak words. "I am genuinely sorry. I wish I had a better explanation for my behavior, other than me lashing out at the wrong person. I was and am ashamed for how I acted toward you and especially for the things I said."

"Hurt people hurt people, and I knew you were hurting. That's why I didn't whoop your ass. But you best believe I wanted to. I just hung back to give you some space. I know that we have a genuine friendship that can withstand anything. I love you, Avery. You ain't getting rid of me that easy."

"Yeah, but I don't want that to be the excuse. I was wrong on so many levels. I have always admired your ambition. You always made goals and completed them, and I used the most difficult time in your life to hurt you for no reason."

"Not saying that your actions were right. I just don't want to harp on it. There were times when I told Amil I was going to call you, and he insisted I wait because you needed to live in your mess. Sometimes, Amil acts like Anthony."

I smacked my nightstand and snickered. "Oh. My. God. I said the same thing."

Tracy and I never ran low on banter, but I was quiet, and the only sound that came from her was humming to the old-school tunes she had playing in the background.

The lack of words made me feel the need to apologize again. "No matter what I was going through, Tracy, I didn't have the right to speak to you the way I did. I can't apologize enough, and I'd like to make it up to you."

"Of course you can make it up to me, and I have the perfect idea."

"Do I even want to know?"

"Probably not, so let me hear what lame plan *you* have first."

"I was thinking of a spa day. I haven't been out of the house for fun in forever."

"I know. You've been cooped up in that hellhole sleeping your life away. A spa day will work too. But I have something better than that."

"How do you know what I've been up to?"

"Your brother has been my primary source. He runs his mouth worse than a girl. I call him or Dr. Booker."

"They never mentioned that to me." That explained how Amil knew Tracy would be receptive to me.

"Because I told them not to. I wanted to wait until you were in a better headspace."

"Well, what have they told you?"

"Plenty," she said and started laughing hysterically. "Dr. Booker told me to keep you in prayer. And Amil said you've lost so much weight that you look like a skeleton, but your head is still big, and your neck can't handle it."

"He's such an asshole."

"I hope you haven't lost that Georgia peach." Tracy chuckled a little, referring to my butt. Every girl in the South wanted a big booty except for me. Girls paid for what I had, and while Tracy talked about getting hers enhanced, I talked about getting a reduction. I hated the way my butt protruded in my scrubs and jiggled when I walked.

That wasn't the first comment I heard about my weight. The devil thought it was a good thing. She commented recently, "I guess something good is coming out of this. You're not as chunky." I ignored it like I did most of her insults. The fact that I took showers in the dark left little room for me to notice any changes in my appearance. I only noticed a change in my weight because my clothes fit differently.

"So, Avery, before we get into the logistics of our outing, raise your right hand."

Even though she couldn't see me, I knew where this was going, so I did it. "Raised."

"Do you swear to tell the whole truth and nothing but the truth so help you God?"

Tracy went way back. An oath that we hadn't used on each other since going off to college. It meant no matter how bad it was, we had to tell the truth. "I swear," I said and lowered my hand.

"How has the thirty-day no contact with Lloyd been going?"

"You know about that too?"

"I've been keeping up. It's almost over, so give it to me straight. How is it *really* going?"

"It's going," I said. "I've seen better days."

"Elaborate, please. The whole truth, remember?"

Although I shied away from telling my dad anything, the softness in Tracy's voice stroked my vulnerable side. There was no hint of the anger that I stirred up in her weeks ago, which made me comfortable divulging the whole shebang without reservations. "Oh, my God, this has been the worst." I shook my head in disbelief. "Pure misery from living in this house, dealing with the devil, and missing both you and Lloyd. I feel like I am burning in hell."

"Think about him a lot?" Tracy asked.

"I do." The oath mattered, but the reservations were in effect. I didn't want Tracy to judge me if I told her that I thought about Lloyd every minute I was awake, and in my mind, we had sex. Sometimes I pretended that Oakley and that kid didn't exist. Sometimes I wished . . . I hated myself for even wishing they'd somehow die and Lloyd would be so distraught that he'd come to me to mourn. There were times when I pretended that Lloyd and I had gotten married and how lovely our honeymoon was. I probably needed to see a shrink, but I couldn't risk them tapping into my mind, discovering I wished death on other humans, including a child.

Tracy's next question cut into my warped thoughts. "Has Lloyd tried contacting you?"

"I have no clue. A lot of random numbers have shown up on my phone, but I don't return the calls, nor do I check any of the messages."

"So absolutely no contact? No emails, secret meetings? Nothing?"

"None whatsoever. I have not communicated much with anyone outside of my family. Anthony will drop in and call with some of his wisdom. And you know Anthony. Sometimes it sticks, and sometimes it goes over my head. And one can only take Amil in small doses."

Tracy laughed. "What about your mom? How has she been?"

"Is that a trick question?"

"Well, I was hoping things had changed."

"The devil is the devil. Who knew hate could be a supersized serving with extra calories? She is so petty. When I see her, she'll either insult me or walk past me like I'm invisible. She'll speak to my dad and only my dad. On the days when I match her petty, I'll purposely talk to her only to receive a one-word reply or silence in return."

"Wow, Avery. I am so sorry you're going through all of this. What do you think her issue is now?"

"Hell if I know. I assume she's still embarrassed about the wedding. Shit, I am too."

"Her attitude has always baffled me. I wish I had some words of comfort." Tracy sighed. "Have . . . Never mind."

"Say whatever you want to say. I promise I won't flip out like last time."

"Are you tempted to reach out to Lloyd?" she asked.

I paused a long pause, thinking about how to answer. Truthfully, of course, but the matter of how truthful was up for debate. No holding back. "Very much so. And if I'm all the way truthful, there is not a day that goes by when he doesn't cross my mind." There. I admitted it.

"So what happens after the thirtieth day?"

Tracy wanted an answer I didn't have because I didn't know what I wanted myself. Even though she couldn't see me, I shrugged. "Honestly, I don't know. I have asked myself the same question. I am afraid that once day thirty hits, I will consider it a 'get out of jail free' pass and go running back to him. I don't want to relapse, but I don't think I'm strong enough just yet."

Lloyd had no way of contacting me, but I didn't delete a single picture of him from my phone. Sometimes I'd stare at the one where he was down on bended knee, proposing to me. Then I'd play the video where he asked me to be his wife. Lloyd barely got the last word out before I screamed, "Yes!"

"Earth to Avery," Tracy called out, snatching me out of the past.

"Huh?"

"Girl, where did you zone out to?"

I chuckled over my craziness. "What did you say?"

"Have you considered keeping him blocked past thirty days? More like forever."

Again, I shrugged, and again, Tracy couldn't see me. "I don't know what will happen when the thirtieth day hits."

The music on Tracy's end disappeared. "Do you feel like you've made any progress?"

I sarcastically laughed at the word "progress." "Let's see. Most days, I lie in the dark. I have forgotten about the sun and its purpose. My blackout curtains are worth every dollar spent. Unless I'm looking at a calendar or clock, I couldn't tell you if it was Monday, Wednesday, Sunday, morning, noon, or night."

"Avery, that's not like you." Concern replaced the softness in Tracy's voice. "You haven't stepped outside at all?"

"Quick, dreaded trips to the store."

"Why dreaded?" Tracy asked.

"There was one time when I was in the store shopping for feminine products and stumbled down the baby aisle. I dropped to the floor in tears. I was too distraught to drive myself home and too embarrassed to call my dad or brothers for help. A lady offered to take me home, but I refused, so she ended up calling me an Uber. A few days later, I called an Uber to take me to pick up my car."

Tracy sniffed. "Oh, my God. You are making me cry."

"I cry all the time when I'm not asleep. I have no desire to do anything unless I have to, which will explain the comments about my weight. Food just isn't a priority. I force myself to eat. Every two days, I'll order fast food and inhale it in a matter of seconds. It always results in an Olympic sprint to the bathroom. I think my stomach walks around with a 'return to sender' attitude from the grease buildup. The only vegetables I eat are the lettuce and tomatoes on my burger."

For the next few minutes, Tracy and I shared sobs over the phone.

Through sniffles, Tracy said, "I'm sorry I haven't been a support system. I know last time didn't go so well, and I apologize for the part I played. I'm willing to help you through this. What can I do to make things better for you, friend?"

That warmed my heart, and I too was in the sniffles line. "I wish I knew. There is no need for you to apologize. This is all on me. You mentioned us hanging out. Maybe that's a start. Simply because I'm ecstatic you're willing to pick up where we left off after how mean I was to you, I'm willing to do whatever you want. What do you have in mind?"

Tracy laughed. "What I'm about to request might not go over so well. Remember what you said, though. You'd do anything."

"Aw, shit." After our laughter settled, I cleared my throat and added, "Before you say anything more, thank you, Tracy. Thank you for not holding my shortcomings against me."

"No worries. Don't let it happen again, or I'm going to beat your ass like you stole from me and slapped my momma."

Not only did it feel good to laugh with Tracy, but it felt good to laugh, period. "Now, let me hear this idea."

Without any hesitation, she said, "I want you to go to Tri-Me Dating Agency with me."

"Oh, hell, no. I'm not doing that, Tracy."

"You owe me, Avery, and I think it will be fun. Let me try to hook you up."

"With all due respect, if you can't hook yourself up, how do you expect to hook me up?"

"What better way to get over Lloyd? What better way to buy more time before you potentially relapse?"

"Nope."

"I'm going to be honest with you," Tracy said. "Lloyd has reached out to me."

I jumped up from the edge of my bed, bumping into the nightstand and knocking over a glass of water. "Are you serious?"

"Yes. That trifling Negro begged me to give you a message. He professed his love for you, and I told him he needed to be telling that to the trick he got knocked up."

"Wow." My mouth hung open as I listened to her and watched the water stain my rug.

"He called a couple of times, trying to swindle his way back. At least see what's out there before you settle for Lloyd."

"I don't know what to say about Lloyd."

"There's nothing to be said. I told him if he contacted me again, I would track down his baby momma and tell her what he was up to and unleash Amil on him again. Haven't heard from him since, so that's an indication he's up to no good, or he wouldn't care if I told."

"Or maybe he's scared of my brother." I had to add that in. Even with what Lloyd did, I still was not ready to accept him having feelings for another woman.

"That too."

After a brief pause, I eased out, "Tracy, I have a confession."

"I'm listening," she said with compassion in her voice.

"A part of me wants to hear from Lloyd. Part of me still wonders if there is a way to accept the title of stepmother. People have done it before, so it's possible. Then I feel stupid for even considering the idea. As long as he is still trying to get with me, Oakley doesn't really have him. I know that sounds stupid, but it's the truth, and it's soothing."

"I can't say I understand, because I know you deserve so much better. And I can't let you walk away from your job. Think about it. You haven't been practicing long, but you are one of the most respected sought-after African American ob-gyns in this city. Are you going to let some selfish Negro and tramp ruin everything you have worked so hard for? You're so much stronger than this."

"I don't feel like I am."

"Don't talk like that, Avery. Everything happens for a reason, and the reason for this is Lloyd doesn't deserve you. There is something else out there waiting for you."

"But you liked Lloyd."

"Indeed, I did. That was pre-Oakley."

I laughed at "pre-Oakley."

"So either you're going to try the dating agency with me, or I'm picking you up and taking you to Lowe's."

"Taking me to Lowe's for what?"

"To pick out your rocking chairs, and then we can head over to the pet store and get you a couple of cats. Old-ass cat lady."

"You make me so sick, Tracy."

"Good. Since you're sick, head on over to the hospital to get checked out. While you're there, clock in, because there are so many women who need you. Think about the young black girls who come to you, scared and mistakenly pregnant, yet you convince them it's not too late to make something of themselves. Don't let the gift God gave you diminish because of Lloyd. He's not worth it. And I'm not saying take the guys from the dating agency home. Just develop conversations, get out of the house, and see if it helps take your mind away from everything else."

I conceded. "You're killing me. How does this dating place work?"

"I thought you'd see it my way. It's called Tri-Me Dating Agency because it has three phases. First things first, you only have to commit to one session with a particular person. That's about two hours of your life. If it doesn't work, you send him to the discard pile at the end of the night. In phase one, you and your date are blindfolded to see if there's chemistry from conversation alone. In the second phase, you remove the blindfold and have dinner to see if there's a physical attraction and even more chemistry. In the third and final phase, you decide if you would like to go on a second date with the person outside of the agency. If not, you place him in the discard pile. That simple."

"Doesn't sound simple or interesting."

"It's fun, and it will be good for you to get out of the house. You never know, you may meet someone you like. An Idris-looking brother who will make Lloyd become a distant memory. Just *try* it. Get it, Tri, like the agency?"

"Yeah, I get your corny joke. I'm probably the only chick who doesn't want to take my panties off for Idris. I don't have a flair for dark-skinned guys or accents. I like my men with light skin and kind of fluffy. Plus, dating agencies are filled with creeps, pedophiles, losers, and serial killers, but since I owe you, I don't have a choice."

"Yay! Well, I'm about to come over there to set up your profile for them to match you. And besides, the streets are filled with the same type of people. It's up to you to discern who's who."

"Ugh, just sign me up."

Chapter 11

The first date sucked. I got all dressed up for nothing. Well, there was one exception. It felt good for my skin to have something against it besides sweatpants and holey T-shirts that looked like someone did a drive-by on them. Although the plum-colored bodycon dress with a low-cut back that I paired with taupe heels cost under fifty bucks, it could've been used for something more productive. Hell, based on the conversation, or lack thereof, I didn't think Malcolm would have minded the sweats and T-shirt, especially considering his attire once the blindfolds came off.

At least the ambiance of the place was beautiful. The dimly lit building wasn't that big. About the standard size of a chain restaurant. Each small square table seated two guests and was accented with floating candles and a vase with roses.

Upon arrival, the ladies were given a number and ushered into one section away from the men, who I later learned were given the same number as their match for the evening. The ladies were blindfolded and seated first, and then the men joined, also blindfolded. When our dating assistant, as the agency referred to them, brought my date to the table, of course I couldn't see anything, so we were introduced.

"Malcolm, you will be joining Avery this evening."

"Avery, it's a pleasure," he said through his New Orleans accent that I happened to find attractive.

Major plus.

"I love your accent. Are you from New Orleans?"

"Yeah."

"How did you end up in Augusta?"

"My uncle was stationed at Fort Gordon, and when Katrina hit, he took us in."

"Oh, wow, I am sorry to hear that."

"It's cool."

"Have you ever had plans of returning?"

"Here and there, but I'm cool for now."

Malcolm's phone sounded. I thought because he was on a date he would ignore it, but he answered. "Excuse me one second." Then I heard him say, "Hey, Momma, what's going on?"

She talked loudly, but not loud enough for me to hear what their conversation was about. Malcolm stayed on the phone with her for a while. By the time he remembered I was there, it was time to remove our blindfolds. I'd admit he wasn't bad looking—definitely not what I was used to, but not too shabby. I always went for the light-skinned brothers who looked like Al B. Sure!, and Malcolm didn't fit that color spectrum. He was darker than I was used to, but he had the most beautiful golden-brown eyes that offset his mocha skin tone. His face was bare, not a strand of facial hair other than his eyebrows, which was another thing I liked. What I didn't like was the manifold wrinkles that covered his faded FUBU shirt. Had he taken the time to dress to impress, then maybe I would've overlooked his unique obsession with his momma, at least for a second date.

It was one thing to love and respect your mother, but needing to include her in everything was a bit too much for me. My vibe-o-meter must've been broken, because I didn't pick up on it until midway through the date. Every time a text popped up on Malcolm's phone, he smiled, paused the conversation with me, and responded to the message. I'd never seen a man's thumbs type so fast. His thumbs typed at least sixty words per minute. If I had to guesstimate, Malcolm received about thirteen text messages. One after another. A chime here and a ding there. He continued to respond as if I weren't sitting across from him, looking scrumptious.

He caught my "black girl with an attitude" expression. Head cocked to the side, eyes bucked or slanted depending on the level of anger. I felt as if my eyes displayed both. And let's not forget about the disproportioned lips that looked like I was on the verge of having a quack-off with a duck.

"I'm sorry for being rude. It's my mom. She's at home sick," he said before his thumbs went back to dancing with his keyboard.

That explained his behavior. I felt terrible. He had sacrificed taking care of his sick mother to come on this date. "No, I'm sorry. I shouldn't have been insensitive. We can end the date early if needed."

Malcolm didn't notice what I said. His phone was his focus again.

Surrounding noise from other dates kept me entertained more than my date did. At one point, I had gotten too comfortable with the couple sitting beside us. I laughed at their jokes and commented as if I were with them. I didn't realize I was invading their privacy until the girl gave me the same "black girl attitude" face that I had given to Malcolm. I sat back in my chair with my hands up in surrender.

I waved my hand near his face to get his attention. "Do you need to go?" I whispered when he finally noticed me. Him looking at me didn't mean a damn thing.

When he finally addressed me, he asked, "What'd you say, Momma?"

Attitude again. "Excuse me? Momma?" He didn't know me well enough to give me a pet name, and "momma" was the worst of them all.

He shook his head. "My bad. I was thinking about my momma and accidentally called you her." He giggled to himself.

Potential momma's boy.

I sipped my watered-down soda that Malcolm ordered for us. He requested extra ice. I love ice, but not extra. I went along with it to not emasculate him. "You and your mom seem pretty close." That was my way of alluding to him being a momma's boy.

Malcolm's eyes, nose, and mouth distorted a little. *Is he getting emotional?*

"I get so passionate talking about my momma. She's my heart. I don't know what I would do without that woman. When she dies, they may as well bury me with her. She is my true love, and no one will ever come before her."

Complete momma's boy.

Not that I had high hopes, but I could already tell that Malcolm was not for me. Although, I was curious to know his position with taking on a wife. Maybe he didn't know that his wife must come before his mother. I glanced at my watch. We still had time left on the date, and I already knew he was headed to the discard pile, so for the sake of finishing out the date, I decided to explore his perception of marriage and family order.

"So, Malcolm, have you been married before?"

"You know, I haven't been married before, but I want to be. I have been engaged. Needless to say, that didn't work out."

Wonder why. I was confident it had to do with the unhealthy obsession with his momma.

Malcolm's phone caught his attention again. Instead of him silencing it, he silenced me. "Hold that thought," he said, and he started speed typing with his thumbs once more.

While I waited for Malcolm to socially return to our date, I looked around at the other dates who were smiling and gazing into one another's eyes, phones nowhere in sight. Tracy's bighead ass was around here somewhere. If I'd had a rubber band, I would have popped her for dragging me here and convincing me that I would have a blast.

"Sorry about that. I might have to cut this date short."

Woohoo! Music to my ears.

"Is everything okay?" I only asked because it was the right thing to do.

"Yeah, my momma needs me to bring her some juice and soup."

Hold on. Was that the "emergency escape a date" plan? I had called Tracy plenty of times to get her out of dates, but with valid excuses. Malcolm was going with juice and soup.

I gulped what little soda I had in my glass. "Trust me. I understand if you need to go. It's okay." And it was okay because my ass was past ready to go.

"I can probably chill for a minute. Let me call and ask my momma if she needs it right now."

"No. No. I insist. Take care of your mom. That's important."

Not only did he not listen to me, but he needed permission from his momma, and this dude had the nerve to put the phone on speaker. During. Our. Date.

Sick? Was Malcolm referring to his momma's cough, which blared through the phone every minute? She coughed a lot, but it seemed to come more from cigarettes than anything.

"I think you are going to like this one, Momma. She real pretty. I told you this dating thing would pay off."

This one? How many have there been?

"I'm sure she's better than that one you tried to marry. Anything is better than that heffa." His momma's coughs had to be contagious, because I started coughing.

"Wait until you meet her. Shaquita ain't got nothing on her."

Shaquita?

Did Malcolm realize he was on a date?

We had a little under ten minutes before we moved into the last phase. Maybe if I texted Malcolm, we could communicate.

"You wanna talk to her, Momma?"

This had to be a joke. He was testing me.

"Don't embarrass me." Malcolm held his phone out for me to take. I didn't want to, but I was put on the spot. "Here, my momma wanna holla at you right quick."

The girl with the attitude whose conversation I imposed upon laughed at me when I hesitated to take the phone.

"Hello," I said in a whisper.

Such a shame that Malcolm's mom couldn't match my volume. "Hey there, baby. I can't wait to meet you," she said, yelling into the speaker.

The couple to the other side of us looked over and frowned. I mouthed, "I'm sorry," and then to Malcolm's momma, I said, "Thank you so much." What else was I supposed to say? And meet me? Her son was a no-go.

She coughed. "You should join us tomorrow for Sunday dinner."

Doubt it. Double doubt it if she was cooking. Not with all that coughing going on. "Thank you so much, and I hate that I will have to decline your invite, but I eat at my parents' house every Sunday after church. My mother usually cooks a big meal." Okay, I stretched the truth a bit. We only had Sunday dinner at my parents' house during football season, and it was football season, so that part was true. However, there were the untruths. My dad grilled something every Sunday during the season. My mother seldom cooked for us, and when she did, we were too scared to indulge because we were afraid she had poisoned us. And I hadn't stepped foot into a church since . . . well, since the baby thing.

"Maybe next Sunday, or the Sunday after that," she said.

Just like a loving mother to want the best for her child. There won't be another anything, especially not after what I saw flash atop Malcolm's phone. It was a message from the infamous Shaquita. There were heart emojis and words that said, Can't wait to see you tonight.

What has Tracy gotten me into? Her ass is mine.

This was the perfect exit for me. "Well, ma'am, Malcolm has an incoming message, so I am going to pass the phone back to him. Thank you again for the invite, and I hope you get to feeling better soon."

When I handed him the phone, he continued talking to his momma. I wondered if she knew he was planning to see "Shaquita the heffa," as she referred to her.

"I think so too, Momma. I know everyone at home will like her."

I didn't know what his momma said to him, but I wanted to know who everyone at home was. And how could this man like me and want to take me home to meet his family when he hadn't asked the necessary questions to get to know me? And because I couldn't compete with his phone, I'd been unable to learn anything about him either. Other than he should probably just date his momma.

"I need to get back to this beautiful woman, but what's on the menu for tomorrow?"

I checked the time on my phone again, and there were messages from Lloyd. I had unblocked him on the thirty-second day (yesterday). And since then, I'd gotten messages from him multiple times. I had convinced myself not to read them, not yet anyway. Even though I awarded him access to me, I eventually wanted Lloyd to be the history Anthony taught. That was a lie. I still had feelings for Lloyd, and him begging for my attention appealed to me. It made me feel wanted even though he committed the ultimate betrayal. I planned to respond to the messages eventually, late at night. I could say something like, "I'm just getting home," and he'd want to know where I'd been, and I'd gleefully tell him that I was on a date.

Malcolm rubbed his hands together. "Whew, that menu tomorrow gon' be lit."

Lit. What I want to do to Tracy—light her ass on fire for this.

"You sure you can't come over? I like you and want to get to know you better. We can make our plates and go to my room and watch a movie away from everyone else. Just the three of us."

Did I need to ask who the third person was? His momma would be the third wheel. Hell no, I would be the third wheel. She probably made his plate, cut up his food, and fed it to him. Curiosity got the best of me with "everyone else." "You guys expecting family over?"

Malcolm squinted as if I were speaking a language he didn't comprehend. "What do you mean?"

"You said we could go in your room away from everyone else. I'm asking if you all were expecting family over for Sunday dinner. Is it always at your house, or do y'all rotate houses?"

"Oh, nah," Malcolm said through giggles. "We are tight-knit. We all live in one big house."

I crunched down on the piece of ice that accidentally went in my mouth but wouldn't find its way out when I spit my drink back into my glass. I stared in disbelief but couldn't resist asking, "How many people live with you?"

"Nine." He held up a finger for each person. "It's my uncle's house. Remember? He took us in after the hurricane. Then it's me and my momma. We share the basement."

He shares living quarters with his momma, too.

"Then my grandma and stepgranddaddy, my momma's sister, her husband, and their two kids."

Maybe this was why he and Shaquita broke up.

Curiosity again. "Did Shaquita live there too?" This was one part joke and one part seriousness.

"Yeah, but her and my momma got into it when she suggested we get our own place. She said she didn't have enough privacy. I don't know why not. There was a partition separating the room, so it's not like my momma could see what we were doing."

Oh, dear. The couple next to us looked over again. I could've melted like the ice in my mouth. I shrugged at them. What the hell? I was officially embarrassed anyway.

"So, Shaquita left?"

"Kind of. She gave me an ultimatum. I had to choose between her and my momma, and I will never choose anyone over my momma, so Shaquita had to go."

The same Shaquita who texted a few minutes ago, excited to see him later. Let's see if he was a liar as well as a momma's boy. "So, Malcolm, do you and Shaquita still talk?"

"Nah, not at all."

"Well, you may want to check your phone."

My first date was over, and I knew Malcolm was headed into the discard pile within the first few minutes.

Chapter 12

Date number two. Although I wasn't expecting much, I vowed to be open-minded. When I filled Tracy in on my date with Malcolm, she said I was too critical of him. I felt as if I had to be critical and cautious with every person I met. I didn't want to get hurt again. But because dear, sweet Tracy spent her hard-earned money for me to find happiness, I decided I'd approach the second date with less criticism.

What was she thinking anyway? Three sessions. A different guy every week, and she expected me not to find flaws. I was sure not one of them would woo me in any way nor fulfill the cravings that I still had for Lloyd. Craving him gave me more insight into a person addicted to nicotine. Hard to let go. Promising yourself just one more puff, needing just that slight satisfaction to get by. Only I hadn't been getting by. I'd only been making things worse by allowing Lloyd's messages to entertain me. At times, I wanted to track Oakley down, show them to her, and turn the tables a little.

For this date, I settled on an outfit that was a little more church-ish. A skirt that covered my knees and a long-sleeved blouse, which I tucked in to show off my tiny waistline in case I was matched with someone who had potential. I could hike up the skirt and tie the blouse in a knot to give me a little more sex appeal.

As with the first date, I was blindfolded and seated before Anton was introduced to me. Through his blindfold, he searched out my hand.

"Your hands are so soft. They feel like silk," I said once our skin connected.

"I have a great manicurist," he said.

Okay, that was a little rude. Not a single thank-you for the compliment I gave.

Outside of the lackluster conversation, there were quite a few things about Anton that I didn't like once the blindfolds came off. First, we revisited the topic of manicures.

"Remind me to give you the number to my manicurist," he offered. "He will do wonders with your nails." He frowned a bit when he looked at my fingers.

Since we were still stuck on the conversation of nails, I asked, "So, do you get manicures often?"

"Oh, God, yes, who doesn't?" He looked at my nails again, and that same grimace decorated his face.

What angle was Anton going for with the nails? My nails weren't terrible. My gel polish was only a week old. Technically, I wasn't working, but I said, "In my profession, it's kind of hard to have my nails done as often as I'd like. But I do think it's amazing. I don't know too many men who will go out and get a manicure, let alone keep up with them."

He nodded as he sipped his tea. That bothered me too. I couldn't help but stare at the female ring he sported on his pinky finger. It stood at attention every time he sipped, giving me the impression that he attended tea etiquette classes or frequented some freaky adult tea parties.

Anton put me in the mind of Scottsdale, especially with the dark gray neck scarf wrapped tightly around his neck. It was chilly outside, I'd give him that, but I thought he was going more for fashion than anything. The scarf was color coordinated with his neatly pressed light blue buttoned-down shirt and gray blazer. As much as he pulled and tugged at it, I wished he would have just taken it off.

Speaking of Scottsdale, he had recently devastated my mother when she tried to go behind my back and talk him into asking me out since Lloyd left me at the altar. Scottsdale had finally revealed his sexual orientation to her. My mother didn't tell me about it. Scottsdale told me himself. I didn't know if the thrill came from her being wrong or the satisfaction in me being able to say, "I told you so," if the opportunity ever presented itself.

Anton and I were clearly not compatible. The more I studied him, the more I was convinced he'd be better suited for someone of his own gender. But, for the sake of being optimistic, there was no harm in going out on a limb, a tiny one at that, and making small talk.

"That's a beautiful ring. Is it symbolic?" I asked.

He slurped from his mug, adjusted his scarf, and said, "Yes, it is."

"What does it symbolize?" I didn't know why, but I too toyed with the neckline of my blouse.

Anton twisted the ring around his finger a few times, but he never answered the question. He looked around the event like he had become uncomfortable because I asked about his ring. I had no intention of robbing him. I was simply making conversation.

"Is everything okay, Anton?"

"Yes, it is."

Oh, my God. Were there any other words in his vocabulary? *Let me try a different approach.* "What do you do for a living?"

"Chef."

Okay. Still not a complete sentence, but at least it's more than, "Yes, it is."

"What's your specialty dish?" The perfect question since our meals had arrived.

"Pancakes."

"I love pancakes. I bet you have some secret recipe." I smiled and playfully winked.

"No, I don't."

"What makes your pancakes better than others?"

He shifted in his chair and adjusted his scarf again before saying, "The batter."

Even though he wasn't saying much, at least we were conversing. He was going to the discard pile for sure, but if he opened up some more, I could at least vet him for Scottsdale.

"What is the name of the restaurant you work for? I'd love to try those infamous pancakes."

"IHOP."

I choked on my water. "IHOP? As in International House of Pancakes? IHOP?"

"Yes."

I was not knocking anyone's profession, but the way Anton talked and acted, I thought he was an actual chef at an upscale restaurant. It was an income, but he was a cook, not a chef.

Silence passed the time between us as we ate our meal. Certainly wasn't pancakes. I opted for the salmon and asparagus while Anton ordered chicken wings. His scarf served another purpose. It collected the chicken wing sauce and grease from his hands.

I reached over and handed him a stack of napkins.

"My scarf is a lot thicker than those cheap napkins," he said and sucked chicken wing juice from his thumb.

Who does this guy think he is? He criticized everything except for his minimum-wage job. He was too bougie acting and flamboyant to work at IHOP. I didn't say a word. I had lost my appetite, watching what was going on in front of me. The elegance while sipping his tea was immediately gone when the plate of wings hit the table. Anton chewed and smacked, and the once-solid-colored scarf that he used to accentuate his outfit was now multicolored.

I glanced at my watch. We still had about twenty minutes before I could toss him into the discard pile.

Anton guzzled his water. "Whew, these wangs hot. We need this on our menu at work."

Mr. Bougie just said "wangs" instead of "wings." Maybe I looked at this all wrong. Perhaps Anton worked at IHOP part-time to supplement his income while he paid his way through school. "How long have you worked at IHOP?" I asked.

He slurped in air, trying to cool his mouth. "Eight years."

Okay, wrong theory, unless he's in med school or law school.

"What do you like most about your job?"

He slurped again. "It provides for my kids."

"I love kids." I still did, but I just didn't want to be around them right now. "Maybe I will be fortunate enough to have a couple one day." *Whenever I move on from wedding memories, if ever.*

"Yeah, well, I'm done. I have enough. They take all my cash. Providing for them on an IHOP check ain't cutting it. I have one side gig, and I'm thinking about starting a mobile manicure business." He looked at my nails again, reached into his pocket, and handed me a business card for mobile car detailing. "Five dollars off for you as a first-time customer."

I stared at the card, not because I was interested but because I was shocked that he was trying to secure a sale instead of a second date. Before things got out of hand, I changed the conversation. "How old are your kids, if you don't mind me asking?"

"Two of 'em fifteen, then the others are eight, six, three, one, and one on the way."

Those were the most words he'd uttered since we had met, and I gulped at what I heard. *Dare I ask?* I did. "You have a set of twins? That seems fun. I always wanted to be a twin."

He frowned. "No, I don't. Regular brothers."

"Oh, okay." I started doing the calculations in my head. "When is the new baby due?"

He looked at his ring. "She in labor now."

My mouth dropped. "And your ring tells you that?"

"Yes, it does, actually. It's a ring clock."

"Well, shouldn't you be there in the delivery room instead of out on a date?"

"I don't think the kid is mine. Until that is proven, she kind of on her own."

I shrieked. I should have taken him home to my mother and given her a heart attack for the fun of it.

Date number two. Disaster. Was this all that was out there? And how did I mistake him for being gay when he was clearly a ladies' man? Anton was like a chameleon. His vocabulary and personality steadily changed throughout the date.

His phone rang. He answered. *Not another Malcolm.* When he hung up, he said, "Ay, I'ma scoot out. My cousin up at the hospital, and she said the baby looks just like me."

I raised my glass. "Congratulations."

Maybe taking Lloyd back and working through our issues wouldn't be so bad, after all.

Chapter 13

Lord knows I dreaded the third round of Tri-Me. I was convinced they had nothing in their database that I wanted to try.

I'd been punctual with my arrival the last two times, but for the final date, I took my time. I didn't focus as much on my appearance, nor did any nerves flutter throughout my body, causing me to wonder what my date would think of me. Quite frankly, I didn't care anymore. This was all a joke. A waste of time. A way for some greedy entrepreneurs to make a buck off of desperate people looking for love. It didn't exist. At least not with the people they greenlit.

No body-hugging dress this time. No Laura Ingalls–looking attire either. I threw on some distressed jeans, a white tank top that I covered with a blazer, and a pair of heels. I kept it casual. If I were to magically find someone, this was what he was going to have to accept outside of scrubs *if* I decided to return to work.

Because I was late, my date was already blindfolded and waiting for me. As usual, the dating assistant introduced us. "Avery, this is Nate, your date for the evening."

He greeted me, but the scent of his cologne took my breath and words away. The smell was familiar yet rare. It was delightful. It was so Lloyd. "I'm sorry, what was your name again?" I only asked because I had to make sure this wasn't some elaborate scheme that Lloyd was using to see me since I still hadn't responded to his messages.

"I'm Nate. It's Nathaniel, actually, but everyone calls me Nate."

His tone seemed frigid, like it lacked the warmth of confidence. This was definitely not Lloyd. He exuded confidence on so many levels, specifically when speaking.

"There's a rarity about your cologne," I said.

"I hope that's not a bad thing."

It was and it wasn't, but there was no need to go into the particulars with Nate. "I like the smell."

"Thank you, Miss Avery. I am somewhat of a kitchen chemist. I play around with smells to create something different. I hope to launch a fragrance line one day."

The ambition was sexy. "Wow, that's an amazing goal. I tried that once with lotion, and it was a disaster. I think every potential customer, who happened to be my family, ended up with some kind of rash. Good thing it was free and they were just my test dummies."

Nate and I laughed. That wasn't the only thing we laughed about. We shared a lot about ourselves in a little amount of time. I didn't want to speak too soon, but this date felt different from the others. I felt like once the blindfolds came off, there'd be a frog staring back at me that a kiss wouldn't be able to fix. Things were going way too smoothly. Too good to be true, maybe. When the MC announced that it was time to remove our blindfolds, I hesitated. I didn't want his looks to expose my shallow side. I was okay with Nate and me being pen pals, never having to put a face to the voice that had warmed up to me.

I slowly untied my blindfold and let it sashay from my face. It wasn't until I heard, "Wow, you are absolutely stunning," that I opened my eyes to see if I would feel the same way about Nate. I wasn't disappointed at all. He was one of those light-skinned brothers who excited me.

I think Tri-Me may have finally gotten it right.

"Excuse me for staring the way that I am," Nate said.

I blushed. I had no problem with him taking in all of me because I was doing the same to him. From what I could see physically, I liked everything about him. His muscles, specifically his man pecks, protruded through the button-down shirt that looked like George Jefferson himself professionally pressed it. And because I was a stickler about facial hair, I was glad that he only had a thin mustache, which was neatly trimmed. The bald head added extra points.

We both sat staring and smiling at one another for so long that we barely noticed the dating assistant when he set our food down.

"So, Nate, besides mixing concoctions of fragrances, what else is it that you do?"

After he finished chewing his food and dabbing the sides of his mouth with a napkin, he politely answered, "I'm an entrepreneur. I own my own landscaping business. If things go well between us, maybe I can get you to help me sometimes. I bet you'd look even more astonishing pushing a lawnmower or planting some flowers."

I chuckled. "I doubt that. I am highly allergic to grass. In fact, I have an EpiPen in my purse just in case."

"What is it that you do for a living?" Nate asked.

That dreaded question. I knew it was coming, and no matter how many times I rehearsed a flattering answer in my head, I would look crazy no matter how it was explained. There was something about Nate, though, and I felt I could be honest without the rehearsed lines. "Although I am on a hiatus, I am a doctor."

"An African American doctor. And I am lucky to be on a date with her. So I must ask . . ."

And here it goes—the why behind the hiatus.

"How is such a beautiful, successful woman single?"

Okay, not the question I expected. If I gave Nate the complete rundown, he would certainly think I was crazy. If I gave him tidbits, he would certainly think I was crazy. What the hell. Either way, I'd be crazy. I'd been humiliated a time or two in my life. I inhaled and recapped in one breath, "I was engaged to be married, and while at the altar, my soon-to-be husband's mistress showed up and announced that she was pregnant with his baby." I shrugged and sipped my water, awaiting Nate to escort himself from the table.

"Holy shit."

"My thoughts exactly."

"I don't know what to say other than to thank him for messing up and giving me a chance to show you how a man should treat a woman."

That left me speechless. The only thing I could do was stare at Nate, hoping he would ask me out on a second date, because I had no intention of sending him to the discard pile.

"Did you come here with someone?" he asked.

"My friend, Tracy. She's around here somewhere. But we came in separate cars." I looked around, but not hard enough. I didn't care about her at this moment.

"Will she mind me escorting you to your car after we make our final decision?"

"I'm sure she won't, but I am grown. And who says I'm not sending you to the pile of rubbish?"

"This." Nate lifted my hand to his lips and planted one of the softest kisses to the back of my hand, which left a lasting impression.

Wherever Tracy was, she could stay there. I'd catch her up to speed later.

Nate walked me to my car, and strangely enough, he had parked one car over from me. Not only was he appealing to me physically and professionally, but he also drove the same car as me. His black BMW 3 Series matched my white BMW 3 Series. A space separated them. Our vehicles looked like his and hers.

I couldn't believe he had a little business about himself and still roamed the planet as a single man.

"Nate," I said softly as if I didn't want anyone else to hear.

"Yes, beautiful."

"I have a question."

"Ask me anything."

"From what I've seen tonight, all impressive. Why are you single?"

He laughed. "Because I was waiting for you."

Any other time I would have called bullshit, but I was enveloped and mesmerized by his charm all at once.

"So, about a second date . . ."

Luckily, Nate asked, and I gladly accepted. I couldn't wait to go out with him again. He was the first man who made me partially forget Lloyd was still breathing.

Chapter 14

Tracy's words vibrated against my eardrums like a catchy hook to a song. *"One way to get over one man is to get under another."* I never believed that because I never had to. While Lloyd still messaged me and periodically found his way into my thoughts, Nate stormed in and pushed Lloyd out of close view. The newness was refreshing. Plus, Nate's obligation to God and the church was magnetizing. With Lloyd, it was damned if we went and damned if we didn't. And most times, it was damned if we didn't. So, we didn't. It became routine, and God slowly evaporated as an essential component in my life.

Nate spoke freely of his faith and encouraged me to give the church another chance. His positive outlook gave me the energy to revisit the idea of repairing my relationship with God. Not church. Not right now. Maybe not ever. The wedding humiliation played a part, and so did my mother. Growing up, attending church was a requirement, and every Sunday, I'd sit on the pew and refute the message being delivered. It wasn't because I didn't believe in God. I did. It was because I watched hypocrites like my mother turn her Christianity off and on like a water hose. Her behavior made me question everyone's authenticity, including the pastor, the first lady, the deacons, the ushers, and even the Sunday school teacher. And if a member wore one of the big fancy hats, big question mark. I always felt like those hats were hiding the evil in a person. My mother wore them faithfully, and she hid multiple personalities.

At times the sermon would engulf my interest and make a home with me. But I hadn't given much attention to church since a few years into dating Lloyd. It grew worse after the wedding didn't happen. Unlike most individuals who relied heavily on God when evacuating storms, I started to doubt His existence. I wouldn't say I turned full-blown atheist, but I was more of a questioner. If God existed, why would He send a tornado to scoop me up, whirl me around, and not place my feet on solid ground? He left me in the middle of a place devastated with rubbish and no tools to dig myself out.

It wasn't until Nate asked if he could pray with me over the phone that I began to reconsider God in a genial way.

"Do you realize that, since meeting, we've spent every night talking on the phone?" Nate asked.

"Have we?" I said and rewound the days in my head.

"I can't wait to see you again, Avery. I have enjoyed every minute of getting to know you."

I blushed. "I can't wait to see you again either, Nate."

"Since we are on the topic of seeing each other, when will you have time for me to take you out?"

"You call it. Now that the Thanksgiving chaos has settled, I am pretty much free. I've already done most of my Christmas shopping online."

"Are you open to allowing me to plan the entire date?"

"Aw, shucks. Absolutely." I was excited to see what he would conjure up.

"And are you open to one more thing?"

I frowned. I didn't know where the question was headed. *It better not be anything inappropriate.* "What's that?"

Nate must've heard the uneasiness in my voice. "It's nothing bad. I just want to know if I can pray for you before we hang up."

The air was sucked from my lungs with a vacuum.

"Avery, you still there?"

"Uh . . . yeah."

"Did I say something wrong?"

"Absolutely not. Of course you can pray for me."

At his request, I closed my eyes, bowed my head, and listened to him bring me back to a familiar place. Other than my dad and pastor, no man had ever asked to pray for me before. I had to start somewhere if I hoped to model Nate's gumption for Christ.

Nate ended the prayer, and we ended our phone call for the night.

Pivotal moments of life replayed behind my closed eyes while the parts of Nate's prayer that I remembered filled in the silence of my dark bedroom. Not dark because I was depressed, but dark because I wanted time to find my way back to God without any distractions.

A feeling hit me. An urge to jump up and retrieve from a box in my closet the journal that Tracy gifted me to detail my wedding. It was black with gold, glittered letters: TAKE ONE STEP AT A TIME. She believed in journaling her feelings and life events. My vantage point of her journals looked more like "fight first, then journal details of the fight, especially who won." I never used it, but I decided to try a revised version of her suggested method. Instead of using it as a feelings tracker, I would write letters to God.

I shielded my face from the LED bulb. The brightness stunned my vision like I had just been snapped in a gloomy alley by unsuspected paparazzi. I rummaged through the box, leaving another mess for Amil to clean up. I grabbed the journal, a pen, and the pink floral Bible that I ordered from Amazon. New Life Version, the only version I somewhat understood, in a sketchy, "don't bet on me reciting a passage" kind of way. The Good Book rested in the palm of my hands as I sat on my bed.

Everything in me was ready to engage whatever scripture I was led to read.

"God, I know it's been a while. I am heavily burdened. Burdened to the max, and I am at a loss on what to do. God, I need some encouragement and a lot of uplifting. Why me? Why this much hurt? As I hold your Word in my hand, I ask that you allow my fingers to find the message for my needs. Amen."

I didn't know why I was nervous. Not nervous like I was about to kiss my crush for the first time. But nervous like I was delivering a commencement announcement in front of thousands of people. I crept into it like I'd defied my parents by running away and now that I was all out of resources, I was crawling back looking for help. That was the type of feeling that shifted through my body. With each inhale, I sucked in the scent of the lavender candle I lit to calm me.

"Befitting," I said as I flipped open the Bible to the perfect scripture. "Psalms 107:1-43. 'God Helps Men in Trouble.'"

Goose bumps traveled along my arms. I certainly had trouble. The words that spoke to me, I read aloud. "'He has brought them and set them free from the hand of those that hated them.'" I thought about the hate my mother had toward me. I interpreted this passage as God telling me that I'd be freed from her rage and Oakley's too.

"'Their souls became weak within them. Then they cried out to the Lord in their trouble. And He took them out of their suffering.'" Tears hydrated my eyes and my Bible. I didn't break my session for tissue. I didn't mind these breakthrough tears. Once they subsided, I started reading again. "'They suffered in iron chains. Because they had turned against the Word of God.'" Guilty. Guilty. Guilty.

I read further. "'So He loaded them down with hard work. They fell, and there was no one there to help.'" It was hard to believe these scriptures were written many moons ago, because they seemed to be about me. "'They had trouble because of their sins,'" I said as I chewed on the pen cap and pondered over every sin I committed. For starters, Lloyd and I engaged in premarital sex. I was not honoring my mother. Instead, I harbored a strong dislike for her and avoided her as much as possible with reason. I looked at these things as possibilities for the hindrance of my growth.

The more I flipped through the pages of the Bible, the more I promised myself that I'd use the words to catapult me through this season of my life. I was proud of myself for not deflecting as I usually would. Holding the Bible in my hand made me feel safe. I felt assured that I could take each moment and let it play out past the closing credits of Mother, Lloyd, and Oakley.

My first letter to God started with the date and "Dear God." Staring back at me was nothing but empty white space waiting for me to tackle the first person on the list. I wrote "Florence Booker" instead of "Mother" in hopes that her being my mother wouldn't distract me from writing the truth. Next, I drew two columns and labeled them as pros and cons. I allowed myself to reminisce from as early as I could remember. Her cons outweighed her pros, but I was determined to air my grievances, leave them at God's feet, and listen for Him to guide me.

I made the same list for Lloyd. He had more pros than cons as far as numbers, not weight. Knocking up another female and hiding it outweighed any good he ever did. My heart worked overtime, contending against the thoughts that bullied me. Lloyd was on top of Oakley. They were under the sheets, moaning, and then I was there, delivering a baby. This trauma was like a stubborn virus. Residual symptoms hit just when I thought it was starting to run its course.

Oakley, of course, had more cons. The only pro was her looks. She was a beautiful woman. And while I'd usually have admiration for a bold woman, not her, because of how she went about it.

To be free, I had to deal with the hand I'd been dealt, but I just couldn't tonight. I eyed the bottle of Ambien, which was the only thing that would give me almost-immediate relief. "Shit." I tossed the empty water bottle across my nightstand. I downed ten milligrams with saliva alone. In about thirty minutes, I'd be asleep and wouldn't have to worry about unwanted thoughts and images.

"Ugh." I kicked the comforter off of me and rolled from my back to my side again. "Damn, it's three a.m." For the past two hours, I'd been trying everything to fall back to sleep. I'd turned the ceiling fan on high. Nothing. Soothing music, still nothing. I'd adjusted positions a million times and more nothing. I even tried watching a black-and-white movie and got nothing. So, I took another pill. Half of one.

"That's more like it," I said when my vision started to double. A sign that sleep was on the way. As with most nights, the craving for food began. I'd been able to control the sleep eating by snacking on a few pieces of candy. Amil found my stash and threw it out. He told me I needed to eat some real food.

As much as I didn't want to go downstairs, I had to satisfy my taste buds, or I wouldn't sleep. I slid out of bed and allowed my bare feet to shuffle me down the hallway. I was woozy. I held the wall and tiptoed down the stairs. By the time I made it to the bottom, my equilibrium was

being assaulted. Before I rounded the corner, I heard my
mother's voice at a whisper. I waited on the last step for
two reasons. One, I didn't want any interactions with her,
and two, I wanted to know who she'd be whispering to at
this time of the morning.

Whoever it was had pissed her off. Her voice rose just
above a whisper. "No, that was not the plan."

I assumed by her sudden pause and quietness that the
person on the other end of the phone had interjected.

"We agreed on a rate, and that is all you are getting
from me. Not a cent more."

What the hell? Now my intention of remaining hidden
was to listen to the conversation.

"I don't care how much it costs you," my mother said
with aggression.

There was that pause again. I heard yelling from the
other side.

A chair slid across the floor, and I staggered into the
den to hide. I could still hear from there, but I didn't
know for how much longer. I struggled to keep my eyes
open.

"No one told you to get pregnant. That baby is your
responsibility, not mine."

What in the hell? Payment? Baby?

"I am tired of your threats. Blackmail me all you want.
I am calling my lawyer as soon as his office opens. And if
you so much as make contact with my family again, I will
have you arrested for stalking. Do I make myself clear,
Oakley?"

I fell back onto the sofa and covered my mouth to
silence my gasps and profanities. Why was my mother on
the phone with Oakley?

"No one will believe the trifling woman who stumbled
into a church and ruined a wedding. Did you forget who
I am? The wife of a prominent doctor. You'll never win
against me."

Part of me wanted to barge into the kitchen and confront my mother, but Ambien had a different plan. The yawns were coming like contractions, and I had no energy to fight them off. Sleep was being born at the wrong time, whether I liked it or not. The quick multiple blinks turned into longer blinks until the last blink turned into a lasting slumber. Seven hours to be exact.

Chapter 15

The love seat in the den cuddled my body, masked my pain, and suppressed my thoughts for the time that I slept. I woke up covered with a blanket and feeling refreshed.

I smelled the aroma of food coming from the kitchen. Something I hadn't smelled in a while. Bacon, my favorite. Even the grease would be pleasing to my tongue and eyes. There was nothing like staring at a napkin saturated in bacon grease. And since I'd been eating better and regularly, stomach issues were a thing of the past.

I followed the scent and slowed my pace when I saw my mother behind the stove.

"Good morning, sweetheart," my dad said over his newspaper.

"Good morning. How'd you sleep?" my mother asked with a smile as she transferred the bacon from the pan to the paper towel.

I traded glances with my dad. He was just as surprised as I was. I didn't know whether to answer that or even how to answer it.

"Good morning," I finally said. "Thanks for the blanket, Dad."

"What blanket?" he asked

"Your father didn't cover you. I did."

My mouth and eyes opened to the same size. She was never this nice to me, and the feeling that rotated within me said to run. Was she planning to kill me? Kill my dad?

Blame our deaths on a burglar? Was this murder-suicide? I could see the story in the newspaper my dad read. MOM COMES HOME FROM A BOOK CLUB MEETING TO FIND HER DAUGHTER AND HUSBAND DEAD. And all along, she was the killer.

"That was nice, honey," my dad said to my mother. "Avery, sweetheart, I think it's about time you start to wean off the Ambien. I'm concerned with your episodes of sleepwalking. Besides, memory loss is more prevalent the longer you take it. And not just short-term loss." He returned to his newspaper, looking unbothered as if that were my mother's normal behavior.

I sat down and kicked his leg underneath the table. When he looked at me, I thumbed in her direction and frowned, my way of silently asking him what was going on with his wife. He shrugged and continued reading.

Things became even more strange when she approached the table with two plates in her hand. She set one in front of my dad and the other in front of me. My dad was used to this treatment. My mother usually served him when she cooked. But not me, never, which made my dad fold his newspaper and lock eyes with me.

"I'm scared," I whispered to him when my mother walked to the cabinet for a bottle of syrup.

Even though the look on my dad's face was expressionless, he knew something was up too.

I fiddled with my fork, scraping it against my plate, trying to decide if it was safe to eat. Saying grace wouldn't be enough to save me from whatever this woman's motives were.

Motives.

I twirled the fork around like I was gathering pasta.

Payment.

I rearranged the food on my plate.

Oakley.

It clicked. I thought. My mother was having a conversation with Oakley. *That doesn't make sense. My mother doesn't even know Oakley. It had to be a dream.*

I tapped my nails against the table and stared at my mother as if eyeing her would solve the mystery. She tugged at her collar: the first sign of guilt. I didn't break my stare. She cleared her throat: the second sign of guilt. "Let me get you something to drink, dear," she said as she got up to pour my dad some juice. The third sign of guilt: distraction.

Judging by my mother's behavior, I thought I had stumbled upon some information she planned to take to her grave. She was trying to butter me up so I didn't spill the beans. Then again, I could be wrong. It could've been a dream, and I would look like a fool against the devil if I said anything. One thing about that medication, it sometimes took a minute to recover information.

A little test wouldn't hurt.

"Dad," I said and eyed my mother for added pressure.

After he finished chewing, he said, "Yes, sweetheart?"

I never took my eyes off my mother. "About this Ambien . . ." I paused for dramatic purposes and watched my mother fidget in her seat.

"What about it?"

"I think it may be causing me to have hallucinations."

My mother's usual bronze skin tone matched the white mug she held to her lips to disguise her nervous energy.

I think I got her.

"What happened?" my dad asked.

I parted my lips to respond, but my mother jumped in. "I agree with the hallucinations. I came downstairs for some water and saw her walking around downstairs. When I got her to lie down on the sofa, she mumbled something." She shrugged and fanned her hand. "I couldn't make out what it was."

"Sleepwalking, hallucinations, and dementia are not uncommon. That's why you need to wean off. Temporary, remember?" My dad jammed a forkful of eggs in his mouth. He took the bait, but I didn't.

If I didn't know any better, my mother tried to conceal a smirk behind the mug that I wanted to purposely but accidentally break. "I don't know. It seemed real."

Instead of pretending to sip, she set the mug down, folded her hands, and glared at me. I was silently being threatened because she thought she'd won. She thought it would be written off as a side effect. The flag wasn't waved yet.

My dad stuffed some more food in his mouth and didn't bother to swallow it before he said, "All right, let's talk it through. What happened?"

"Are you really going to entertain this nonsense, Henry?"

Another indication to prove that what I overheard was, in fact, as real as the long salt-and-pepper tresses that grew from her scalp.

He nodded.

"I came downstairs around three-ish for a snack and overheard Mother on the phone arguing with someone that she referred to as Oakley."

That evil laugh of hers roared through the kitchen like thunder. "That's nonsense."

My dad chuckled too. "Why would your mother be on the phone with a woman we all despise? That was definitely the medicine." My dad shook his head. "Maybe break it in half and see what that does." He piled more food in his mouth.

Little did he know, I was already breaking them in half.

"How dare you, Avery? This is the thanks I get after getting up and making breakfast for you and your father. I did that to apologize for not receiving the olive branch you extended to me with dinner and a book discussion."

"Avery, I know your mother cuts a fool, but she is not capable of committing such a sinister act. Your accusations are disrespectful, and you need to apologize."

She seemed sincere, but you never knew with her. There was a possibility that I was tripping. It may have been the medicine. Or maybe I was trying to convince myself to retreat because my dad seemed to be on my mother's side.

"Save your apology." My mother grabbed a napkin and dabbed the corners of her eyes.

The only thing that changed with that napkin was the folds. "An attempt at a fake cry. Your napkin is still dry."

"Avery!" my dad barked. "What has gotten into you?" He slammed his fist against the table, rattling the salt and pepper shakers that made their home in the middle of the table. Even the spilled grains that surrounded the shakers moved.

My dad had never been this pissed at me. I never gave him a reason to be, but I didn't care. My gut told me I was right. I was going to prove that she was, in fact, the devil in disguise and take her down.

I succumbed to the omnipotent feelings and grabbed my mother's cell phone lying face down on the table. I ran to the half bathroom and locked the door. She was at my wedding and should've been prepared for the grab and dash. She was the only person in history who didn't have a lock code on her phone. "It takes too much time to conduct business," she'd say. It took a swipe, two taps, and scrolling to discover something I was not ready to know. Something that would destroy us all. The truth hit me like a linebacker desperate to stop a touchdown. Life seemed to run in slow motion until I let out a wail of emotions.

They didn't have to break into the bathroom this time. I willingly floated out. The half bath was too small to hold the weight of the truth.

My dad's lips moved, but his words never reached my ears. My mother's did. "Avery, please don't."

An imaginary defibrillator must've been used on me, because life jumped back into my body. My surroundings were no longer silent or blurry. "No! No! No!" I yelled out.

"Please, Avery. I'm begging you." The devil rested her cold fingertips on my elbow, but I pushed them off.

"Don't touch me."

"What is going on?" my dad asked. He was clueless and had been for over forty years.

My mother made one more attempt to persuade me to keep quiet.

"Ask your wife why she never told you or her other children about her firstborn child named Oakley."

Chapter 16

If my life were a TV show, it would be an uncensored version of *Jerry Springer*. I thought I had reached my lowest point, but I was wrong. More hurt latched on to me like a spray tan, turning me Smurf-blue somber.

Oakley was my half-sister. Was I saying that right? It tasted like vomit in my mouth. The same mouth that coached her through delivering my neph . . . I couldn't say it in a complete sentence. Nor in bits and pieces.

The door to my bedroom creaked. My dad stuck his head in. "Hey, sweetheart." There was sadness in his slow greeting, and rightfully so. He had just found out his wife was a liar.

I kept my head buried between my knees. I didn't want to look at my dad because I didn't want to see what I heard. Shame painted my face like makeup from a mall counter run by a clown. I was ashamed because I just had to prove a point that caused more devastation.

I thought maybe my mother paid Oakley to stay away from me. But then again, she would have never been gracious enough to do that on my behalf.

A sister.

A baby.

That baby belonged to my ex-fiancé. Imagine if we had gotten married. I would be a stepmother and an aunt. Forget Jerry. We needed our own reality show.

"I'm so sorry, Dad. I should have never looked in her phone."

"This is not your fault. You hear me?"

I didn't believe him, so I lied. "Yes, sir."

"Your brothers are here. Come downstairs. You can express yourself all you want."

There was no need to express my feelings. I wore them. At least, that was what I saw when I looked in the mirror. My hair was disheveled, eyes practically bloodshot and swollen, and snot ran from my nose like it was the spawn of Usain Bolt.

After I'd exposed the devil, she followed my dad to their room, begging to explain. Yelling had come from their locked bedroom for about three hours. I'd run to my room and three-way called my brothers. Anthony had quoted some philosophical passage, and Amil had dropped the F-bomb, the S-bomb, the A-bomb, the D-bomb, and if he could have, he'd have set off roach bombs, because he'd referred to the devil as a roach during his rant.

I descended the staircase the same way I felt—heavy. Burden increased my weight and caused a thunderous echo to follow each time my foot connected with a stair. When I rounded the corner, Anthony and Amil sat side by side on the sofa, carrying the same weight. My dad sat in his usual spot, a rocking chair that had lost its rock. He never sat in that chair that still. His head drooped like a plant, days shy of total dehydration. The devil looked frazzled. Strands of her hair pointed in every direction. I'd never seen her cry before, but her bottom lip quivered as she dabbed her tears with a wad of tissue.

I didn't speak to her or my brothers, nor did they speak to me. We all sat in silence, staring off at a random object. I followed Anthony's eyes. He stared at the Buddha statue on the mantle that he'd given to my parents. I wondered if he was silently questioning the statue's failure. There was no good luck. No positive energy. The only thing that circulated within this home and family was an abundance of the contrary. Amil seemed to be looking at the clock on the wall. I was sure he was ready to go, because it took some convincing to get him here. As for me, I watched my family, wondering if they were mad at me. Everything that had happened was because of me.

My dad cleared his throat. "I called this meeting to discuss . . ." My heart broke when he paused and reached for the tissue on the end table next to his rocking chair. I'd only seen him cry one time, and that was when his mother died. His tears caused my and Amil's tears, and all of our tears caused Anthony to grunt and pound his fist into the palm of his other hand. He never knew how to express his anger other than using violence. It took him a long time to channel that into something else—reading, which was why he always quoted shit we could hardly comprehend.

"Pops, we don't have to talk about it." Anthony moved closer to our father and patted him on the shoulder.

"We have to, son." My dad nodded. "We have to."

Anthony roamed over to the mantle and stood in front of Buddha like he'd magically change our circumstances.

I rolled my eyes. "That shit ain't working." Everyone looked at me. I'd never cursed in front of my parents before, and I had no remorse for the slip.

Disgust riddled Anthony's face as he turned from Buddha to the devil. "What do you have to say for yourself?" Anthony pounded his fist in his palm again. He churned it like our mother's face was there instead of his skin.

Through pauses and tears, the devil revealed the past she'd kept hidden. "When I was fifteen, I became pregnant. Because my father was a prominent pastor, my parents felt it was best to spare the family the embarrassment, so they sent me away until I delivered and then forced me to put the baby up for adoption."

The typical old story, which made me question its validity. If she lied by omission, who was to say she wasn't lying again for sympathy?

"And we are just supposed to believe this?" Anthony beat me to the question. "You believe this, Pop?"

My dad was hardly at a loss for words, but the only thing he gave was a shrug.

"How did she find you, Florence?" Amil asked.

Not Mother. Are we on a first-name basis now?

My dad broke down again and then answered for his wife, who seemed lost for words, which was surprising considering she always had something smart to say. "Technology. The internet." He wiped his face and blew his nose.

"This is my mess. Let me explain, Henry."

Wow! Ownership.

"Married church members adopted Oakley just before moving to an unknown location. I had no information, not even her name. As soon as she was born, they carried her away from me. I never even got to hold her." The devil cried into her hands, but none of us tried to console her. She gathered herself and continued, "Once Oakley got older, she started asking questions and searching. She was given my father's name, and that's how she found my name and where I live."

"How long have the two of you been in contact?" Amil asked.

The devil caught a falling tear with her knuckle. "Since spring of last year."

The three of us gasped.

I hoped Anthony believed me now. *That statue ain't helping shit.*

Words didn't seem appropriate, but I mumbled, "That long? And you never thought to say anything to us?"

"I'm sorry," the devil repeatedly cried out.

I was so tired of hearing that word.

Then it was like we had all been shot with a tranquilizer. No sound. No movement. Only uncontrolled breaths and faint heartbeats.

Finally, I broke the silence. "What about Lloyd? Does he know?" I still cared about him. He still reached out to me, and I still read his messages without responding. Nate was enough to fill a little bit of the void for the time being.

The devil shook her head. "I don't think so, unless Oakley has told him." She uninvitedly moved to the empty seat beside me. I tensed up and refused to make eye contact with her while she addressed me directly. "Lloyd was a casualty of war, Avery. Oakley made several requests for hush money, and regretfully, I complied. But then she demanded a house and a car, and I pushed back. Oakley didn't like that, so she threatened to turn up the heat and ruin not just me but my family. I didn't believe her, and somehow she sank her teeth into Lloyd to prove just how far she was willing to go."

"Let me guess, Oakley must've been watching the house and following everyone who came in and out?" Amil suggested, putting his policing skills on display. I wondered why he never noticed anything suspicious, but I didn't bother to ask.

I saw the devil's nod from the corner of my eye.

"And Lloyd was dumb enough to fall for her," I said.

"Unfortunately, yes. Oakley said she saw Lloyd leaving our house one night and followed him to his place. She wasn't sure who Lloyd was, so she followed him for a couple of days to learn his routine. Apparently, she staged car issues, and in a conversation they had, she learned Lloyd was engaged to you, the daughter her mother kept. That further fueled her anger."

We uttered, "Wow," at the same time.

Well, at least Lloyd told the truth about how they met.

"This is some Lifetime movie shit," Amil said.

I turned to the devil. Hope filled her eyes until I shouted, "You, Oakley, and Lloyd are fucking cowards." I couldn't believe my language or disrespect, but she needed to know how I felt, and I didn't care about the delivery.

"Avery!" my dad yelled.

The devil held out her hands to calm my dad. "No, Henry, she's right. I am a coward. I want everyone to say whatever they feel. I deserve this."

Amil laughed. "Man, all the shit you talked about us for years like you're just this perfect saint. Meanwhile, you birthed a whole muthafucking human and hid it from your own husband."

"I understand you all are upset with your mother, but I will not tolerate this disrespecting of parents."

I scooted to the edge of the chair and aggressively asked, "What about how she disrespects us? She gets a pass?"

My dad nodded. "That stops today too." He glared at my mother. "Is that understood, Florence?"

She nodded, apologized profusely, and added, "After I was forced to give up Oakley, I harbored a lot of resentment for all things baby and parenthood."

That hit close to home. I couldn't stomach anything baby related either.

"Well, why did you procreate three times over then?" Amil asked.

"Because your father wanted kids, and I didn't want to deny him that," the devil answered through sobs again. "Even though we were married, when I got pregnant with Anthony, I always felt in the back of my mind he'd be taken away too. Same with Amil, and you, Avery." She paused and took a few deep breaths before she continued.

"If I shielded my feelings, I wouldn't hurt as much as I did when I lost Oakley."

"Sounds like bullshit," Amil said and took a swig from his YETI. I was pretty sure whatever was in it was spiked.

I didn't know what made me touch her knee, but something also forced words of understanding from my throat when I did. "I get it," I said, surprising the hell out of everyone, especially myself. "I know what it's like to lose someone you thought you'd spend forever with." I only understood the baby part. Lloyd, he was an idiot for cheating on me, and he could still kiss my ass in a nonsexual way. But for my mother, I softened a little bit, imagining how I would feel if I were forced to give up my child. "Thank you—"

"What the fuck?" Amil growled.

I ignored him and continued my thoughts. "Thank you for your selflessness. You never wanted kids, but you sacrificed your painful past to give our father three. I wish we knew about your past so we could've worked through it together and received the love from a mother that we deserved." A part of me felt that if a person was forced to give up one child, they would love the others endlessly and unconditionally to make up for that loss, but everyone grieves differently.

My mother melted, fell to her knees, and praised God for the turn of events.

I felt both of my brother's disdainful glares for what I had said.

Amil tapped Anthony, pointed to me, and said, "Your sister is off her rocker."

"I know this is a lot to take in, but if you kids ever want to talk or need anything, I'm always here." Although my dad was hurting, he cared more about what we felt.

"So, what's supposed to happen now?" I asked.

"Your mother and I plan to take some time apart." His voice trailed off before finding its way back. "We need to work on some things through individual counseling and marital counseling. And I hope that the five of us can go to family counseling."

"Oh, naw. Black people don't go to therapy, and if they do, they don't stay."

"Amil, you are always on some anti-empowerment craziness. I think therapy is a great start," Anthony said.

"You would think that, bro."

"You must have forgotten that you had a few therapy sessions," I said.

"And like I said, if we go, we don't stay."

Amil always felt a need to have the last word, but Anthony wasn't giving in to him. "Plenty of black people go to therapy and stay. It's people like you who create stigmas that will keep people from living to their full potential."

Amil shook his head in disagreement.

"Kids, this is not meant to turn into a riot," my dad said. "Just consider it. I think it will be good for your mother to have our support."

I knew exactly what crossed Amil's mind when he frowned. I thought the same thing. She had never supported us, but then I reminded myself of her past. Things wouldn't change overnight.

Our dad addressed us by age. "Anthony, do I have your buy-in?"

"I'm not saying no, but let me think about it, Pop."

Dad nodded and shook Anthony's hand.

"Amil, I know you are against it, but can you at least give your word that you will consider it?"

"Yes, sir."

I looked at Amil because I knew he was lying. He was going to harbor more disgust and become more distant. I bet he couldn't wait to throw the devil's past in her face.

It was my turn. "Sweetheart, I know this is extra hard for you. What do you think?"

"I'll try."

My dad nodded. "The sooner we get into counseling, the sooner we can get the help we need."

Amil raised his hand like he was back in elementary school asking permission to use the bathroom.

"Yes, son?"

"What is going to happen with Oakley? Is Florence pressing charges? Restraining order? What's the plan?" he asked as if my mother weren't still in the room on her knees, praying.

"Right now, there isn't a plan."

"So, she can just continue to do whatever she's been doing without consequences?" Amil asked.

"No. We are going to talk with our attorney. This is a delicate situation. Your mother doesn't want to send her biological child to jail, but she's prepared to if she continues making threats. Oakley is hurt. And I'm not making excuses for her, but I don't think she intended to behave this way. Once Oakley learned her biological mother had other kids, she got angry."

"We've been abandoned by our mother too, and we aren't acting out like her. Florence is only our mother physically, nothing more," Amil snapped.

My dad attempted to speak, but my mother jumped in before he got a word out. "I love each of you. I was just scared to show it."

"To add to things," my dad said, "her father was emotionless toward her but would hop in the pulpit and deliver a powerful sermon on family, love, and togetherness. He paid more attention to his congregation than he did his family."

"Does she realize she is every bit of her father?" Amil asked, still not addressing our mother directly. "She presents one way in front of her church family and a different way to her children."

"The only way I could go on after losing Oakley was to convince myself that she was dead. In my mind, I buried my child along with emotions and feelings. I am not making excuses, but I do want to be completely honest."

"And for the record, I have never been a fan of how your mother behaved toward you kids. I wanted to keep my family together. I'm sorry if I failed you as a father and a protector by not pursuing a change more aggressively."

"What? No!" I bellowed.

To hear our dad think that he had failed us was heartbreaking. The three of us ran over to him, hugged him tightly, and cried.

"I am going to do everything in my power to change." We ignored my mother's promises. She was wrong if she thought she would get the same type of comfort as we gave my dad during his breakdown. I'd become angry with her all over again simply because she made my father feel as if he were a failure.

"You could never fail us, Pop," Anthony said, speaking the truth.

"Man, Pops, don't talk like that. You have been the best." Amil squeezed my dad's shoulder.

"Not only have you been an admirable father, but also a best friend," Anthony added and started pacing. "Pops, may I have the floor?" He didn't wait for an answer before diving into his thoughts. "I think it's a little too late for an attorney."

"Agreed," Amil added.

"This girl has shown how unstable she is. She found information and used it to get close enough to Lloyd and ruin my sister. Who knows what else she's capable of?"

"I understand your concerns, Anthony. All of these things will be brought up."

Amil started pacing the floor with Anthony. "Bringing it up does little to keep everyone safe, especially Avery."

"I'm fine, son. And I will make sure your sister is protected. Before we create a lot of scenarios, let's see what the attorney says."

"Just to be on the safe side, I'll crash here for a while," Anthony said as he continued pacing the floor, moving outside of the den.

"You don't have to do that, son. Your sister and I will be fine."

"I'll stay too," Amil said. "I'll get my supervisor to adjust my schedule so when you can't be here, bro, I can. We have way more questions than answers right now. And with all due respect, Pops, I'm not taking no for an answer."

Although my dad objected, Anthony and Amil continued formulating a plan to make sure we had around-the-clock bodyguards. I agreed with my dad. I loved my brothers, but sometimes they forgot they were my brothers and acted like my father. And with this Oakley thing, they were going to be extra protective and extra annoying.

I remained quiet, but not on the inside. I broke down the debacle. My fiancé cheated on me with my mother's firstborn child I didn't know about and got her pregnant. She then started blackmailing my mother, who was cooperating to keep it a secret. During my wedding, this same girl exposed my fiancé, then went into labor, where I was tasked with looking at her vagina to deliver a baby. A baby who happened to make me an aunt. *I should be an author. My life reads like a novel. Hell, I find it hard to believe that it's my reality. Wait until I tell Tracy.*

"Avery, are you going to let Lloyd know?"

I rolled my eyes because I thought Amil was trying to be funny. But the more I thought about it, the more I realized the question had some validity to it. "You know, I hadn't thought about it. As of right now, I don't plan to contact him. He didn't tell me about her, so why should I tell him?"

"My girl." Amil crouched in front of me and gave me a fist bump.

I couldn't help but laugh. My life was a hot-ass mess.

Chapter 17

I jumped up, sweating and panting. A nightmare with potential relapse effects. Since putting effort into my appearance and recovering what little social life I had, I'd slowed down on the Ambien. Mainly because before the explosive drama with my mother, my nights were spent chatting on the phone with Nate, which left little time for sleep. And when I did take it, I'd only take half a pill. The nightmares happened, but not to this extent.

I stood at the altar in a wedding dress different from what I wore when I was about to marry Lloyd. Although pretty, it was a colorful dress that I never would've chosen.

Johnny Gill was there. How crazy was that? I knew a few of his songs but wouldn't call myself a fan. I hadn't listened to him since his "My, My, My" days, but he was there. His voice soothed our ears as we watched the mysterious groom walk down the aisle. When he made it to the altar, he was faceless. He was like the Headless Horseman, but human, and with a hat that floated above where his head should have been. Weird.

There was an insurmountable sense of peace. Who'd be happy marrying a faceless person? His chocolate-covered hand interlocked with mine.

I'd gazed into his invisible face as he delivered his vows without a mouth. I was still trying to figure out how that happened.

Right when we exchanged rings, chaos ensued. The church's doors ripped open, and a blinding light hit my eyes. I guarded my eyes against the light, trying to make out the three bodies approaching. I looked over at my faceless groom, who also shielded his eyes from the light. But why? He didn't have a face.

The door slammed shut, startling me. The faces of three bodies floating down the aisle appeared. I dropped my bouquet and backed away as my mother, Lloyd, and Oakley held out their hands and repeated, "Marry me."

I screamed, "No!"

Oakley handed me a crying baby who appeared out of nowhere. Tracy walked from behind me and took the baby. Then my mother, Lloyd, and Oakley caught fire and disappeared. I turned back to my groom just as the female minister said, "You may now kiss your bride." Whoever I married that didn't have a face or lips kissed me.

When I awakened from the horror that played behind my eyes, I knocked over my lamp, trying to grab a bottle of water. "That was some freaky shit."

"What was some freaky shit?" Amil asked as he and Anthony burst into my room.

I forgot they were here. "Just because the two of you hired yourselves as fake security guards don't mean you can come in my room without knocking. What if I was naked?"

Amil dove across my bed and deepened his voice. "This is our house now. We don't have to knock. And don't think about locking doors in our damn house."

I laughed at his comical impersonation of our father anytime my brother got into trouble. Amil played too much, but his sense of humor put a smile on my face most of the time.

"Our apologies for not knocking," Anthony said. "We thought we heard a ruckus and came to check it out."

I pointed to my overturned lamp and then eyed Amil. "Why can't you be more like Anthony? He apologized, and he has sense enough to pull out a chair instead of getting on my bed."

Amil rolled over my legs and tried to grab my head to put me in a headlock, but he pulled back when he felt something oozing from my pores. "What the hell?" he said, wiping his hand on my comforter. "Your nasty ass pissed in the bed?"

I kicked him. "Shut up, stupid. How can it be pee if it's covering my entire body, dummy?"

"I wouldn't put anything past you."

"It's sweat. I had the craziest dream. A nightmare rather."

"Would the nightmare happen to be your face? It scares me every time I look at it." Amil punched my leg.

Anthony shook his head. No matter our age, Amil and I always carried on like kids. For Anthony to be an undercover thug, he had an old soul and was studious. "What was the nightmare about, Avery?"

"It was crazy! Let me tell you this first. I dusted off my Bible and had a moment with God, but I don't think He heard me. I read a passage on God helping in times of trouble. I asked to be freed, not reminded." I scooted against the headboard and filled Anthony and Amil in on the dream.

When I finished, Amil threw a pillow at me and said, "Lay off that shit. That's something a high person would dream."

Anthony nodded and wouldn't stop nodding. "Dreams have a lot of meaning. Let's break yours down."

"Aw, shit. Here we go. Professor Nerd is in the building," Amil said and tossed my throw pillow in the air and caught it.

"What's that supposed to mean?"

"I love you, bro, but you be going deep with it. Outer-space-type shit."

Anthony crossed his legs like a girl would. "And your point?"

Amil sat up and scooted toward the edge of the bed. "Go 'head, bro. I kind of want to hear this analysis."

Not that Anthony was a dream expert, but he was analytical, always reading, always studying, and I hoped whatever he said made me feel better.

Anthony uncrossed his legs and zoned out for a minute. "Your dream was not bad news, Avery."

"The hell it wasn't, bro. You need to sage this girl."

It was rare for me to agree with Amil, but maybe I did need a sage cleanse.

"I don't see a problem," Anthony said. "You were given the answers you were seeking. God showed you your life."

Amil and I sat deadpan.

"Let me show you." Anthony got up and pushed the chair back under my desk. He fumbled around, looking for something. "Avery, where are your markers for this whiteboard?"

"In the desk drawer."

Amil leaned over and whispered to me, "This man takes his profession way too far. He is about to play school with us as if we weren't adults."

I whispered back, "I hope all the markers are dried out."

"I can hear y'all." Anthony wrote and talked. "Okay, let's take the wedding." He wrote "wedding" on the board and circled it. He did the same thing for every word he felt was relevant. "Your dress was different yet colorful." He scribbled "dress, different, colorful," and drew the equal sign. When he finished writing his interpretation, he turned to Amil and me and read it to us. "Think. You are going to marry someone different from what you are used to. The color represents someone outside of your race, or maybe the person has a colorful personality."

Well, this was fun while it lasted. I wasn't saying that I had plans to marry Nate, but if things progressed between us, there might be a chance. I'd only seen Nate one time in person, but he was nothing like Anthony described. Nate was my typical type. "Okay, well, why was Johnny Gill there? I haven't listened to his music in years."

"Easy," Anthony said, turning back to the whiteboard and writing, "J. Gill."

I wanted to snatch that marker out of his hand.

"Johnny," Anthony said as if he knew the man personally. What person didn't call a celebrity by their first and last name or stage name? "He has a song called 'Soul of a Woman,' and in it, he sings about having a strong connection to the person you're in love with. You said you couldn't see his face, but you were the happiest you've ever been. That's God's way of telling you to look for a strong connection with someone opposed to the physical."

"Okay, but I want to be physically attracted to the person. Plus, the guy I've been talking to is my type, and I happen to like him. We have a date Saturday if I go."

"Just because he's your type doesn't mean he's your one. An attraction to the soul lasts longer. Physical appearances shouldn't be the most important thing when selecting a mate. You know that, Avery."

"Shhhiiiittttttt," Amil said. "Yo, bro, you straight buggin'. I'm out of here."

I laughed as I watched Amil hop up from my bed, trip over one of the pillows he kept tossing around, and exit my room like he was a firefighter rushing off to douse flames.

"As I was saying," Anthony said, "an attraction to the soul surpasses anything else."

I wasn't sure if I believed Anthony's analysis, but my antennae were up, aluminum foil and all. "What do you think the baby means? And what about them catching fire?"

That zoning out that Anthony did happened again. It was like someone was talking to him who only he could see. "Them burning could be one of two things. God could remove them from your life, or He could be showing you that the negative memories of them will eventually burn from your memory. And the baby being passed to Tracy, isn't that what you would do at work? Deliver a baby and pass it to her? That means you're going back to work."

So informative. So believable. Yet, I remained a nonbeliever.

"Avery, you have to start looking at things from a different perspective. Life isn't always black and white. But if you asked God for something, you have to believe He will deliver. Your dream wasn't bad. It was answers." He set the markers down on my desk and walked over to my bed. "You are going to be fine. We all are. Think about what I said, and when it happens, I will be right there to say I told you so." He leaned over and kissed my forehead. "By the way, Pops made breakfast. It's probably cold by now."

"Thank you."

"You are going to be fine. Better than ever, and I can't wait for you to see what I already know." Anthony turned to walk out but stopped. "You should go on that date. You need to get out to take your mind off of life. I have a feeling something good is going to come from it."

Chapter 18

I usually wouldn't do this, but I gave Nate the address to my dad's house to pick me up for our second date. I made sure he knew my dad had guns, my oldest brother swore he was a militant, and my other brother was a cop. I didn't tell him that I lived with my dad. Not a good look, but as soon as I could rid myself of the mortgage with Lloyd and figure out work, I would find a place of my own. I wasn't in a rush, though. I loved being around my dad. Being with him left me with fewer responsibilities, which I needed, and time to figure out my life without added pressure. And with the devil gone, it was much easier to concentrate on making logical decisions.

It was even peaceful being in my room, which was still decorated like in high school. Then, I didn't have adult problems to worry about, only acne, braces, and puppy-love crushes. Posters of my old heartthrobs still hung on the wall: New Edition, BBD, and although I hated to admit it, Hulk Hogan. I had a serious thing for him at one point in my life.

I lay across my bed, talking to Nate, trying to guess possible places he was taking me. He and I had been in regular communication since I drove out of the parking lot of Tri-Me Dating Agency a few weeks ago. I felt comfortable enough talking to him about Lloyd, the wedding, and a snippet of my mother. None of it scared him off.

His original idea was a picnic, and I was sure I would have loved that if it weren't for my severe grass allergy.

Whatever he finalized, he wouldn't give me any particulars, only to dress cute but comfortably.

"Comfortable for me is scrubs, and most of them are pretty cute," I told him.

Nate laughed. "Okay, well, if that's what you want to wear, as long as you're comfortable."

"You are making this so difficult. Give me one clue."

"One clue?"

"Just one."

"Okay. You are going to have fun. Good night." He hung up.

Pickup time was initially at 3:00, but he texted early the morning of our date and asked if he could move the time up to 2:15 because he had to make a pit stop before our date. I blushed at the thought of what the pit stop was. I thought he just wanted more time with me.

I was dressed and waiting on the porch when an old beat-up work truck pulled up at precisely 2:15 carrying a trailer on the back loaded with lawn equipment.

They must be lost.

I squinted, trying to make out the name on the sign plastered on the passenger side door—NATE'S LANDSCAPING & MECHANIC SHOP, with a telephone number that I recognized.

That's odd. Why would he pick me up in his work truck?

Nate hopped out of the driver's side and ran up the walkway to meet me. "You look cute," he said.

Too cute to be riding around in this work truck. I could've just worn my scrubs, but instead, I went with a floral thigh-high dress and Converse.

"Please excuse my appearance. I have a stop to make before our date officially gets started."

I hoped that the stop was for him to change cars and clothes. The Jason Voorhees jumpsuit that he had on was not going to work. And who wanted to ride around in a truck with a trailer and lawn equipment hitched to the back?

I wasn't in Nate's truck more than five minutes before I started sneezing.

"Sorry to throw this in at the last minute."

I scratched my arms. "No problem."

I didn't know what ran worse: my eyes, my nose, or me running away from him in my head. "Is there a pharmacy nearby?"

Nate looked over at me. "You are swelling. Are you okay?"

"I told you I was highly allergic to grass."

"Oh, that's right. But we are in the truck."

"There must be grass particles from your clothes or something."

"I'm sorry, Avery. We're almost there."

Never mind that I was dying. Nate was more concerned with getting to this pit stop.

The remainder of the ride consisted of sneezing and scratching the rash that had taken temporary residence on my skin. We wouldn't have been able to hear one another anyway. The windows were down because the AC was out on his truck. So much for my hair, which blew every which way the wind blew.

We arrived at a gated community. For a minute, I thought this was Nate's house because security greeted him by name and let him right through. My dad was one of the top cardiac surgeons in Augusta, and we didn't live in a community like this. *Nate must cut a lot of grass to afford such a lovely home.* Wraparound front porch and a three-car garage that put me in the mind of a farm-house.

"Wow, Nate, this house is stunning," I said through an itchy throat.

"Yeah, I think so too. This is one of my top clients, so when he calls and needs special favors, I deliver."

"This isn't your house?"

"I wish. My pockets don't run that deep. He called last minute, and I couldn't turn it down. This is how I eat and how I'm paying for our date."

When he said that, I noticed the same BMW from our first date. "Your client allows you to leave your BMW here?" I said it and left it out there, not really expecting an answer because I knew it wasn't his.

"Oh, no, the BMW is his too. I was doing a little maintenance on it."

Can we say bamboozled? "And he was okay with you taking it out for a spin?"

"Yeah. He's actually a pretty nice dude. Different, but nice."

I started to ask what he meant by "different," but I started drooling, and it wasn't from allergies. The only chocolate that I liked was in the form of candy, but the chocolate that emerged from inside the house and descended the staircase was . . . I was speechless. There were no words to describe him. He was nothing that I would've gone for, but I was in awe.

God made this?

"What's up, O?" Nate said.

O? What does the O stand for? Obsolete because they don't make them like this anymore. Open? Open to the possibility of him and me being together. I'd even take the O standing for "obedient" because that was what he would get from me—obedience.

I'd heard of love at first sight but never believed it existed until now.

"I hope it's okay that I brought someone with me. We have a date after," Nate said.

"Not at all. You are one of the hardest working men I know. Brought a date to work, huh?" Then O looked at me and asked, "How are you doing?"

I detected an accent. *Makes sense. There is no way something like him could have been made in the United States.* I wanted to answer his question, but it felt as if my throat was closing. Good thing this chocolate prince noticed. Nate didn't. He was unloading a riding lawnmower from his trailer.

"Sweetheart, do you by chance have an EpiPen with you?"

I nodded and pointed to my purse.

"I am going to reach in your purse and grab it."

He stabbed my thigh and explained his next move. I could barely hear what he said over the lawnmower. Nate hadn't realized that I was inside of his truck practically taking my last breath while he cut grass.

O scooped me up and carried me inside, where he laid me on his sofa. Our eyes locked, I thought. Hell, I could barely see out of them. Through silence, I still found him to be intriguing. He cared for me, a complete stranger, like he *cared*. He delicately laid a cold cloth on my forehead and rubbed Benadryl cream over my skin.

Meanwhile, the sound of that stupid lawnmower was still going, but I could hear the sirens over them. The medics checked me out, but I refused further treatment. I was a bit drained and just wanted to sleep.

As the paramedics wrapped up, I could see Nate's bighead ass looking scared from the archway. He inched closer. "Let me take you home," he said as if that weren't the worst idea.

I rolled my eyes. I hoped I did. I wasn't sure if it turned out right with them being swollen.

"Do you want me to call you an Uber?"

If he doesn't stop talking . . .

"She shouldn't take an Uber in this condition, and even if you use my car to take her, you've been cutting grass, and that may trigger another flare-up. I will make sure she gets home safely," O said.

"Well, since you are in good hands," Nate said, "I am going to go ahead and knock out another job. I will call and check on you later."

This time my eyes bucked with horror. Now he was abandoning me. I didn't necessarily mind it. I wanted him out of my sight and to look at what I was being left with.

After Nate left, I told O, "You don't have to go out of your way. I can have someone pick me up."

"It's no trouble at all. The break is much needed anyway."

Now that I could see a little more, I looked around the room. "Exquisite taste for a man. The paintings are breathtaking."

"Thank you."

"You're an artist?"

"I dabble."

One of his dreads swayed in his face. Dreads had always been a deal breaker for me, but I was willing to make an exception for him. His were different. They were neat, pinned up, and his tapeline was fresh. God made him, but he looked like he was made in a lab with all the perfect assembly parts. And he had a beard, which was another deal breaker, but his was neatly trimmed and turning me on. It wasn't just a physical attraction. It was something more. Something I couldn't explain.

The ambiance itself was something that I never wanted to leave. The incense burning nearby calmed me and so did the jazz music that escaped from another room. Nate was right. O was different.

"Let me know when you're ready to go home."

I don't think I ever want to leave. I wanted to stay and learn more about this man. "I assume O is short for something," I said.

"It is." His accent was a little stronger. "Obasi is my name."

"I'm Avery. And thank you for taking such good care of me."

"My pleasure, Avery. Sorry your date left you." He chuckled a bit.

I shrugged. "It is what it is. What do you do besides paint? You play the piano?" I asked when I noticed the black Yamaha piano and music sheet sitting in the corner.

"I dabble. Mainly paint and write. I'm a little entrepreneur." He shrugged as if his resume weren't impressive. It must have been paying off.

"Write? As in an author?"

"Yes, as in an author."

"I love to read. What are some of your books? Maybe I've read them before."

"Are you into poetry or spoken word?"

"No. More like thrillers and serial killers."

He laughed. "Well, I can assure you, you won't find my name attached to anything like that."

"You must sell a lot of books and paintings. You have a beautiful home."

"I do pretty well for myself. Enough about me. What do you do?"

That dreaded question again. "It's complicated."

"How so? Unless you have somewhere else to be, then I have time. I have time anyway because I think I'm your ride."

I laughed until I snorted. Embarrassing.

"To make a long story short. I was at my wedding, and before the ceremony ended, I learned that my ex-fiancé had impregnated someone else. She crashed the wedding and announced it." I shook my head, thinking of the additional details that I was in no mood to share. "Anyway, the girl went into labor, and because I am an ob-gyn, I ended up delivering the little sucker right there in the church. Not sure if I want to go back to that field."

"Are you sure you don't write books? You have to be making this up."

"Maybe you can ghostwrite it for me."

"You might need a drink. Can I interest you in some wine?"

"I would love some, but I only drink a certain kind, so that's okay."

"What do you like?"

"2014 Bond Vecina."

"Coming right up."

"No way. You have that?"

"I happen to like it too. I keep a bottle handy and sip on it when I'm in creative mode."

"Wow."

"I'll be right back."

When he disappeared into the kitchen, I got up and started looking around the room. Everything was neat, different, and in its own place. The artwork that lined the walls captured my attention even more. I had never been fascinated by art before. I didn't know if it was because Obasi painted it or because it was intriguing.

"I have paintings all around. I can give you a tour if you'd like."

I jumped at his voice. "You startled me. I'd like to when I'm able to see one hundred percent."

He snickered. "I'm sorry, I don't mean to laugh. But did you tell my man about your allergies?"

"I did. More than once."

"Well, let's toast to bad dates and good eye health."

"What the hell, might as well."

Our glasses clinked. We stared at each other as we sipped.

"Can I get you something to eat?" It was as if I could see his accent roll off his juicy lips with all seven words.

"No, you've done enough. You've nursed a stranger back to health."

"It's no trouble. You caught me on a good day."

"What's a bad day?" The more we talked, the more questions I had.

"Not really bad days. I'm just swamped most of the time."

"I understand. It was the same for me when I was running my practice." I held up my finger and added, "But I don't want to talk about it."

"Fair enough. I'll just say what you experienced was pretty traumatic. A mental-health break is okay."

Finally, someone who got it. Even if he was pretending to get it, I needed what he offered. Understanding. Just because I had credentials behind my name didn't mean I was immune to struggles in life.

"And for the record, Avery, if you care to hear my opinion?" His eyes were asking for permission to continue.

I raised my glass and shrugged.

"Nothing but respect for your profession. The whole idea of a woman carrying a life inside of her is the most beautiful thing I've ever seen. Whatever you choose to do with your life is your choice. Just make sure you're happy doing it."

I saluted his statement and hoped that by me not adding words, he'd move on to another topic.

"Don't get me wrong, I love my man Nate. He does wonders with anything I ask of him, but how did you end up with him?"

I laughed at his laugh. I didn't know what it was about Obasi, but I felt an instant connection.

"I'm ashamed to admit it, but it was a dating agency," I said.

"Has Nate even called to check on you?"

I looked around. "I don't know. I don't even know where my phone is."

"Nate said he brought it in. What's your number? I'll call it."

"Is this your way of asking for my number?"

"No. I was going to get that anyway." He winked at me.

"Cocky much?"

"More like confident. I go after what I want, and I usually succeed." Obasi pulled out his phone, prepared to dial my number, but then my phone rang.

I laughed. "Looks like you failed." I backed away from him to my ringing phone. None other than Tracy calling to be nosy. I silenced it. I'd call her later.

"Is that your boyfriend calling? Is it Nate?"

"Shut up. No, it's not Nate, and if I had a boyfriend, I wouldn't have gone out on a date with Nate. Where's your significant other? She's not going to drop by unexpectedly and try to beat me up, is she?" My way of checking on his relationship status. He had to be taken, but I needed confirmation.

"Single. And before you ask what's wrong with me, nothing. I haven't found anyone I vibe with or who is as ambitious as I am. I'm all about building my own empire, and I need someone to match that energy."

"Gotcha. I respect it."

"Did Nate at least plan to feed you on the date?"

"I have no clue. I think this *was* the date." I snickered. "Me watching him cut grass." Maybe it was the wine and my adrenaline settling, because I started feeling a bit loopy.

Obasi must have read my mind. "With the allergic reaction and a few glasses of wine, you need to at least put something on your stomach."

"It's okay. I'll eat when I get home."

"I've got the perfect dish for you. Come on." He started walking, and I followed him into the den. He handed me the remote. "What do you ladies like? Lifetime or Hallmark Channel? Watch that while I make you something. It will make you feel a lot better."

Lifetime? Little did he know. I flipped the channel to a college football game.

"Yeah, right. You know you are not about to sit and watch this game."

Perfect timing. "Pass interference," I said in unison with the ref.

His eyes grew bigger as he threw his hand over his heart.

I smirked in his direction. "I love football. I watch it with my dad and brothers every week."

"Get out, a chick who loves football. And it doesn't hurt that she's easy on the eyes."

While he was giving me audible compliments, I gave him silent ones like *chocolate thunder drop* and *chocolate that can melt in my* . . . I stopped myself from completing that thought. *Focus on the game. Focus on the game.*

"I'll join you as soon as I feed you." He disappeared into the kitchen before I said anything else.

A couple of hours later, I jumped up out of my sleep and started looking around.

"Hey, sleepyhead. How you feeling?"

I felt around for my phone. "What time is it?" I asked, my voice groggy.

Obasi pointed toward the cable box. "A little after 8."

"I am so sorry for taking up your day. I didn't realize I had fallen asleep. I need to get home."

"It's no trouble. I started to wake you, but you seemed peaceful, and after the allergy attack, I knew you needed the rest."

I stood and folded the throw blanket that he covered me with.

"Your food is in the microwave. Let me get it for you."

"That's okay, really. I can just take it to go."

"Then I won't know if you liked it. Or you can just text me the results."

"Which means you'd have my number from that."

He was halfway to the kitchen when he yelled, "I told you, I am not worried. I will get it. But since I don't have it yet, you'll just have to stay here and eat it while we watch the Georgia game."

A delightful aroma hit my nose as I heard the microwave ding. Obasi emerged from the kitchen carrying a food tray. If I was curious about the density of his muscles, they flexed as he held the tray and carefully walked it over to me.

"You did not have to go to all this trouble," I said.

"Sit down, please." He nodded to the seat directly next to where he was sitting when I woke up.

When I sat, he placed the tray over my lap, and I silently prayed that there was nothing in this food to harm me. "This looks and smells amazing. What is it?"

"A delicacy from my country. Pepper soup."

"So that explains the accent."

"I am Nigerian. Since we weren't properly introduced, let's start over. I am Obasi Adebayo. Most people call me O." He extended his hand to shake mine, but I was too busy stuffing a spoonful of soup in my mouth.

"Sorry." I wiped my hands on the napkin he had folded on the tray. I shook his hand and said, "Avery Booker."

"That's not your name," he said.

I frowned.

"*Dr.* Avery Booker. That's your name, and don't let anyone take that away from you."

My God. This man. This experience. This food. "This soup is delicious." *Wait until I tell Tracy that I met the perfect African prince she's always wanted. The only problem, I'm keeping him for myself.*

"Thank you. It has medical benefits to it, so eat up. There's more if you want it. I'm thinking about adding it to the menu at my restaurant."

I couldn't snatch the spoon out of my mouth fast enough. "Wait a minute. You own a restaurant, too?"

"Something like that. I own a spot. We are kind of famous for our wings, and every Friday night we have spoken word."

"Wow. That's impressive. Is there anything that you don't do? You are a bit modest with your accomplishments."

"Sure there is. If you stick around long enough, you'll learn more about me."

I plan to. "Do you have family here?"

"No, it's just me for now. I am trying to get my sister here."

"You miss home?"

"I miss my family, of course. But this is my home now."

"Where is your spot located?"

"Downtown on Broad."

"I wonder why I have never heard of it. No offense."

"None taken. Do you get out much?"

"Well, I did when I was dating my ex."

"None of the guys you met at that dating place took you out?"

I laughed. "Nope. Your yardman was the first who made it to second base. We see that turned out to be a bust. Wish I had known before I had given him my number."

"And he still hasn't called?"

I looked at my phone and shook my head. "Not even a text." But there was one from Lloyd. I'd read it behind closed doors like I usually did.

"Well, at least you know his work ethic is amazing."

"Ha-ha, very funny."

"I know. That's why I said it."

"Wise guy."

"You should call him."

A pained look covered my face. "For what? He should be the one calling me. This disastrous date was his fault."

"Make sure he didn't get run over by his own lawn-mower. I heard of that happening before at a farm somewhere in Idaho."

I just stared at him, and when I started laughing, so did Obasi.

"You, sir, are getting on my nerves. Let me shut you up. What team are you going for?" I directed my attention back to the large flat-screen TV mounted on the gray wall.

"Georgia, duh."

"Okay. I'd usually pick Georgia too, but I'll let you have them."

"Nah, I'll be a gentleman. You take Georgia, and I'll take LSU."

"Cool," I said. "If I win, and I know my team won't let me down, you have to make me some more of this soup."

"I can do that."

"What do you want if you win?"

He rubbed his hands together. "Your number."

Chapter 19

LSU took the win, Obasi took my number, and I took the time to read the text Lloyd sent. Finally, a conversation worth having with him. The townhouse we purchased. The only problem was that Lloyd didn't want to have the conversation via phone, text, or email, and it was my preference to have a paper trail. He was adamant that he needed to speak with me in person. He even went so far as suggesting we meet at the townhouse to talk some things over. Tempting. I was eager to develop a solution and even more anxious to find out if he knew the truth about Oakley. If I met him at the townhouse, I would have wanted to take my father and brothers with me, but then that home would have ended up as Lloyd's grave.

I told Lloyd no and would have my legal representation reach out to him. Scare tactic. I learned through my Realtor that with both of our names on the mortgage, my hands were pretty much tied. We were both still responsible for paying the mortgage until we agreed to place the home back on the market and it sold, or one of us bought the other out. I wasn't willing to pay the mortgage. It was his breach. I'd rather accept subpar credit due to a foreclosure on a home I never got to live in.

In the meantime, I filled my thoughts and time with Obasi. I finally made it to his sports bar. Those wings he said everyone raved over were worth raving over—every one of the eight flavors. I wondered if the chocolate covering his skin was as flavorful as his wing recipe.

No matter how much I wanted to shout Obasi's name from every rooftop and carve our initials into every tree and picnic table I saw, I kept knowledge of his existence minimal. A smile and a shrug when anyone inquired.

During breakfast once, Amil asked, "Who are you always on the phone with?"

"None ya."

My dad looked over the top of his newspaper with one eye as he usually did when trying to be inconspicuously nosy.

"Things must be going well with Nate. He is giving a phosphorescent element to you that I've never seen before." Anthony nodded. "I like it. I'd like to meet Nate."

I gave Anthony a deadpan look. The same look I always gave when he said something that went over my head.

"The only thing Nate gave—"

Amil smacked the table. "Please don't say an STD."

I hit Amil and pointed to our father. "Watch your mouth in front of my daddy," I said through clenched teeth. "As I was saying, the only thing Nate gave me was an allergy attack and an excuse." He had reached out via text two days after the incident at Obasi's. He apologized for his absence, saying he was giving me time to recover and that he felt because of his profession and my allergies, it was best we didn't see each other again. I didn't respond. I had moved on already.

"Well, whoever it is, you are absorbing the positive energy that is radiating from him or her," Anthony said.

Amil laughed. "You dating a girl? You're the female Scottsdale."

"No, I'm not, and I don't know why Anthony would say that, but if I were, so what?"

"I agree with Avery. Amil, you need to grow up. Your outlook on societal norms is extinct. Love isn't determined by dating a person of a different gender anymore.

Personality is key. The world is changing, and you will get left behind if you don't catch up."

"Man, bro, what the hell are you saying?"

I felt like the sigh Anthony let out was calling Amil a dummy.

My dad shook his head. "Whoever this fella is, I'd like to meet him too. Does he like sports?"

I nodded.

"Bring him by for the Super Bowl. That way, we can all meet him." My dad surprised me with the invite.

"Or her," Amil said and started laughing again. "I'd love to see who has you smiling all the time and spinning around this house like a damn four-year-old ballerina."

Things were going great between Obasi and me. Better than great, which made me nervous. How could such a good catch not be caught? He filled the void that Lloyd left. He dotted my i's, crossed my t's, uplifted me when I was down on myself, and politely put me in check when I got beside myself. Because of Obasi's schedule and Oakley's unpredictable behavior, we didn't go out much, but we talked often. Last I heard of her, they were trying to find information to serve a warrant for extortion. I rarely thought about her or Lloyd anymore. I had Obasi. Every morning began with a text filled with sweetness, and every night ended with me hearing his accent-filled voice.

I dreaded inviting him over for the Super Bowl, but he agreed without hesitation. I wanted him to come, but I knew my family. There would be indirect threats, shady remarks, and a lot of trash talking. When I warned him, he laughed and said, "No worries. Only a disingenuous person would have concerns. They are showing how much they love you by vetting me. It's all good, babe. It's a rite of passage in a sense."

"There's just one other thing." I scrunched my face together in a way that would make the perfect Halloween mask.

"What's that?"

"I learned my mother will be there, and since I haven't spoken to her much, I am not sure how the vibe will be."

"Okay, no problem."

"Well, I wouldn't want you to be in a place with thick tension."

"It isn't a problem for me. Your parents are still married and are working through their issues. I'm sure your father wants her there. And it's not my business, but I think now that your mother has revealed her skeletons, you'll see a different version of her. You just have to be willing to give her a chance. Of course, in your own time."

When the Super Bowl came around, the jovial atmosphere was replaced with tension when the alarm lady announced, "Front door open."

"Hi, everyone." My mother smiled and crept in like she knew she wasn't wanted. Her presence silenced us all except for Tracy.

"It's good to see you, Mrs. Booker," she said as she got up and offered my mother the seat she was in next to my dad.

"You too, Tracy." She inched past us, and as Tracy walked away, my mother grabbed her hand. Amil jumped up like he was about to break up a fight. I looked on in horror. I stumbled to find footing to help him. My mother hugged Tracy for the first time in the history of our friendship. "Thank you for being a good friend of the family, especially to my daughter."

"Which daughter?" Amil asked before walking away.

My mother nodded. "I deserve that."

I eyed Anthony, who shrugged and continued sipping from his red cup. Tracy made the punch, and it was strong, so maybe we were seeing things.

For a split second, I felt sorry for my mother. Sympathy instantly turned into fright when the doorbell rang. "I'll get it," I said. Amil tried to beat me to the door, but Tracy stepped in front of him to slow him down. I flung the door open, excited to see Obasi but nervous for him to meet my family. I glowered instead. "Oh, it's you."

"What do mean, 'it's you'? Like I'm nobody," Scottsdale said and wiggled his fingers in my face. "You better act like you're delighted to see me, honey. Mrs. Florence didn't tell you she invited me?"

"Nope. She sure didn't." I loved Scottsdale, but I shoved him aside when I saw Obasi walking up the stairs looking good and, the closer he got to me, smelling good.

"Hey, babe. I hope you don't mind I brought a few things." He shook the pans of food that hid his hands.

"Hi." Being that all of my teeth showed, I felt like my greeting came off a little creepy. "You know you didn't have to do that."

We held hands as I went around the room and introduced him to everyone. Anthony and Scottsdale were first. They were standing up, talking about the game. Anthony sized him up while Scottsdale spoke and smiled wide like he liked what he saw. I did too, so Scottsdale had better back off. Tracy and Amil were passing out cups of a liquor potion they concocted. Amil gave a head nod and a frown. Tracy hugged Obasi and tapped me on the arm. "Okay, girl. I see you."

It was my parents' turn. I had mixed emotions. I wanted to introduce my mother as my dad's wife, but I promised I'd try to put forth more of an effort to repair our relationship. "Obasi, these are my parents, Dr. and Mrs. Booker."

My mother was the first one out of her seat to shake his hand. "It is such a pleasure to meet you."

I looked over my shoulder, and everyone had identical confused expressions.

My dad shook Obasi's hand and then hugged him. "Whatever you're doing that has restored the smile on my daughter's face, thank you."

So dramatic. A simple, non-embarrassing greeting would've been just fine.

Judging how my dad and brothers high-fived and fist bumped Obasi during the game, I'd have said they liked him just as much as I did.

I followed my dad when he excused himself. "Thank you, Dad." I hugged him tight from behind while he poured a drink.

"What's that for?"

"Because you are a good dad, and I appreciate everything you've done for me."

"Sorry to interrupt."

I looked at my mother but didn't verbally acknowledge her presence.

"I'm heading out. I just wanted to thank the two of you for having me." Since she and my dad separated, she had moved into a secure building somewhere downtown, compliments of Dad.

My parents embraced.

I waved. "Good night."

I fiddled around with the uncovered pan of spinach dip, taking the time to draw hearts in it with a spoon.

"What's going on, sweetheart?"

I smiled before the words formed.

"I love seeing that beautiful smile. You must really like this African fella."

"I do. Can you please tell Anthony and Amil not to bully him and scare him off?"

"They seem to like him."

"Keyword: seem. You know how they are. Two D-list actors."

My dad laughed. "I will make sure they behave. But are you sure he's not one of them Facebook scammers? They are all African, own oil rigs, and need you to send them money because something catastrophic happened and their money is tied up."

I laughed. "He's legit."

"Good."

"But what if I'm making a mistake again? I'm scared. What if he turns out to be a creep like Lloyd?"

"I wish I had the answer, sweetheart. You can never tell these things until you go through them. But I will say don't punish him for the mistakes of Lloyd. Give this African fella a fair chance. If something is wrong with him, the flags will emerge."

"That's the problem. I don't want to walk around flagging everything because of Lloyd."

"And I understand. I want you to be happy, and I want you to have someone who will care for you when I am no longer here. But you have to start somewhere. Not every man is Lloyd, and every other man shouldn't have to pay for what Lloyd did. In every relationship, there will be problems. You have to decide if that person is worth working through those problems with."

"It's not that easy working things out. I'm surprised you are."

"It's not. I stay married to your mother because I am too old to start over, I'm settled, and it's just cheaper to keep her."

We laughed at his joke.

"Believe it or not, your mother is turning into the woman I first met and fell in love with. We've been communicating effectively. There is so much we are learning in therapy. I wish you and your brothers would come, but . . ." He gave a half shrug.

"Thanks, Dad."

"Anytime. And just try to have some fun. Enjoy the moment at least. Laughter is the best medicine for a broken heart."

The night was a success, and so were Obasi's wings and pepper soup. The only snag was Amil mocking Obasi's accent.

And can we talk about the kiss that we shared at the end of the night just before we became an official couple? Breathtaking. It was the kind of kiss that made me as giddy as a high school girl kissing her crush under the bleachers for the first time.

Obasi was leaning up against his car while I stood in front of him. "Thank you for inviting me. Your family seems cool," he said.

"Thank you for coming." I rocked from side to side and looked up at the stars and every car that passed by so Obasi couldn't see me blushing.

He shifted his weight from his car and was directly in my face. If he didn't back away, he might have witnessed the steam coming out of my pores like a pressure cooker.

I took a step back. He took a step forward. I took another step back, and he took another step forward. Thanks to the nippy night air, I slipped on a jacket to walk him out but failed to zip it. Obasi gripped one side of my jacket and pulled me closer to him. He leaned down and pecked my lips a few times before latching on. When we separated, he licked his lips and said, "In my country, a first kiss symbolizes a commitment."

"It doesn't quite work that way in America, but I am okay with your country's way."

"I'll call you on my drive home. Good night." He kissed me again.

I raced back inside and grabbed my cell phone because I didn't want to miss his call. When I got to my room, I dove across my bed and started singing, "I got a boy-friend, I got a boyfriend." I squeezed one of the pillows on my bed and replayed the moment.

Within minutes my phone rang and jolted me out of my replay. I didn't even look at the name on the screen because I was sure it was Obasi.

"Miss me already?" I said instead of hello.

"I've been missing you, baby."

Ewwwww. This voice didn't have an accent. I looked at the name on the screen. This was old news.

"Lloyd? I thought you were someone else."

"Damn. That hurt."

"What do you need?"

"I just wanted to know if we could meet in—"

"I told you already that I was not interested in meeting."

"You win, Avery. I just wanted to meet in a public place to talk over some options for the townhouse. We can give it up."

"We don't need to meet to do that."

"We don't, but I also need to talk to you about some-thing else. Give me one meeting, and I won't bother you anymore. I promise."

"Fine."

Chapter 20

About that meeting with Lloyd, I canceled it. It wasn't that I didn't want to finalize things with the townhouse or find out if he knew particulars about Oakley, but there were scheduling conflicts. I promised Lloyd I'd call him when I had a break in my schedule. Same thing I told Tracy, to which she replied, "What schedule, Avery? You don't work." Anthony seemed to think that I subconsciously wanted Lloyd back, which was why I was dragging my feet. Trust me, Lloyd had a better chance of dating Michelle Obama than me.

Since meeting my family, Obasi and I had been hanging out more. Tracy and I were making up for lost time, and since I was under the same roof with my brothers, we too had been spending more time together, complete with music video parodies. We even had Scottsdale over a few nights. He had been coming around more since the Super Bowl. I thought he was trying to steal my man, but I wasn't going to let that happen.

What Obasi didn't know about me was that no matter how much I aged, I would always think I was a performer. It was a one-woman show because my backup talent, Tracy and Amil, were in denial at how bad they sucked compared to me. Tracy had pipes. She even plugged her ear like Mariah Carey, but she was a horrible dancer. And well, Amil was Amil. There was nothing more that could be said about him.

One night, we decided to have a contest—girls against guys. Anthony was a prude, so he was a judge along with the fabulous Scottsdale. My dad looked on because we had taken over the den where he was watching TV.

Anthony picked the songs. "TLC, 'No Scrubs' for you and Tracy."

We high-fived because we had this.

"All right, Amil and Obasi, y'all got 'Poison' by BBD."

They got excited and started doing the Kid 'n Play.

"I don't know why y'all celebrating. I hear the crowd booing y'all off stage already," I said.

Amil pushed my head and asked, "Who's going first?"

"Let Pops pick," Anthony said.

After my dad stuttered and prolonged the order, he finally said, "Ladies first."

Tracy and I stepped onto the makeshift dance floor and gave our all. Scottsdale sang along. My dad clapped and cheered for us. It was Amil and Obasi's turn. They stepped up to the stage and . . . let's just say, Scottsdale's bottom lip touched the floor, Tracy's bottom lip touched her thighs, and mine touched hell because of the nasty thoughts that developed in my head. Obasi gyrated, rolled every part of his body, and lifted his shirt to show off his defined abs. I didn't remember all that shit being in the video.

During their performance, Tracy leaned over and whispered, "Damn, he must be good in bed."

I whispered back, "I sure hope so."

Our expressions didn't change until Amil jumped in our face yelling, "Y'all lost."

Any other time, I'd be a sore loser, but I felt like a winner sitting in the front row watching Obasi move. Moves I hoped he planned to use on me during our dinner date at his house.

***

He insisted on cooking for me, and I insisted on eating. Obasi showed me another part of his dwelling.

"What in the HGTV is going on back here?" I asked when I arrived at our dinner date. He had the most amazing backyard I'd ever seen in person.

He laughed, and I would've reacted the same had I not been captivated by the scenery. He grabbed my hand and led me to an oversized wicker egg chair. It faced the outdoor fireplace and mounted TV that was surrounded by hues of brown stones.

I followed Obasi's finger. "You think you'll be okay out here since the patio is covered? If not, we can eat inside."

My head was still tilted upward, looking at the motionless ceiling fans hanging from the dark-colored pergola that covered me, the hot tub, and the swimming pool. "Outside is fine."

"You sure?"

When I looked at him, he had a stupid smirk on his face.

"Shut up. What little grass you have is way over there." I pointed across the pool at the grass surrounding the guesthouse. "Besides, you've proven you're capable of saving me. I guess I trust you."

The crackle from the fire stole my eyes from Obasi. "This is beautiful and so peaceful."

"Thank you." He bent down and grabbed a beer from the bar cart. "Want one?"

I shook my head. I wanted a beer, but I'd much rather taste it from his tongue.

"If you change your mind, help yourself." Obasi lifted the hood of the grill. The smoke teased two of my five senses. "Salmon, right?"

I nodded. And there we were, playing the staring game again. Of course, I cut my eyes first. "I assume red is your favorite color."

He took a swig from his bottle. "What gave it away?"

"Just the millions of red and white monogrammed pillows." Each decorative pillow had an A and a different shade of red. I began imagining what my nickname would be once we married. *AA, Double-A, Avery Booker-Adebayo. ABA.* If he didn't stop looking at me like I was the main course instead of what was on the grill, the red blush lightly powdered across my cheeks was going to brighten and blend in with the color scheme of his patio.

I looked over at the pool for a distraction.

"It's heated if you want to get in."

I'm heated if you want to get in. I did want to get in. More so with Obasi. Without swimwear. The pool wasn't working. "Do you use that hammock?" Another distraction.

"All the time. You want to get in it?"

With you—yes, but I'd had my one and only terrible experience with one of those deadly nets. "No, thanks," I said. "Me and Tracy tried once when we were at cheer camp, and it was a disaster. It overturned in the grass. She ended up with a broken arm, and I ended up having my first-ever allergy attack."

"It will be different with me."

I was sure it would be. Shit. How could a person turn a hammock into something sexual? Another distraction. I pointed to the three easels that lined the pool. "What do you plan on painting?"

"Not sure yet. When it hits, it hits."

Shit. Shit. Shit. I imagined him painting me naked. Better yet, me painting him naked. I needed to go home.

"Food's done." And just in time for *The Favorite Son* airing on BET. I'd read the book and couldn't wait to see the movie. "Wait until you taste my cooking, girl. You are going to fall in love." He leaned over and kissed me before going inside to make our plates.

Too late to fall in love. I'm already there. I didn't tell him because I didn't know if he felt the same. I was okay with waiting for him to say it first.

Commercial. I was stuffed, and if I didn't unfasten my pants soon, I was afraid a button would pop off and aim straight for the TV. I leaned back for some relief, which must've sent pheromones to Obasi. His fingers fondled mine with the hope they'd do the same to other areas. The fireplace wasn't the only thing blazing. I heated up like I was two feet away from the sun.

Instead of watching the movie, we watched each other. I'd always equated intimacy to sex with no regard for the atmosphere. This felt different. I'd never experienced the non-sexual kind.

"Do you mind?" Obasi held the remote toward the TV, and when I nodded, he powered it off and filled the space around us with music.

I gasped when Johnny Gill started singing "Soul of a Woman" through the speakers. My dream. It was happening. Johnny Gill's voice faded out, replaced with Tamia. I sucked in air, ready to sing the first line to "So Into You," but I tasted beer. Obasi's tongue was in my mouth. Tamia would have to wait for the chance to sing alongside me. I wrapped my arms around his neck like a necklace, allowing my white gel nails to lightly scratch the nape of his neck. Ecstasy. I wondered if the drug gave the same euphoric feeling. I moaned every time his tongue entered my mouth. And even though it was for a short time, I missed his tongue when he pulled it out.

I collapsed underneath his weight. My body was flaccid from the involuntary quivering. He stopped and stared at me while his thumb caressed my cheeks. My hands moved from his neck to his back. I lifted his shirt and traced over his muscles. Without seeing his back, I knew it was sculpted just as fine as his abs. He nuzzled my neck and nibbled on it. I'd never been a fan of passion marks, but I wouldn't stop him if he tried. He transferred the same amount of passion and pressure to my breast, using his nose and teeth to move my shirt around. Light kisses while he squeezed my thighs. I grabbed his shirt again, this time pulling it over his head and tossing it aside. Obasi was so invested in what he was doing, and I was invested in what he was doing. Suddenly, he stopped.

"What's wrong?"

He stood and pulled me to my feet. "Turn around."

Aw, shit. Gladly.

"Sit down," he said, motioning toward a bench next to the chair he was sitting in.

Okay. Not what I expected.

He turned his chair to face me and rested both hands on my knees. "Avery, I—"

"What's the problem, Obasi?" No wonder he was single. *He's about to tell me some bullshit. Like he has libido problems. That can't be. I felt the umbrella when he was on top of me.*

"Nothing bad."

"Well, why did you stop?"

He blew out a breath. "Believe me, I want this as bad as you do, but . . ."

There's a but.

"I have to honor the deal I made with God."

Confusion dotted my face like freckles. "I'm not sure I understand."

"I promised God that if he sent me a woman I connected with, I'd honor her body and wait for her to become my wife. And . . . I feel like . . ." His voice trailed off as he nodded.

I knew exactly what he meant. I was her. The one. The wife. The one who had the body he was honoring. I loved that he thought so highly of me, but shit, he could mess up one time and repent. An unnoticeable sigh escaped my lips. "I respect you more for respecting my body and our future." I leaned in and pecked him on the lips.

"Can I at least hold you?" Obasi asked.

"Of course."

If intimacy were an Olympic sport, Obasi was deserving of the gold, silver, and bronze medals. There was passion, romance, body temperature changes that intensified with every kiss, every touch, every whisper. I finally understood what Tracy and Amil meant when they told me about their colorful escapades. Most of the time, my black-and-white escapades felt like a chore. When I shared my views on sex with Tracy, she always said, "Lloyd must have a small peen and a whack stroke game." I never made a big deal about it because I was with him for love, and when the physical faded, love was all that was left.

As I lay in Obasi's arms in the hammock, looking at the sky, I reflected on Anthony's analysis of my dream. I silently whispered, "Thank you, God."

Chapter 21

Curiosity is one of those things that only goes away after satisfying the urge. What Lloyd wanted to talk to me about plagued me more than what he planned to pitch regarding the townhouse, especially since he'd messaged me every day, saying it was urgent. The very thing that I'd been stressing over somehow vanished into the pile of "get to it whenever."

Finally, our schedules aligned. I agreed to meet him over dinner.

I arrived at the restaurant twenty minutes late, on purpose, of course. And just like with any woman, I added an extra touch of pizzazz. I knew Lloyd still wanted me, and even though I had a man, I wanted him to realize what he was missing out on since we had broken up. I'd admit I had caught a bit of the complacency bug while Lloyd and I were together. Scrubs had become my entire wardrobe, and so did the professional clogs that I wore, even if I just needed to make a quick trip to the grocery store. In a nutshell, I had let myself go. I saw that now.

Either I was feeling myself a bit in the sleeveless red minidress that hugged my curves, or the men at the restaurant who had trophies attached to their arms for the evening were checking me out. Whatever the case, I smirked, which I was sure made my red-painted lips add a little more seduction and arousal to whatever they were thinking.

I strutted past them like Sandra from *227*.

"Welcome to Saints and Sinners. Will you be dining alone?" the hostess asked.

Dining alone? Not looking like this.

"No, I am actually meeting someone," I said. "He should be seated already. The section near the bar." I pointed as if she didn't know where to direct me. Lloyd told me where he was seated when he texted and asked if I was still coming.

"Yes, right this way," she said and led the way with a menu in her hand. Saints and Sinners was a restaurant whose name spoke for itself. Many saints came here with sinful desires. Remember the men at the entrance? I was sure that, on Sunday, they served the Lord, but Monday through Saturday, they served those ladies on their arms who looked young enough to be their grandchildren. I'd eaten here before. There was an aura in this building that guaranteed a hookup afterward. I was sure that was why Lloyd picked it.

I could see his bighead ass from a distance as the hostess escorted me to the table. Our greeting was awkward. This would be the first time that Lloyd and I would see one another since the day after the wedding. I planned to sensually strut in and twist my booty extra hard as he watched me take my seat. It was a strut that should have said, "You'll never touch this again," but when Lloyd stood to greet me, his body language said he was going in for a hug. I had to do a move on him that I learned in a self-defense class that left him standing with his arms out, looking stupid.

"You look amazing, Avery." He placed his hand over his heart. "He is a lucky man."

Although I said, "Thank you," I was thinking more along the lines of, *I know.* And yes, Obasi was a lucky man just as much as I was a lucky lady. I wanted to tell him that, but he might've gotten mad and changed his mind about the townhouse.

"I didn't think you were going to come. I'm glad you did."

"So, what's up? How are we going to do this? And what is it that you need to talk to me about?"

"Straight to business, I see." Disappointment colored his face.

"This is a business meeting, is it not? And yes, straight to business." I could be with Obasi right now. He had a little free time and wanted to spend it with me. He said he had someone he wanted me to meet, but I told him I had an important business meeting and would call him after.

"Good evening, good folks. I'm Sean, and I will be taking care of you tonight. May I interest you in some wine this evening?" The waiter handed Lloyd the wine list, but he held up his hand.

"I already know what the lady likes," he said. "Let me get a bottle of 2014 Bond Vecina."

"Good choice, sir. Please don't take this the wrong way, but I like to make all of my patrons aware of the six-hundred-dollar price tag for the bottle."

Lloyd didn't flinch. "I'm aware. She's worth every penny plus some." He stared at me like there wasn't a sea of people surrounding us to distract him and cause his eyes to divert.

"My favorite wine. You remember?"

"There is not a single detail about you that I don't remember."

I laughed. "Nah, there's one major detail that you forgot."

While Lloyd pondered, the waiter returned, filled two wineglasses, and left the remaining in a chilled bucket in the center of the table. With the smile that spread across his face, he must have thought that I was about to crack a joke. "Okay, let's bet," he said. "Ask me anything about you, and if I answer them all right, I get another date with you."

"And if you get it wrong?" I asked.

"I'm not worried about that because I'm not going to get it wrong."

I agreed because I had something up my sleeve, even though I didn't have sleeves. "What's my favorite color?"

"That's easy. Pink."

"How tall am I?"

"Another easy one. Five two."

"What is one thing I wish I could do as my profession?"

"Super easy. Sing, but you cannot carry a tune to save your life."

That was true. My singing voice was that of a door in need of WD-40. I was getting a thrill out of Lloyd thinking he had this game won. "Not too bad. Another question. What is my biggest fear?"

He cocked his head to the side because he thought he was going to have the correct answer.

Trick question.

"Depending on the angle you are going here, it can be a couple of things. If it's career-wise, you have a fear of failing. If it's in general, you fear mice and roaches." He pumped his fist in the air in celebration of what he thought was a victory.

I let him celebrate a moment while I sipped my wine. It was good, too. And what was even better would be the look on his face when I revealed he was wrong. I took a few more sips of wine first.

"So, are there any more questions you want to ask me, or can we go ahead and plan our next date?"

"There won't be a next date. You didn't win." Oh, the excitement in my voice when I said that.

The smile faded from his face. His mouth was agape. "I had all the right answers."

"Nope, you didn't. You got the last one wrong."

"Quit playing, Avery. You have always been afraid of mice and roaches."

"That part is true, but that's not my biggest fear."

"Then what is?"

Ah, now we were getting somewhere. "Being cheated on."

Lloyd sat back in his seat, defeated.

The smirk of confidence on my face when I first got here had returned. Silence floated around our table like a ghost until the waiter approached us to take our orders. Lloyd suddenly lost his appetite, and I never had one.

I poured myself another glass of wine. "So, what do you need to talk to me about, and what options do you have with the property?"

When Lloyd didn't answer, I looked at him and noticed a weird look on his face. My eyes followed his gaze. "Obasi," I said and gasped. The shock of seeing him standing at our table paralyzed me.

He pulled up a chair from an empty table nearby and joined Lloyd and me. "I spotted you when you first walked in. I thought to myself, that looks like my girl, but it can't be, because she's at a business meeting, and when I think of business meetings, I think of pantsuits and blouses, not Julia Roberts *Pretty Woman* dresses and a face full of makeup."

He didn't have to embarrass me in front of Lloyd like that. I held my hands up. "It's not what you think."

Obasi looked from me to Lloyd, who remained quiet, and then back to me. He demanded more of an explanation without moving his mouth to ask for one. It was all in his eyes, which were squinted from anger.

I didn't know what else to say. It looked as if I were caught cheating, but I wasn't. Maybe I went overboard with the attire and the reason behind it. The whole time

I told my brain to say something to save what I was developing with Obasi, but I was catatonic.

Obasi looked at Lloyd. "Are you in the medical field? Her business partner or something?"

My eyes pleaded with Lloyd to help me the same way his voice pleaded with me to help Oakley when she went into labor.

"Not exactly," Lloyd said.

"Okay, well, I'm Obasi, and you are?"

"Lloyd."

Obasi looked at me. His eyes were tighter than before. "Lloyd? Lloyd as in the ex-fiancé Lloyd?"

"Hopefully not for long. I am trying to win her back."

"Lloyd, shut the hell up," I yelled and silenced the whole restaurant. Now all eyes were on me. I was humiliated all over again. This time, it was because of my own actions.

"Obasi, please listen to me. This is not what you think. There is no way we are getting back together."

"I know me and you aren't. I can't say the same for you and my man here." Obasi extended his hand to shake Lloyd's. Lloyd returned the gesture. "Good luck, my man. Y'all make a cute couple." Obasi walked away and didn't look back.

Chapter 22

"Hello." Tracy answered the phone with questionable behavior in her tone.

"Tracy, I messed up," I sobbed.

She seductively giggled. "I think I'm messing up too, girl, but it feels so right."

A man's whisper came through the phone, telling her to hang up.

"Tracy!" I screamed her name as loud as I could. Nothing but dead air on the other end of the phone.

My sobs were more intense. I weaved in and out of traffic like a maniac leading the police on a high-speed chase. Cars honked at me, and I laid on my horn in response. I zoomed through every yellow traffic signal and even ran a couple of red lights trying to make it to Obasi's house.

I turned in his neighborhood at about forty-five miles per hour and slammed on the brakes to avoid running into the back of another car. "Shit, shit, shit. Security. They will let me in." Since Obasi and I had been dating, they always let me in. I was third in line, and by the way I cried on the drive over, I knew I'd alert the guard that something was off. I pulled the mirror down and looked at the smudges of makeup that had smeared across my face. I looked like a clown. I popped open my glove box and grabbed the baby wipes I used to hold the nozzles when pumping gas. I scrubbed my face as fast as I could. Second in line. Still looked like a clown. I scrubbed faster and harder.

I did one more mirror check. Besides the red irritation circles, I looked a bit presentable. My favorite guard was on duty. "Hey, Brandon, how's it going?" I made small talk as I usually would. I didn't want to alert Brandon that things were off.

"All is well, Dr. Booker."

I cringed at "Doctor." Yeah, I worked hard for it, but it left a stain. "I told you to call me Avery."

"I'm sorry, Dr. Booker," Brandon said, overlooking what I asked of him. "Mr. Adebayo advised me not to grant you access."

"I see." What I saw was the opportunity to ram my car through the gate, kick my heels off, and run the mile to Obasi's house.

"Dr. Booker, I'll have to ask you to make a U-turn here and exit."

I watched where Brandon pointed. That was new. I had never been turned away before. Humiliation was the story of my life. I did as I was told because although I had an elaborate plan to break through the gate, I didn't want to add a mug shot to "jilted bride." I could see the news headline above my jail portrait: RECENT JILTED BRIDE GETS BUSTED ON DATE WITH EX, THEN CRASHES THROUGH SECURITY GATE OF NEW BOYFRIEND'S RESIDENCE.

It really was a business meeting. I dialed Obasi's number numerous times to try to tell him that. He wouldn't answer. In fact, he sent me to voicemail. That was the same treatment I had given Lloyd, and I knew how much it annoyed me that Lloyd would reach out to me anyway. I decided to accept defeat and leave Obasi alone. Maybe when he'd had time to calm down, he'd want to talk.

I redialed Tracy's number.

"Avery, you better be dying, because you keep interrupting something important."

"Obasi just dumped me. I'm picking up a bottle of wine and coming over."

"Nooooooo. You can't come over here, not right now. Not tonight. I mean, I'm sorry about Obasi, but . . ." Silence lingered, and then I heard, "Dammit, shit. Go ahead and get the wine. I'll see you when you get here."

Tracy must've thought she had hung up the phone because then I heard, "You gotta leave. Your sister is on her way over."

I gasped. I sped up and weaved in and out of traffic the same way I did when I was headed to Obasi's. I bypassed the liquor store. I wanted to catch Amil coming out of Tracy's house. It had to have been Amil, because Tracy and Anthony were total opposites and had nothing in common.

I banged on Tracy's screen door.

She swung it open with an attitude. "Heffa, ugh," she said as she walked over to the couch and plopped down. "You're empty-handed. Where's the wine?"

I looked around. He was already gone. "Why are so many candles burning?"

"Because I like candles. And this better be important, or else I might toss one on you and set your ass on fire. Now, where's the wine?"

"I thought you would have had some left over from your sex session with Amil." I rolled my neck and bucked my eyes, waiting for her reaction.

"Oh, my God, Avery, I was . . . we were going to tell you. I swear we were."

"I don't care about you and Amil. Just next time, make sure your phone is hung up before you start talking if you are going to be sneaking around. I saw that coming a mile away." Then, I burst into tears and fell onto Tracy's lap, but I wasn't crying because of Amil and Tracy. I was crying because of Obasi. "I don't want to lose him. It was an honest mistake."

Here I was, crying on my best friend's lap over a man again.

"Try to calm down, Avery, and tell me what happened." Through bouts of ugly cries and snot pouring from my nose, I recapped the whole night. "It was honest, Tracy, I promise."

"Why in the hell would you do that? I mean, for Lloyd's tacky ass."

I shook my head, thinking about the stupid reason. "I read a magazine."

"What the hell are you talking about, Avery? What kind of magazine?"

"I saw an article in a magazine. 'How to Make Him Miss You.'"

Tracy raised her hands. "Hold up. You mean to tell me you risked all of that African meat for Lloyd's tacky ass?"

Pain uttered. "It was stupid, Tracy."

"Yeah, it really was."

"I just wanted to hurt Lloyd back. I wanted him to see me looking and feeling good. I wanted to make him regret what he did even more."

"Oh, Avery. I love you, friend, but you have got to stop falling apart over these men." Tracy lifted my face. "Look at me. Obasi will need to understand that it didn't take you overnight to fall in love with Lloyd, and it won't take you overnight to fall out of love with him. Think about it. You were going to spend the rest of your life with this man. As much as I despise Lloyd, feelings don't just immediately disappear because he mistreated you. This would've been so much easier had you given us permission to kill Lloyd and bury his body like we wanted to."

"Obasi won't even answer my calls."

"Do you want to call him on my phone? Maybe he will answer."

"I'm scared, Tracy."

"What's the number? I'll call him."

She tried too. No answer.

"He's probably just upset right now, and he has every right to feel that way. Remember, as you were going through your thing with Lloyd, you needed time to process every emotion. Give Obasi that and try to reach out to him in a couple of days."

"A couple of days without speaking to him is too long, but I understand. I'm in love with him, Tracy. I don't want to lose him."

"I understand. The same thing I feel toward your brother."

"Why have you never said anything?"

"Well, for starters, your momma wasn't accepting of anyone. And I didn't want to risk it ruining our friendship."

"But it's okay to potentially ruin our friendship now?"

"Girl, you owe me."

"No, I paid you back with that dumb dating agency."

"I don't feel like I have been paid in full yet."

"You are creeping with my brother. Now you owe me."

"Okay, you win."

"How long has this been going on anyway?"

"Officially since the night of the Super Bowl."

"Gross." Then I started crying again. "That was officially when Obasi and I became a couple."

"Avery, Obasi is just mad right now. I see the way he looks at you. The two of you will work this out."

"Are you sure?"

"I'm sure. Give the man some time."

Chapter 23

Tracy lied to me. Weeks passed, and every attempt I made to contact Obasi failed. What was even worse was I went by his restaurant on a Friday night during spoken word because I knew he'd be there. When I walked in, I saw him hugged up with another woman. I put so much effort into my appearance, prepared, and practiced my speech, and there he was with his arms wrapped around a Nubian goddess. At least that was what she looked like to me. Her skin was sunkissed and hydrated. She had an aura about her that told me I didn't stand a chance. She glowed, hell, he glowed as they buckled over in laughter. I cried the whole drive back home.

Life was back to where it was—stale. The depression weighed down my spirit with as much darkness as an unlit alley. Days and nights ran together. I barely ate, and I looked forward to swallowing anything that would put me into a long, deep slumber. I was at the point where I didn't want to feel again.

Tracy had less time for me in between her new job and cuddling up with Amil. They finally told my parents they were an item. Dad, of course, was thrilled, and surprisingly so was my mother. I guessed therapy was working for her.

One day I had a crazy, spur-of-the-moment idea, and I found myself back at Tri-Me Dating Agency. Solely my decision. I thought I was hoping to run into another one of Obasi's laborers who would've taken me on a date to his house so I could at least see him and explain. Not Nate, though. Some man he would've been. But because of the Tri-Me losers, I found a winner in Obasi, and maybe that would happen again.

Nope. Two dates. Same shenanigans.

Same process. I was already blindfolded and seated when the dating assistant escorted Keith to the table.

"Keith, we have matched you with Avery for the evening."

"Avery, what a beautiful name for a beautiful lady."

What? He couldn't even see me. I didn't even know what to say back, so I said nothing. Not even a thank-you.

"Do you mind if I shake your hand?" Keith asked.

"Sure."

We couldn't see, so we felt around the table until our hands connected. He did the Ray Charles thing on me, felt my wrist, and worked his way up my arm until I snatched it away. Creeper alert.

"So, what do you do for a living, Amanda?"

"It's Avery." That dreaded question again. *How do I answer that? I'm an unemployed ob-gyn.* I played it safe. "I work in the medical field."

"That's what's up. What in particular, like a CNA, medical office receptionist?"

I knew it. More details. "I'm actually a doctor."

"Woah. Look at you. Dr. Amanda."

"It's Avery," I said for the second time, but who was counting.

"My bad. Dr. Avery."

"No. It's Dr. Avery Booker-Peter . . ." I stopped shy of finishing "Peterson." I couldn't believe I was about to refer to myself as the name I rehearsed from the moment Lloyd had proposed to me. I'd been rehearsing Avery Booker-Adebayo too, so why would Peterson half roll off my tongue?

"What's your specialty, Doc?"

"Ob-gyn."

"That's what's up."

According to Keith, everything was up. And his time would be too in about an hour. "Thanks," I said.

"I think the birthing process is amazing."

I used to think the same.

"I have a four-year-old daughter. It's some crazy stuff to look at without vomiting or passing out. I can't believe I'm on a date with a doctor. Let me put some respect on your name. Dr. Amanda Booker-Peter."

I cringed, and through clenched teeth, I said, "It's just Booker. Avery Booker. Not Amanda. Don't even call me a doctor."

"So, who is Peter?" Keith asked.

"Peter is no one. Forget I said that."

I imagined Keith looking perplexed. "Are you really a doctor?"

I nodded. "Why would you think I wasn't?"

"I've never seen a doctor not want to be called a doctor."

My insides churned. "I just want to separate the professional and personal."

"Okay, cool. Y'all hiring at your job?"

"Excuse me?"

"I work full-time, but I am always looking for something better paying or something part-time to go along with my full-time job."

He was so enthralled with touching me and inquiring about my profession that I failed to ask about his. I became curious since our date had turned into a job interview. Before I could ask, he went on about his background.

"You wouldn't go wrong hiring me, Dr. Amanda. I can do it all. I can even deliver a baby if you needed me to."

Still the wrong name. He found humor in his comment, but I didn't. I felt around for my glass of water and took a sip. "You know, delivering a baby takes a lot of schooling, Keith."

"It does. I read up on it while I was in prison."

Leave it to Tri-Me. "Prison?"

"Yeah. You'd be surprised what you can learn doing ten years behind bars. I mastered a lot of things."

"Wow. Ten years is a lot of time." *I need a clock. How much time do we have left on this date?*

"Yeah, being young and dumb."

Surprisingly, I understood that excuse. Amil went to jail for being young and dumb, although he didn't serve but a day.

Keith continued talking, as he'd been doing since the date started. "I was thirty when I went in, served ten, and been out six years now."

This time I coughed to avoid choking. Thirty was too old to be taking the "young and dumb" approach. I was over this date already. I no longer cared about what he did for a living. He was going to the discard pile for sure.

As if it couldn't get any worse . . .

"Amanda, do you mind if we hold hands until the blindfolds come off?"

"I'd rather not, sorry."

Keith got upset. "I see why you single."

I wanted to snatch my blindfold off and run away. "Um, you're single too."

"That's because of stuck-up sistas like you. With a name like Amanda, you might not even be a sista."

Forget the name correction once again. He could call me whatever he wanted to at this point. "I am not stuck-up. I just don't want to sit and hold hands with a stranger."

"You need to be glad someone wants to hold your hand."

"Excuse you. Maybe if your hands weren't so rough, then I wouldn't mind holding them."

"Yeah, well, your arms feel like you need to work out a lot."

"There is something definitely wrong with you. Must be all the years spent behind bars."

"I can get any girl I want. You will see once the folds come off. It's your loss."

I cannot believe I am arguing with this man. "If that were true, you wouldn't be here."

"That's the difference between me and you, Amanda. I am here to add more desperate ladies like yourself to my rotation. But you, you can forget it."

The countdown started to remove the blindfold. I wanted to save myself the trouble of looking at the idiot in front of me, but a part of me couldn't wait to see the idiot in front of me.

We both snatched our blindfolds off.

"Damn, you fine," Keith yelled, which brought all eyes toward our table.

He was a puny little runt with nickel-sized warts on his hands. I was certain not even his cellmates wanted him. I stood to leave. Forget the next two phases. Forget the discard pile. He could go straight to a trash dump.

"Sista Amanda," Keith yelled as I walked away from the table. "I was just joking with you."

I looked back and yelled to him and the dating assistant. "Discard pile!"

Chapter 24

"Any luck?" Tracy asked when I told her I went crawling back to Tri-Me without her since she was all into Amil now.

"I made two more attempts of *trying* Tri-Me to find love, and I won't be *trying* them anymore if this last one doesn't work out."

As we walked and talked around the Savannah River, I filled her in on Keith. Of course, she thought that was the funniest thing in the world. "What about this last date, Amanda?" Tracy jokingly asked once her laughter subsided.

"Please don't call me that. I heard it enough in one night. The second date was with a guy named Theo. He has potential, I think." I shrugged. "We hit it off and exchanged numbers, but for some reason, I haven't heard from him."

"Have you tried reaching out to him?"

"I have. No response. I don't know what went wrong. The date went well, and he seemed cool. He smelled amazing. He came in rocking Dolce & Gabbana cologne."

"Isn't that what Lloyd wears?"

"It is, and while we had the blindfolds on, I was thinking, what if this was Lloyd? It wouldn't be the first time I wondered that."

Tracy stopped and looked at me. "Are you sure that's not the reason you are worried about him? Because he reminds you of that trifling Lloyd?"

I kept walking. "For your information, his conversation had substance to it. I learned a lot about him."

"What did you learn besides his cologne preference? First, does the Negro have a job?"

"Yes. He runs an import and export business."

"Importing and exporting what?"

I shrugged. "I don't know."

"You didn't ask?"

"Unlike you, Tracy, I was not trying to be all in the man's business like that on the first date. The answers will come as we get more acquainted."

Tracy stopped again. "By what you are saying, it doesn't seem like you are going to find out."

"I found out enough to grant him more of my time."

Tracy mumbled under her breath, "Doesn't seem like he wants it."

I stopped walking and lightly pushed her. "I heard that."

She laughed. "Seriously, I think you need to stay away from Tri-Me and fight for Obasi."

"Now you're all of a sudden opposed to the dating agency? And besides, Obasi has moved on."

"I told you what to do, Avery. You should have broken up that hug and claimed your man."

"I am not you. I don't want a criminal record."

Tracy slammed her fist into her palm. "Punching a girl in the face is not really criminal."

I looked at her like she was an alien. "You went to jail. That's criminal."

"That was a long time ago." She dismissed it with a wave.

"Three years is not a long time, and it was all over a man you are no longer with."

"And neither is she, which is what you should have done to Lloyd's baby momma and whoever this chick was who was on Obasi's arm."

"Whatever. It doesn't matter. I will take this as a lesson, open myself up more, and step outside my comfort zone. I will probably never meet anyone as magnetizing as Obasi, though."

"Don't say that. It may not be too late for you and Obasi. He has had enough time to process what happened, and I know that he will be open to talking if you reach out to him. Trust me. I feel it in my spirit."

"Your spirit isn't right, and you sound like my dad. He has been telling me the same thing. Anyway, I am not taking any more advice from you. You give the worst."

"Show up at his bar and tell him how you feel."

I waved my hand in her face. "Hello, tried that, re-member? It backfired."

"Try again and again if you have to."

"What if she's there?"

"It's not disrespectful to tell him how you feel. You don't know if he is on the verge of marrying this woman. All you know is that they were hugged up. It may be a love interest, and it may not be. You won't know unless you try. Trust me with Obasi."

"I will not trust you with holding my sandwich."

"And you shouldn't because I have been extra hungry with my increased workouts, but damn, it's like that?"

I nodded.

"Well, if you won't listen to me, then at least listen to Dr. Booker. It must mean something if we are saying the same thing."

"Moving back to Theo. I made one more attempt with him this morning. I called, and it went straight to voicemail. Then I sent a text asking him to call me, and I haven't heard back from him."

"What else did y'all talk about since you thought the conversation went so well, and he's seemingly ghosted you?"

"Everything from his profession, my profession, politics, future desires."

"I see what it was. You don't have a profession. He sensed that lie."

I gasped. "Tracy, you are starting to act like Amil."

"Maybe his ass is a magician since he disappeared." Tracy laughed at her stupid attempt at a joke.

"Ha-ha."

"If he is that much of a professional, maybe he has a LinkedIn profile. Have you tried looking that up or import-export businesses in the area?"

"You know I don't go surfing the internet trying to find out stuff on people. I like to build genuine connections."

"Well, I do. Genuine connections have gotten you cheated on and ghosted. What's his name? Theo what? And is Theo short for Theodore or something?"

"Tracy, why are you so mean all of a sudden?"

"I didn't say it to be mean. I said it to wake you up. Everyone lies, and those lies can be discovered with one click. Sometimes it takes a little more than that, but it's doable. What is Theo's last name? Is it Huxtable?" Tracy made a drumming noise and buckled over in laughter. This thing with her turning into my brother was going to ruin our friendship.

"Again, not funny. Stick to being a nurse. He said his last name was Wilson."

Tracy's face was glued to her phone. A part of me hoped a pole was coming up and she'd run into it.

"Speaking of nurse, when do you think you are going back to work?" Tracy asked.

"I don't know. I doubt that I will return to the medical field. I may go back to school and take up something else. Law school or something."

"Do you know how silly that sounds?"

"Maybe this is God's way of pushing me into the path that I need to be on."

"Hmm."

"What was that grunt for?"

"You wouldn't make a good lawyer."

"Thanks for believing in me, friend."

"Lawyers have to be able to gauge people at all times. They need to know when people are bullshitting them. You don't have that characteristic, and that's okay. You have to be able to read people. That's not something you learn. You are born with it."

"How do you know what I have and don't have? Lloyd got one over on me. I'll give you that. But that doesn't mean that everyone will."

"Theo Wilson did too. Well. It wasn't Theo, per se. Theo is the alias he uses. Marvin Trotter is his real name."

"What are you talking about, Tracy?"

"I told you it only takes a few clicks to find out who people are. If they give you a smidgen of information, you can find a lot."

"So the whole time you've been walking with your face planted in your phone looking him up?"

"Yep, and you are gonna wanna see this."

"I don't. I am not snooping through people's private lives."

"Technically, you aren't. I am. He gave you a fake name, and his mug shot on the news makes this public."

"It's not a crime to give fake names. Maybe it's a nick-name. How many times have we've been out and given fake names, Gina?" I said to Tracy, using her fake name that she'd give every man who approached her. For a while, I forgot her name was really Tracy.

Tracy turned her phone around, and I caught a glimpse of a recent mug shot of Theo. Light skin, mustache, low haircut.

"Wow!" I said.

"I agree that it's not a crime to give a fake name, but it is an arrestable offense for trafficking narcotics. That explains the import-export part. Not to mention, the police seized three guns."

"I give up on men, dating, love. All of it."

"I am about to call Amil and ask him about it. While I'm doing that, you need to call Obasi and win that man back. You were the happiest with him. There is nothing else out there. He's it. Call him."

Chapter 25

I took Tracy's advice, kind of. I agreed with her that there was nothing else out there, but instead of calling Obasi, I called Lloyd. I'd been avoiding him since Obasi caught him and me at Saints and Sinners. The townhouse still lay in wait, and so was whatever Lloyd wanted to talk to me about. I was sure it was nothing concerning Oakley, because if it were, he would've texted it to me by now.

I sighed at my life. A hot damn mess again. I was all over the place, behaving like I had daddy issues, but mommy issues counted just as much.

Obasi had clearly moved on, and I didn't want to disrupt that. I knew what it was like to have a woman come in and cause confusion in your relationship, and that was definitely not the person I wanted to be. It was crazy to say that while I was considering taking back the man who allowed a woman to come into our relationship and cause confusion. I didn't want to be lonely, but I would probably be in jail if I had listened to Tracy.

Lloyd was surprised to hear from me. We agreed to meet for dinner later that week. I missed dressing up for date night in general. But when I was with Lloyd, on the days when I was too tired to go out from bending, pulling, tugging, and performing acrobats delivering babies, he'd drop by my house with takeout and definitely wine. He'd throw on some light music, and his hands would rub out the tension in my sore muscles.

Lloyd must've learned from the last dinner meeting we had. He didn't try to hug me this time. "It's good to see you," he said as he pulled out my chair.

"Thank you." It was awkward. I glanced around the restaurant in case Obasi was there. There was nothing special about my appearance this time. I wasn't trying to make a statement. I wasn't sure that I even wanted to be there.

"Thank you for calling me. How have you been?" Lloyd asked and slid me a menu.

Should I say I have been miserable since I lost my man? Not you, Lloyd. The good one. Instead, I shrugged and studied the menu.

When I closed it, Lloyd asked, "What does that mean?" Before fixing my mouth to say anything, the waiter approached the table for our orders. An innocent-looking young man. He couldn't have been any more than 20. It made me wonder what LJ would be like when he got around that age.

"Are you ready to order?" he asked.

Lloyd folded his menu. "I'm ready. I already know what I want, and I'd like to order for the lady if she allows it." Lloyd and the young waiter I still viewed as Lloyd's son looked at me for approval.

I nodded the go-ahead.

Lloyd proceeded to order my favorite. "For the lady, salmon with asparagus and a salad, and for me, I will have the steak, medium well, with the same sides."

I held up my glass of water to salute him on a job well done. "That was perfect."

"I've missed you," Lloyd said.

"And I have been miserable, but that's life."

Lloyd nodded in agreement. "I can understand the miserable part. I have been miserable without you."

His comment irritated me. I wanted to throw the glass of water sitting in front of me in his face. "You have no idea what miserable feels like. Miserable for you is waking up in the middle of the night to feed your crying baby or to change a diaper. Miserable for me is the movie that constantly plays in my head of a woman confessing a secret that shredded my heart, and just like Humpty Dumpty, it can't be put back together."

"Avery." Lloyd's voice was calm. "Honestly, I haven't seen LJ. Oakley will call when she needs money. She won't come around, so I Cash App her. That's pretty much it. I don't even know where she moved to. She won't tell me anything."

Interesting. Probably because she has a warrant and is scared we are working together to catch her. "How much do you know about Oakley?"

"Nothing really. Enough to know she's not worth losing you over."

I laughed inside. I thought Lloyd really was clueless about Oakley and who she was.

"I know I hurt you," Lloyd said. "I'd like to change that. If I had my way, I'd marry you right now. I would have married you when I was supposed to. I know I screwed up, and I cannot change what has already happened. I know that now, and I knew that then. I was hoping after dinner we could walk along the river and talk. That would be a better environment for us to discuss details and the townhouse if you still want to get rid of it."

Yeah, we can walk along the river so I can push you in. "I still want to get rid of the townhouse."

"I hate to hear that. I was hoping you'd have a change of heart. Please, let me prove to you that I will be a better man." Lloyd tried to reach across the table to grab my hand, but I moved it.

Silence lingered until I spoke. I wanted to find out if he was as clueless as he was leading on. "How's work going?"

"Work is going well. Working lots of hours."

"I can understand. Two extra mouths to feed."

"One."

"Two. The momma counts."

"Not on my dime."

"Whatever."

"Are you going to have an attitude toward me for the rest of my life? What can I do?"

"More than likely."

"I don't want to be with anyone else except for you."

"That's some bullshit, and you know it." I hushed when our food came out. My temperature was hotter than the sizzling plate that Lloyd's steak came out on. As soon as the waiter walked away from the table, I started again. "If that were true, there is no way you would have a kid with another woman right now. And there is no way this finger would be bare." I held up my hand and did the Beyoncé "Single Ladies" wave toward him.

"I want to place a ring back on your finger."

"What about Oakley?"

"I told you already. I don't want anyone but you."

"I want more details. We are past the broken-down car and help. I want to know about the sex."

Lloyd stopped chewing. "Can we talk about that when it's just the two of us and not a restaurant full of people?"

The restaurant had started to get thick with people. I looked over Lloyd's shoulder at the servers pushing tables together for a large party. "Since you are so good at pretending, pretend it's just us two and tell me where it happened and how many times?" I angled my fork so that the prongs faced Lloyd. I was prepared to stab him if I felt the urge.

Lloyd set down his knife and fork. "Oakley was a one-night stand. She invited me to the sports bar where she worked to thank me for helping her. I had a little too much to drink and . . ."

Sports bar? Obasi owned a sports bar. *Please tell me it's not the same one.* My heart was working overtime. I was nervous about what I was about to hear. "And?" I asked.

"And." He shrugged his shoulders. *He doesn't get to shrug.* Shrugging was my thing, and that was not going to give me the visual I was looking for.

"You had too much to drink, and what else? Don't expect me to use my imagination to fill in the blanks when your words will do just fine. I don't care how uncomfortable it is for you." And it was uncomfortable, because he was sweating hard under dim lights.

"I don't want to hurt you, Avery."

"Too late for that."

I hadn't touched my food, but I still had my weapon aimed his way, ready to prick him a few times.

Through a whisper, he said, "She and I hooked up that night."

"Where?"

He hesitated. "In the bathroom of the sports bar."

If I had an Adam's apple, I would've swallowed it. I reached for the cloth napkin that held the rest of my eating utensils to dry the stream of tears that poured from my eyes. Lloyd tried to reach for me again. "Don't touch me."

"This is why I didn't want to talk about this. I hate seeing you cry."

"When you were getting busy with Oakley, did me crying cross your mind?"

He didn't respond. He just sat looking like he'd seen his puppy get run over.

"I already know the answer. I was the furthest thing from your mind as you were having sex with a stranger without protection. How dumb are you?"

"I'm sorry."

The critical question. I tapped my foot under the table, trying to control my nerves. "Where is this sports bar? And you better tell the truth."

"In Grovetown."

"Are you sure it's Grovetown and not downtown?"

Lloyd tugged at the collar of his Polo shirt. "I'm positive."

"What kind of establishment is this that y'all can do that in the bathroom? How do you even know this is your baby, dummy?"

"I guess because the dates add up."

"'I guess because the dates add up,'" I said, mocking him. "And you don't think she's capable of hooking up with other dudes in bars like she did with you? You don't think she purposely baited you?"

"Like I said, I had too much to drink. All I know is that I want to be with you. I want more with you."

"So you want me to be a stepmother before I am a mother, especially when the title of stepmother could've been avoided? Not only did you cheat, but you created a life with my sister."

Lloyd's face scrunched at my confession.

"See, so you can't want more with me when you already have more with someone else. Capitalize on that and make an honest woman out of her." And for the sake of it, I added, "You have my blessing, and I'll even get you a wedding gift. I may even be there. I may even keep my nephew while the two of you are on your honeymoon."

"I'm not asking you to be a sister wife. I don't want Oakley. I want you, Avery."

He didn't get it. "Oakley used you as bait to get back at my mother, her biological mother. And you fell for it."

Lloyd's eyes grew, and his already-light skin turned white. "That's impossible. You're making that up."

I cocked my head to the side. "Am I? If Oakley was bold enough to pull a stunt like she did at our wedding, you don't think she'd be capable of revenge?"

The more I sat with Lloyd, explaining the situation to him, the more I thought of Obasi. I couldn't stop saying his name in my mind. I missed him, and I missed how secure he made me feel.

Lloyd sat silent and in shock. I watched the large party gather behind him. Looked like some type of celebration. Then I noticed the couple sitting next to the large party. They held hands and gazed into each other's eyes. They looked to be in their late teens. The love that floated around them reeked of new love, and it made me wonder what kind of problems they'd face in their relationship. I looked at Lloyd again and remembered when we first met and developed new love like that.

We were in high school. Lloyd had transferred to one of my classes during the second week of school. When he walked in, I groaned. He had a reputation for being an asshole.

"Hey, what's up, girl?"

"My name is Avery, not 'girl,'" I said and pushed my falling glasses up on my face.

"How often do the trains come?"

"What are you talking about?"

"Those train tracks on your teeth. How often does the train come?"

"Have you know, my braces come off in two months, so your joke is dumb like you," I said.

He laughed and reached for my paper. "Let me see your notes."

"For what? Why are you even in AP Calculus?"

"Avery, is there a problem?" the teacher asked.

I was humiliated. I had never been called out in class before. I stumbled over my words. "No, um, no, Mr. Herrington. I . . . I was—"

"She was trying to catch me up on the notes, Mr. Herrington. It's my fault, and it won't happen again."

Lloyd looked at me and winked.

"Very well," Mr. Herrington said. "You two will have as much time as you want to talk and compare notes around class because I am assigning you as partners for the upcoming project."

"But, Mr. Herrington, you can't be serious. I've taken your class for three years, and I've always worked with Ishmael."

"Oh, but I am very serious. You and Ishmael present the same concept with each project, and while your work is great, I want to see something different from the two of you."

Lloyd looked at me with a smirk. He leaned over and whispered, "So, basically, Mr. Herrington thinks you're boring, and he wants me to add some flavor in your life."

And Lloyd did add flavor. Brought me out of my shell, which had been great until he added the wrong mix of flavors—a baby momma and a kid.

The sudden, loud "Happy anniversary" from the large party caught my attention. They gathered around an elderly couple. The restaurant was dark. However, I knew they were celebrating their fiftieth wedding anniversary because of the jumbo neon, glitter-covered number fifty candles. It seemed like the number five and number zero helium-filled balloons moved extra hard to get my attention to remind me that I would never celebrate a fiftieth anniversary with the man sitting before me. Fifty years was a long time, and it made me wonder what type of problems they faced over those fifty years. With all of the people standing around, I wondered if those were their kids and if any of them had been conceived outside of the relationship. If so, how did they get over it? I replaced their faces with Lloyd's and mine after conquering relationship demons. That felt wrong. I traded out Lloyd's face for Obasi. Maybe that could be us one day.

Each face had a smile on it. It made me smile. It made me reach for Lloyd's hand, thinking he was Obasi. I held it until I noticed another couple. The husband stood behind the wife, rubbing her pregnant belly. Their fingers interlocked. I saw their wedding rings. Their faces faded and were replaced with Lloyd's and Oakley's.

A sick feeling swept through my stomach. Then a stabbing sensation within me. Lloyd needed to feel what I felt. I motioned for him to turn around.

"That's going to be us one day," he said.

"It's already you."

His smile faded like a pair of jeans that had been washed too many times. "I beg your pardon," he said.

"You said that will be us, and I said it's already you."

Lloyd frowned. "I don't understand what you mean."

"See that couple there?" I pointed. "The pregnant lady is Oakley, and the man standing behind her . . . that's you." I let out a deep sigh. "Oakley is my sister, and LJ is my nephew."

"Avery, can we not do this? I know things are horrible now, but I still want to try to fix it."

"I wish we didn't have to do it. I wish none of this had happened. There was a time when having the title of your wife and building a life with you excited me."

"And I still want that with you," Lloyd said.

I shrugged and pulled my hand from Lloyd's. "I'm sorry, but that will never happen. I used to think that, because of the love I had for you, I could learn to move past it, but . . ." My voice trailed off. No sense in repeating myself.

The more I watched that family celebrate, the more
the disgust grew in my stomach. If I were that crazy to
rekindle with Lloyd, I'd never be invited to LJ's birthday
party or anything involving him. Not as an aunt and
definitely not as a stepmother. I would feel out of place.

"Just give me a chance to show you."

"I don't want to deal with Oakley as my sister. You
think I'd deal with her and her baby momma drama for
the rest of my life?"

"You won't have to, Avery."

And just as he said that, his vibrating phone caught his
eye and mine too. Oakley's name appeared on the screen.
He silenced it, but she called right back. He silenced it
again and slipped the phone into his pocket.

"Exactly my point." I double pointed downward. "Even
if she weren't my sister, you cannot make a lifetime commitment to me when you've made one to someone else."

"One chance, Avery."

"I love you, Lloyd, because we have history, but not in
a romantic way. And not enough to put myself in this
situation." I gathered my things, never even touched my
food. "Oh, and when the mother of your child calls, you
should probably answer. It may be an emergency with
your baby."

Seeing that family restored the sense that I had temporarily lost. There was no way that I would serve as
runner-up to anyone, and there was no way that I would
go another day without fighting for Obasi.

Lloyd called my name a couple of times as I walked
out, but my back served as a shield protecting me from
turning around. Even though we never discussed the
townhouse, I felt relieved while waiting for the valet to
bring my car around. Somehow, I would find a way out of
that mortgage.

"Excuse me."

I turned around to see if that voice was summoning me. I instantly recognized that face. The last time I saw her she was panting, sweating, and in labor. Those familiar eyes again. They were from my mother.

"Well, well, well." Oakley inched closer to me every time she said "well."

"What do you want, Oakley?"

"Is that any way to greet your big sister? I came by to give you an important message."

"There is nothing that I need to hear from you."

"I beg to differ. Lloyd and I are getting married, so you need to stay away from him. I hope he told you that over this little dinner y'all had because it will be the last time."

"Congratulations on your engagement and wedding. I am sure you'll make a lovely bride."

"Oh, you trying to be sarcastic?"

"Not at all."

I was done with the conversation. I searched through my purse for tip money and my phone while trying to drown out everything Oakley said.

"That's a nice bag. Lloyd bought me one better than that." Oakley dangled her purse. It was indeed a cute bag.

"Good for you." I kept it short and classy. I could've said more. At this point, eyes were watching. I was not about to do this with her.

"Stay away from him," Oakley demanded. "Stay away from him, or you will be sorry."

Was it worth responding? Was it worth being the bigger person? I couldn't resist. "No worries, future Mrs. Lloyd Peterson." She inched closer to me. She had crossed the imaginary line that now made her a threat instead of an upset lover. I had every right to defend myself by any means necessary. My body shifted into defense mode. Underneath the straps of my purse, my fists were balled. And while I wore heels, I didn't kick them off, not yet. One needed to be a weapon for me against her. My left foot rested just before my right. I'd lead with a left hook and, hopefully, scare her off. She inched a little closer. "Oakley, please step back."

"I'll let it go when you admit that you still want him."

Some prize Lloyd got. What was wrong with this girl? My car pulled up, which allowed me the chance to escape the drama. I tipped the driver and hopped into the driver's seat. When I attempted to pull off, Oakley was standing in front of my car, taunting me. What did Lloyd see in this immature woman?

"Do you want us to phone the police, ma'am?" the valet attendant asked as security restrained her.

Oakley was obviously sick. "Please do. She has a warrant for her arrest. Her fiancé is inside the restaurant. I will call him to come and get her."

Lloyd picked up on the first ring.

"FYI. Oakley, your fiancé, is outside causing a scene. She's been detained by security. The police are on their way."

"What? How does she even know where I am?"

"She followed you before. One thing I forgot. She has a warrant out for her arrest, so you may want to find out where LJ is."

Oakley struggled with security to get to Lloyd when he came out. Before I pulled off, I saw Lloyd through my rearview mirror, standing in front of Oakley with his hands flailing. I grabbed my cell phone and called my brothers and my dad. I didn't follow Amil's advice. I was not staying behind to file a report. I pulled off when I heard the sirens approaching. I didn't want any part of this. She already had warrants that would take care of her. I just hoped LJ was okay.

Chapter 26

My heart thumped double time as I drove downtown to Broad Street. I was going to win Obasi back. Or at least try.

The closer I got, the harder the rain fell. The closer I got, the more red lights I encountered. Maybe that was a sign that I should turn around and go home. But I could hear my dad's voice: *"If you never try, then how will you know?"* I slowed my car looking for parking. Just my luck, there was an empty spot in front of his sports bar. I parallel parked and sat for a minute, waiting on the rain to slack. That was the excuse that I used not to go inside. I had an umbrella.

The longer I sat, the more I thought of how I would look like a stalker if he came outside and saw me sitting there. I turned the car off and slowly opened the door to get out, but then I closed it again and started the engine. "I cannot do this."

When I thought about how much I missed him, I finally mustered up enough courage to go inside. When I opened the door, a stream of light traveled in his direction. There he was, and there she was. The same girl he was hugging was standing beside him, drying glasses. Their energy was electrifying. Not only did I see it, but I felt it, or I was allowing fear to make me believe I was. They were staring at me. My mind told me to turn around and run away, but my feet wouldn't let me. Love allowed me to slowly move in the direction of the bar.

I could understand how this girl felt being around Obasi because he made me feel the same way.

They both watched as I crept toward the bar. When I sat, Obasi stopped drying glasses and threw the towel over his shoulder.

She smiled at me. "Hey there, gorgeous, what can I get for you?" Her smile was radiant.

"Hi," I said. I smiled back at her, but my smile quickly faded. If she was here with Obasi, they must have been serious, and I didn't want to ruin that. I didn't want to be the girl who came between love, but I had to do this. *If they are serious, I will respect it, walk out of here, and never return.*

"Obasi, can I talk to you for a minute?" I looked over at her and said, "In private if that's okay?" I looked back at him for approval.

"Jules, can you finish up here?"

"On top of it."

I watched as he walked from behind the bar and stood at the edge of the counter. "Can I get you anything? Water, margarita, Coke, wine?"

"No, I'm good."

"You hungry? Want some food?"

Nope, I just want you. "No, I don't want anything, thank you."

"Follow me." He led me to a booth tucked away in a dim corner.

We sat, and he dove right in. "What's on your mind?"

I should have taken the water, because my mouth seemed stuck together. "A lot is on my mind."

"Such as?"

"You. Us." I couldn't believe that came out as easily as it did.

"What about me and us? You came here to talk, so talk. I am not going to sit here and try to pull information out of you."

"Can I get that water after all?"

He looked over his shoulder and yelled toward the bar. "Jules."

"Yeah," she yelled back.

"Water, baby, just one." He signaled with one finger.

Baby? I knew this was a bad idea.

Even though I didn't want his "baby" touching my water, I guzzled it as soon as she placed it on the table. It was only an eight-ounce bottle, so it didn't make me seem less ladylike.

Obasi pulled two napkins from the holder. He nodded toward my shirt. "Waterdrops. You seem parched. Want another?"

Those waterdrops gave me an instant flashback of the stains on my wedding dress. I knew Lloyd was a place that I did not want to go back to. I needed to speak up and tell Obasi how I felt. *I feel sorry for this girl at the bar. I hope she understands that I at least have to try.*

I fiddled with the empty water bottle.

Obasi put his hands on top of mine. "Why are you so nervous? Just talk."

I took a deep breath and then released a long sigh. "I'm sorry to pop up on you like this." I looked over at the woman behind the bar. "And I'm sorry to do this with your girlfriend nearby."

Obasi let out the most hysterical laugh.

"What's so funny?"

"Nothing, please continue." He sat back against the seat and crossed his arms. Even though he had the biggest grin on his face, I was just going to say what I had to say.

"I'm smitten with you and have been for a while. I know that sounds crazy because you saw me out with Lloyd, but it's not what you think. I have been all over the place with my emotions, but I can't stop thinking about you. My timing is bad, I know, and I understand if this comes off as disrespectful with your girlfriend being here."

My mouth was covered with Obasi's mouth. I pulled back and looked at the bar where the woman was clapping. "Are y'all some kind of swingers or something?"

"Woman, no. I don't share." He scooted out of the booth and pulled me by the hand toward the woman. "Remember I told you I have a sister I hadn't seen in a while? This is her. Jules."

I felt like a relieved fool.

"It's nice to finally meet you. I've heard a lot about you." She extended her hand to shake mine. It was warm and welcoming.

Now that my nerves floated away like a dead fish with a wave, I heard her accent.

"You've heard about me?" I asked.

"Often. My brother speaks of you often."

"He does?"

Obasi chimed in. "I do. You are not the only one with feelings. Remember I told you that I needed someone to match my energy? You do that. And I am sure your ambition will display once you figure out what you want to do with yourself."

"But you refused to speak to me."

"Had to teach you a lesson. Plus, I am a firm believer that if it's meant to be, then it shall." Obasi went back to drying glasses with his sister.

I silently thanked God.

"Now, is Lloyd out of your system? Tracy and your dad seem to think so. Are they accurate?"

"Completely. Except for the townhouse. I don't know what to do to get rid of it. Wait a minute. You've been in contact with Tracy and my dad?"

"They called me and explained the whole Lloyd thing and the reason for the meeting. Again, I had to teach you a lesson. As your man, I need you to come to me about those things. I want to be included in stuff like that.

When you do it the way that you did, it makes me feel like there's something more, or you have something to hide."

I nodded in agreement. "Neither Tracy nor my dad said anything."

"And they weren't going to. It had to be up to you to do what you did today, not because anyone forced you or tipped you off. I needed to make sure you were serious enough about a relationship to make yourself uncomfortable enough to make an effort." He set his towel down and walked around to the stool where I was sitting. He lifted my chin so that our eyes were connected. "And don't worry about the townhouse. It will be taken care of."

I cocked my head to the side and frowned. "What do you mean?"

Obasi pulled a business card from his wallet. "Call my attorney. He's a miracle worker and will get something moving as soon as you call. I have a buyer right now, cash."

"Who?"

He nodded toward his sister. "Jules and I went by the townhouse, and she loves it. We have some things in the making where she plans on staying to help me out around here."

"I love the townhome," Jules said.

"How did you find it?" I asked. "Let me guess, Tracy?"

"Yeah, she told us where it was. We've been making moves behind your back. We only peeked through the windows and walked the perimeter."

"Well, that means I can move into it. No offense, Jules."

She smiled.

Obasi tapped me on my shoulder to take my attention from his sister. "You can't afford such an expensive place without a job."

"Where am I supposed to live?"

"With your dad, like you have been, or go back to work and rent a place. If things go right with me and you, then you'll be living with me in my home. If you don't want to do that, then we can move. Your choice."

"Your home? Will Brandon let me in the gate this time?"

"I stand corrected. Our home if it comes to that." He shrugged. "Be the woman I fell in love with and your gate privileges won't be revoked." He laughed. "I bet you were pissed off. I asked Brandon, and he said you handled it well."

"That was not very nice."

Obasi wrapped me in his arms. In between every kiss to my cheek, he said, "That was your one mess-up. Don't let that shit happen again."

I blushed. "So, what now? Are we okay?"

"We are good. Now, you can stay and help because you need a job."

I laughed. I didn't know if it was more at the joke or that I was in a good mood because I had my man back. "Don't do me like that."

"I'm serious, babe. I need to put a dent in some things around here because I am going fishing with your pops and brothers tomorrow."

He was back to calling me "babe," which did something to me when I heard it roll from his mouth with his accent. "I cannot believe my dad invited you on a fishing trip."

"Indeed, he did. I have that effect on people."

"Whatever."

"Maybe you, Jules, and Tracy can hang out tomorrow while we are gone. I'm sure she'd love to see the inside of the townhouse."

"That's not a bad idea," Jules said. She put her hands together like she was praying I'd say yes. "Please."

"Of course." I tugged at Obasi's beard. "We need money for a spa day, too. If you don't surrender a charge card, I am going to pull harder."

"Okay, okay. I got you."

"You got the three of us?"

When he nodded, I let go.

"Nate told me to tell you hi, by the way."

I punched him. "Since you think you are so funny, you should do standup." I pointed to the stage. "Go ahead, get on the stage."

Obasi got excited. "Jules, can you bring us two glasses of 2014 Bond Vecina? This woman here just gave me a brilliant idea."

Confusion rushed through me. "What did I say?"

He kissed me. "I hadn't thought about comedy acts coming in until you just said that. That is another way to grow business. Write this down, Jules." He tossed her a pen, and she started jotting down his thoughts on a napkin. "We will leave Friday as spoken word, add Saturdays for comedy night, which we will have to work around college football, then we already have Sundays dedicated to football during the season." He squeezed me. "That was a brilliant idea, babe. Now, if you aren't doing any work, then you need to leave after our glass of wine, or I will be sitting and staring at you and kissing on you all day."

I batted my eyes. "I wouldn't mind that, but what can I help with?"

"Finish drying these glasses, please. I need to figure this out."

After we toasted to restarting our relationship, I took the towel from Obasi and did what he asked.

Before he walked off, he stood behind me, wrapped his arms around my waist, and said, "P.S. Thank you for coming back to me."

Chapter 27

I lay across Obasi's lap. We were deep into a movie when an unrecognizable number flashed across my screen.

"I have no idea who this is," I said to Obasi.

"Probably your boyfriend," he said playfully.

I returned the banter. "I don't see a phone in your hand."

He pointed to my ring finger and started tickling me. "That's because I'm not your boyfriend, remember?"

Never would I ever forget Obasi proposing to me six months ago. The proposal happened on a Friday during spoken word. His restaurant was packed to capacity and had been since the addition of Jules, the soup, and the Saturday night comedy shows. Obasi's book released with excellent reviews the week prior, and Jules, with my help, surprised him by throwing him a launch party. Little did I know, he had a surprise for me too. When he took the stage to thank everyone for coming out, he called me up with him.

"Y'all see this woman right here?" He spun me around to cheers from the crowd. "She has been everything I could ever ask for. My life was pretty damn cool before her, but now that she's a part of it, it has been pretty damn amazing. I look forward to her presence. If we go hours without speaking, I find myself missing her, needing to talk to her, wanting to talk to her." The crowd was in an uproar.

I knew he had a way with words, but I never heard anyone publicly confess them toward me, not the way he did. I felt like I mattered. I felt included. I thought he was finished. I started to walk off the stage when he pulled my hand and turned me to face him.

"When I saw you, there was an aura about you, nothing that I'd felt before. Your circle of light, although dim from hurt and an allergy attack, still managed to peek through the dimness." He and I both laughed about the allergy attack. "I didn't know much about you other than you had some serious allergies." Everyone laughed. "But what I did know was that I wanted to get to know you better. Now that I have, I can't see you not being a part of my life." He dropped to one knee and pulled out a box. Not a blue one. He went to Jared's. "Avery Booker, will you please be my wife?"

You would have thought there was an earthquake with how the excitement shook the building. I thought I fainted a couple of times, but I said, "Yes, yes, yes. Hurry up and put my ring on."

Obasi was still tickling me when I answered the phone through laughs. They subsided the moment I heard Lloyd's voice.

"It's so good to hear you laugh."

I covered the speaker of my phone and whispered to Obasi, "It's Lloyd. What do you want me to do?"

"See what he wants."

"Do you want to talk to him?"

"No. He didn't call for me. He called for you."

"Lloyd, now is not a good time. I'm watching a movie with my fiancé." *Emphasis on "fiancé."*

Obasi got up to leave the room, but I tugged on his shirttail and motioned for him to sit back down.

"Hold on, Lloyd." I muted my phone.

"The two of you have history, and I am secure in what we are building. If I weren't, I would have never asked you to be my wife."

"No. As my future husband, I want you here with me. No secrets."

He sat back down, and I unmuted the phone and put it on speaker. "What's up, Lloyd?"

"You're engaged?" he asked.

"I am."

"Wow. I will admit that stings a little."

You had your chance.

"So, I guess the reason for my call won't matter then."

"Depends on what you were calling for."

"You've been on my mind, and I wanted to once again say that I am sorry for everything that happened and for the pain that I caused. It took having my life turned upside down to realize the caliber of the woman I had. I messed up. I lost the woman of my dreams being selfish, and I'm sorry."

"Thank you, but you don't have to keep apologizing. I have forgiven you, and you need to forgive yourself. How's LJ doing anyway? I bet he's gotten so big."

"I wouldn't know."

"I'm sorry. I assumed he was in your care since Oakley is still in jail."

There was silence before Lloyd dropped a bombshell.

"I had a DNA test done. He's not mine."

Obasi and I gasped. His eyes widened larger than a tarsier's. Obasi slapped my shoulder, and I almost dropped my phone. He was reacting like a girl hearing the latest juicy gossip.

"Wow!" I said, my voice full of disbelief.

"Oakley isn't even her real name. It's Tamika Oaks. She uses Oakley for the sophistication of it. But I'm assuming you knew that already."

"Yeah. I did. We learned of her real name during her arraignment. However, we weren't privy to LJ's location."

"When she got arrested, I had to hire a lawyer in an attempt to get custody. That's how I found out Oakley wasn't her real name. I found out a lot more. Apparently, she had a boyfriend all along. I wouldn't be surprised if he helped her swindle money from Mrs. Booker."

I contained my composure, unlike Obasi, who was now pacing the floor with his fist in his mouth. "Oh, wow. I am so sorry. I know how much you wanted kids, especially a son."

"Yeah, but I wanted them with you."

I looked at Obasi and shrugged my shoulders. I knew he had to be uncomfortable listening to this. "You're still young, Lloyd. I'm sure you will meet a wonderful woman who will bless you with the family you want."

"I don't want another woman. I want you."

I looked at Obasi again, hoping he'd intervene. I covered the speaker of my phone and asked, "Do you want to take over?"

Obasi shook his head. "You got it, babe. I trust you."

"I'm getting married in six months. I'm happy about building a life and family with my fiancé, and nothing will change that."

"Just reconsider, please."

"I'm sorry, Lloyd. I have to go. I wish you the best. And sorry again about LJ. Take care." I disconnected the call.

Even though Lloyd hurt me, I felt terrible for him. I would never wish this pain on anyone. I felt bad for Obasi for having to sit and listen to his future wife's ex-fiancé, minutes shy of being her husband, plead for her back.

"I'm sorry, Obasi. I hope that wasn't disrespectful."

"You don't need to apologize to me. Thank you."

"What are you thanking me for?"

"Because you handled that well, which further proves I am marrying the perfect woman."

"I don't get it."

"It's internal, hard to explain."

I nodded. "But can you try to explain?"

"You and Lloyd have a ton of history. You were about to marry this man. The main reason you didn't want to take him back was because of the baby. Now the baby isn't his. You could have decided to take him back and work through the cheating, but you held committed to us."

"How do you know I won't?"

"I don't know, but I do know that when I first met you, your spirit was down. And even through that, I knew that if I nourished it a little, it would spring back up. You are in a different headspace. I doubt you want to go back to that."

"If your ex called, I'd be freaked out."

"That's because Lloyd took something away from you that I never will. Trust. No doubt there are times when I pay for his mistakes, but I will remain patient and believe that one day I will no longer have to. I haven't given you one reason not to trust me. You have access to everything, including my phone. I grew in love with you for many reasons, and one was your ability to rise above your circumstances. You have had my back and encouraged me on days when I've been uncertain. I am sure you are not taking him back."

"Women are fools when it comes to stuff like this."

He shrugged. "Yeah, but consider these two things: one, you asked about the child he had on you, which is something no woman will do unless she's completely over it. And two, compare your peace now versus then. That alone puts me at peace. However, if Lloyd or anyone can win your heart, it wasn't mine to begin with. If that is God's will, then so be it."

"Just like that?"

"I know I will never do anything to hurt you. Now can you hush so we can get back to this movie?" He pushed my head. That was Amil's behavior, and I hated it, but when Obasi did it, it made me blush.

"Oh, so now you want to watch the movie that I had to pull teeth to make you watch?"

"Lifetime movies aren't that bad. But don't tell anyone I told you that. I have a reputation to uphold," Obasi said.

"I tried to tell you."

"It's either the movie distraction, or we are going to consummate this marriage before our wedding night with those little-ass shorts you have on."

"Obasi Adebayo."

"Avery Booker-Adebayo."

I melted hearing him call my soon-to-be new name. "Guess what?"

"What?"

"I love you and thank you for being so patient with me."

"I love you too, babe."

Chapter 28

It was just another day of our usual Saturday morning chilling. Almost. My dad had the nerve to come waltzing in the door after staying out all night like he wasn't grown.

Tracy helped me finalize the seating chart to hand over to Scottsdale, who Obasi and I hired as our wedding planner.

"Pops, man, where have you been?" Amil asked and put both of his hands on his hips like he was somebody's momma.

My dad shook his head and kicked his shoes off. "Good. You are all here."

"We've all been here since last night. We slept here like we normally would, minus you." Amil shifted his weight from one foot to the other. "We want answers."

"Boy, I told you when you called last night that I'd be home in the morning. Now sit down. We need to talk."

"Yes, sir."

I sighed. "Not another family meeting." We have had so many of them since Tamika's court date, and quite frankly, I was tired of meetings.

We all turned toward the foyer when we heard the alarm lady announce, "Front door open."

My mother strolled in. "Good morning."

"Good morning," I replied.

"Good day," Anthony followed.

Amil said nothing.

"Your mother and I want to talk to you."

"So, is this some kind of ambush?" Amil asked, clearly not happy.

"Good morning, Dr. and Mrs. Booker. It's good to see you." Tracy nodded toward my mother. "I'm going to leave you guys to it. Avery, call me, and we can finish this later."

"What's going on?" Anthony asked.

"Your mother has some things she would like to say to you three, and since none of you has responded to her texts or phone calls, I told her she could come over and talk with you in person."

Anthony turned to the mantel, staring at that fake-ass Buddha again. He didn't do anything the last time, and he sure as hell wasn't going to do anything this time. If he couldn't make these problems disappear, then what was he good for?

Amil looked off. He was in the room with us, but he wasn't.

I chose to pay attention.

"How is the wedding planning going, Avery?"

I smiled. "Good." Nothing could knock me off this high.

"Do you need help with anything?" she asked.

I shook my head. Even if I did need help, I wouldn't know how to ask her.

My dad gave my mother the floor. "Go on, Florence."

"I'm sorry to barge in on you guys, but I didn't know what else to do."

"I just want to say I'm sorry for everything. The way I spoke at times. The way I criticized you all and made you feel like you weren't good enough. I am sorry that I missed sporting events and debates. I'm sorry I didn't teach my boys how a woman is supposed to love a man or how a mother should love her sons. I failed you, boys." She paused and then turned her attention toward me.

"And, Avery, I apologize for not being there to go dress shopping with you for prom or have those mother-daughter moments where we'd go and get pedicures together. I'm sorry for not developing enough as a woman to teach you anything." She swiped her heavy tears. "There is so much I could've done. I regret it all."

"Do you regret not being around for the birth of your first grandchild?"

That question shocked us all. Anthony's back faced Buddha when his usual small voice roared with anger.

"I do regret that, yes. And I hope I never have to miss anything else."

Not a peep from anyone.

"I know this will take time and a lot of work, but I am prepared to do whatever I can." My mother walked near Anthony. "Son, I am sorry for not being the mother I should've been to you. I know it will take some time, but I am asking for your forgiveness." The closer she inched toward Amil, the more he backed away. "Amil. Son, I am sorry for not being the mother to you I should've been. I hope that one day you will forgive me." Then she turned to me. For some reason, I tried to look at that powerless Buddha Anthony had so much faith in. All I could see was Anthony's back. I looked at the floor. "Avery. You got it worse than your brothers because I had already lost one daughter, and instead of embracing you, I pushed you away. I'm so sorry, and I hope one day you can forgive me, and we can take those mother-daughter spa days and shopping trips."

"Have you kids given any more thought to family therapy?" my dad asked.

I'd given some thought to personal counseling only because I understood the pain of losing a child. Not that I'd been through it. I'd had to deliver stillborn babies. The pain from the mothers, fathers, and grandparents was something that I'd always take home with me. It always made me wonder how my mother's parents were comfortable giving up their firstborn grandchild just to save their image. Wasn't the church meant to bring in lost sheep? Not turn their backs on them. My mother was a lost sheep.

It all made sense, though. I'd always asked about my maternal grandparents because I had never seen photos of them. I'd never met them. They died before Anthony was born. I wondered if they were physically dead or just dead in the eyes of my mother. Even when I had to complete a family tree for class, my mother was tightlipped with information. She gave me the basics.

"I do have a question."

Everyone turned to me. My dad had a glimmer of hope in his eyes. Amil and Anthony shot daggers, and if I wasn't crazy, Buddha did too. "Is it true about your parents? Were they deceased before Anthony was born?"

My mother nodded. "Yes. They were. I had been sent away to an all-girls school. Before I graduated, they were both killed in a house fire. That's why I don't have any pictures. Everything was destroyed."

"Any siblings?"

"No. I was an only child. Everything I've told you about my past was true other than your sister. I promise."

I nodded my understanding. "I have one more question. On the day of my wedding, when I asked Dad about taking me to the hospital, you convinced him to take me, but why? If you were trying to keep Tamika a secret?"

"I knew your father wasn't going to do that. And as bad as it sounds, I didn't want to alert anyone to anything. I tried to act as normal as possible. I am so sorry."

I nodded again.

"Boys, you have anything to add, and have you given any consideration to counseling?" My dad looked at both my brothers.

Anthony answered, "No, I'm still processing," to Buddha, and Amil just stood in the corner, looking like he could be on an episode of *Snapped*.

"No pressure," my mother said through a cracked voice. "I understand there's a lot to resolve and time needed to process everything that has taken place. If and when you are ready, I will be waiting for the chance to prove myself to you."

"Well, as a matter of fact, I do have a question," Anthony said. "You really paid her over twenty thousand dollars to go away?"

My mother nodded.

After an eternity of silence, my dad asked, "Amil, do you have anything to say to or ask your mother?"

"The only thing I regret in this situation is not being the one who arrested Oakley that night."

Again, my heart hurt for my mother.

Once the door shut, Anthony asked, "What do you all think about that? Have either of you given any thought to counseling, forgiving her, anything?"

"Man, bro, hell nah. While she was talking, I was thinking about what I was going to eat for lunch. What parts I heard, if I had a violin, I would've played it. Nah, a violin is too elegant. I would have played the guitar and smashed it when I was done."

"What do you think, Avery. Any thought?"

Shit. The spotlight was on me. I honestly thought she was sincere, but how would I look telling my brothers that when we were supposed to have an alliance? I shrugged. "I don't really know. I listened like I was asked to do, and that's all I have to say about it."

"You asked us, what do you think?" Amil asked.

Anthony turned back to Buddha like he was waiting for that fake-ass thing to speak for him. He stroked the doll's face and said, "They say forgiveness holds power.

Forgiveness is a chain. If we cut the chains, it will free us and catapult us away from oppression."

Amil shook his head and plopped on the sofa beside me.

Anthony was on his Anthony shit, and I didn't feel like hearing it. I texted Tracy and told her to head back over. I pulled out my wedding book and looked over the names of my wedding party. Who could I replace Anthony with? He seemed to get weirder and weirder after every full moon.

"I think she was sincere," Anthony said.

Amil sat up and looked at me with a scowl.

"You know, Thomas Fuller once said, 'We ought to see far enough into a hypocrite to see even his sincerity.' And George Henry Lewes said, 'Insincerity is always weakness; sincerity even in error is strength.'"

Amil jumped up from the sofa. "Man, bro, take a day off, and be normal for a change. I'm out of here."

"I agree with Amil, weirdo."

Chapter 29

Obasi and I arrived at Augustino's arm in arm for our biweekly date night. I was excited for him to see me in something sexy. Lately, I'd been busy with wedding stuff, so he hadn't seen me in anything but sweats, my old scrub pants, and a T-shirt.

While we waited to be seated, I felt his hand caress my booty, which poked out of my tight dress. I loved it when he did that. He was super touchy and packed on the PDA like no one was around but us. He groped me again, "Damn, girl. You don't know how bad I want to get you out of this dress."

I marveled over his compliment. What woman wouldn't want her man gushing over her? "Thank you." My cheeks felt on fire, and so did the thing in the inside of my panties. But we were waiting for the wedding night, according to Obasi. I was ready to cave, repent, beg for God's forgiveness. "Just one time? Don't you want to sample the goodies first?" I groped over the bulge in his pants.

"Of course I do." Obasi looked at me like he was about to throw me on one of the tables and have his way with me. If he did, I wouldn't stop him. I wanted his nightstick to give me a beating, and I made it no secret.

"So do it." I made a few circle movements and even turned around to brush my ass against his package. I was practically throwing myself at this man, and he was calmly resisting.

"Avery, stop playing with me, girl."

"Who says I'm playing? There's the door. We can always leave."

Obasi eyed the door like what I said was a possibility. I held my breath, hoping he'd change his mind. The way I felt, we wouldn't make it very far. I'd probably straddle him on the drive over.

"Adebayo, party of two," the hostess called out on the microphone.

Obasi raised his hand. "That's us."

"Right this way."

We maneuvered through a sea of tables. Not one person there seemed disappointed. I wasn't disappointed until I saw my view. Lloyd spotted me at the same time I spotted him. He turned pale, and I imagined I did as well. Everything within me felt like it was shutting down. Lloyd was on a date. That explained a lot. He gave up the townhouse without any more fighting. And since then, he hasn't contacted me. This town was small, but Lloyd was here on a date of all places. And I was here on a date, but we weren't dating each other.

"Something wrong?" Obasi asked and sipped his water.

Obasi's back faced Lloyd. Maybe he wouldn't notice. I couldn't not say anything. The last time I omitted the truth, I lost him. I didn't necessarily want to tell him that Lloyd happened to be dining with us in a way. I didn't think Obasi would turn around, but if he did, he would see Lloyd and probably come up with the wrong idea.

"Don't turn around and look, okay?"

"Okay," Obasi said and immediately turned around. "What are we looking at?" Lloyd's date repositioned her head at the right time.

I lightly smacked the table and leaned forward. I didn't know why I felt compelled to whisper in an establishment where chatter swirled around my ears. "I said don't turn around."

"Telling someone not to turn around is the same thing as telling them to turn around." He turned again. "What am I looking for anyway?" His attention was back on me.

"Lloyd is here." I nodded now that the path had been cleared.

This time Obasi didn't turn around. "He's not with you, so I don't give a damn. You worried about something?" Obasi's stern look made me feel like he would make me confess to a crime that I didn't commit.

I am innocent, right?

"Good evening, I am Dexter. I will be assisting you guys for the evening. Would you like to start with an appetizer?"

"You want an appetizer, babe?"

I shook my head. I eyed Lloyd and wondered if he'd purchased a $600 bottle of wine for his date. Shit, why did I even care? I was happy with Obasi, but for some reason, I kept taking peeks at Lloyd and his date. It was just that I'd never seen him with another woman. It kind of stung a little. Just a little. Not enough to shed a tear. Not enough to flip this table. Not enough to cause a scene. Not enough to do the Electric Slide with depression. And definitely not enough to lose Obasi again. It was real. I wouldn't spend eternity with my high school sweetheart.

Obasi broke through my thoughts. "How's the wedding planning coming?"

I smiled and reached across the table to squeeze his hand. "Excellent. Don't forget about the cake-tasting appointment Wednesday at Smiles Home Bakery in Graniteville."

"You must've heard some good things about this place since you are making us drive forty minutes to taste cake," Obasi mumbled. "I'd much rather taste you." He sipped his water and peered at me.

"I'm all for that, Mr. Adebayo, but remember . . ."

"Yeah, I remember," he said, disappointment in his voice. "Just be ready for what I am going to do to you after the reception."

"Why after? Why not on the way to?"

He rubbed his hands together and smiled. "I love some freak in my woman, but um, on the way, there isn't enough time. And plus, you won't be able to walk after."

I gulped my water and excused myself to the bathroom to freshen up the areas Obasi was making hot. I held up my finger. "I'll be right back. I have to run to the ladies' room. Watch my phone and my purse."

"I ain't the kind of dude who watches purses. You better take that with you."

I looked back and blew him a kiss but kept walking. *He'd better get used to holding my purse. That's a requirement of being my husband.*

I stared at my reflection in the mirror. Not really stared. More like admired. I loved who was looking back at me. A different version of myself. Better. Avery 2.0. It took many seasons to find this version. A season of naiveness. A season of bitterness. A season of loneliness. Depression. You name it. I went through them all.

My eyes must be deceiving me. I blinked rapidly, trying to blink away Lloyd standing behind me. I spun around. "You know this is the ladies' room, right?"

He shrugged but didn't say anything. I surveyed his body but couldn't read him. His hands were stuffed in his pockets. Did he have a weapon? Was he going to kill me?

"You look good, Avery."

"Thank you." I could have complimented him back, but I didn't want to give him the wrong impression.

An awkward, uncomfortable silence roamed through us.

"Are you sure you're marrying the right person, Avery? Are you sure this guy is what you want, or are you trying to get back at me?"

I shook my head. "What? Do you hear yourself?"

"If you're trying to get back at me, it worked, okay? Now can we just go? Can we just go and figure this out?"

"There is nothing to figure out." Lloyd had started to make me uncomfortable. He blocked the door. I fumbled for my purse. *Shit. I left it with Obasi.* I had Mace in case I needed to use it. I could call Obasi or the police, but I left my phone too.

"Avery, please hear me out."

"Lloyd, I have heard you several times. There is too much irreparable damage for us to ever be a couple again. Besides, I am with someone I love, and I don't see that changing anytime soon. Hell, you are with someone too."

"She means nothing to me. She is something to do to pass the time. I will leave her at this restaurant if you take me back. Please, Avery. It will be different this time, especially with your sister unable to interfere. And her kid isn't mine, so I believe we can move past this. Just let me show you."

I sighed. "You still have some growing up to do, Lloyd. Things get a little rough, and you get selfish. You left me at the altar, and now you are trying to leave your date in a restaurant. Plus, you act like you didn't have a relationship with my sister, conceal it from me along with a whole life. You need to do the work and find out what you want. It makes me wonder how many other women you encountered besides my sister who you were so willing to give me up for."

"Avery, it's not like that. I already know what I want, and it's you."

"You're right, it's not like anything, and I have who I want. Hear me clear. You and I had our time. It's over. Now please move from in front of the door before I scream."

Lloyd took two steps away from the door. "Avery, you're making a mistake."

"The only mistake I made was you. Take care, Mr. Peterson."

"Babe, what's wrong?" Obasi asked when I plopped into my seat, winded.

"I have to tell you what just happened in the bathroom. I want you to trust me and know that I handled it." He nodded his head. "Lloyd came in the bathroom while I was in there." As I told Obasi what happened, veins started throbbing along his temple and forehead.

I grabbed Obasi's hand when he slid his chair back. I probably should have told him in the car, but I didn't want any issues. "Obasi, don't. Please. I handled it. I promise."

"I don't tolerate disrespect, and I don't appreciate him making you uncomfortable."

"I'm fine. I promise. Please, Obasi. Please."

He shook his head. "All right, only because you are here. But a day will come when it will be just him and me."

"Can we get back on the subject of the cake and stay there?" I moved on anyway, hoping to calm him down. "Tracy told me the owner, Gina, makes the best cakes. She's tasted almost every flavor. I checked out her page, and she has stellar reviews."

Obasi picked up his chair and moved it so that he faced Lloyd. "Gina? Have I met her before?" he asked, never taking his eyes from Lloyd.

"Obasi, please, don't act up in this restaurant. Can we just go?"

"We are good, babe. Tell me about Gina. That name is familiar. Have I met her?"

I exhaled an uncomfortable breath and silently asked God to keep the peace. "I don't think so," I nervously said. "I've never met her in person. I only spoke to her over the phone when I set the appointment up." I looked from Obasi to Lloyd the entire time I talked. Lloyd laughed with his date and pretended as if he didn't just try to hook up with me in the bathroom and as if he didn't see the daggers thrown his way.

"Oh, okay. That name sounds familiar."

"Gina is the fake name Tracy uses when a guy she's not interested in approaches her."

Obasi snapped his finger. "Okay, okay. I remember now because she used it when she was helping me pick out your ring, and then again at the bar when some dude shorter than her asked her name." He chuckled. "I love Tracy."

"Excuse me," I playfully said. "Confessing your love for another woman to me?"

"I only have eyes for your dysfunctional ass. But I love Tracy because she loves you. She's a real friend."

All this time, I knew Obasi liked Tracy, but I always wondered how he would receive her once we married. Some marriages don't allow for friends because it's believed that all of your free time should be spent with your spouse. Something I have always disagreed with. Spouses need time to do things outside of one another. Things, not people. But I always missed Obasi when I was away from him.

"Yeah, Tracy is a real friend," I echoed his sentiment. "And she is good to and for Amil. I can't believe she talked him into going to therapy. It's not the family therapy my dad wants, but it's something. Poor therapist. She is going to have a hard time with him and his antics."

"Amil is a cool dude. I like him. Especially when we performed against you and Tracy. We get each other. Then again, the competition isn't good, so it's not hard."

I threw a piece of bread at him. "Obasi, you like everybody. Well, almost everybody." I glanced up at Lloyd, who was eyeing me like he planned to hurt me.

"That's what happens when you are the man like me. I'm famous around here." He popped the collar of his shirt.

I rolled my eyes. "Man, whatever. People don't pop collars anymore."

"That's the thing. I'm not people. I'm O."

"The only thing O makes you is obviously delusional." I'd tell him about the other O words when I first laid eyes on him one day.

"Don't be mean to me, babe. I'm sensitive."

We laughed. One of the things I loved about Obasi was his playful spirit. Anytime we were together was guaranteed to be filled with laughter and a lot of ogling. I couldn't wait for the night of the wedding.

As if he read my thoughts, he said, "What else has to be done for the wedding?"

"Off the top of my head—"

"Well, if you're relying on your memory, we know that ain't gonna work out well." He laughed.

This man was a protector, a friend, and he made me giggle at his playful insults. Sometimes he'd drop some wisdom on me that wouldn't hit me until a week later. Obasi was a portion of my father, Anthony, and as much as I hated to say it, Amil. It tasted like dirt on my tongue. *I have an Amil.*

The noise from the crowd broke through my thoughts. Some kind of celebration. Obasi and I gave in to the distraction. Lloyd was down on one knee. "Is he proposing?" That was a dumb question. Why else would he be down there? The crowd wouldn't be cheering the way they were if Lloyd were just picking up a knife that he dropped on the floor.

"You want to leave?" Obasi asked.

"No. I'd love to see this circus play out."

The young lady's baby bump turned around before she did. *Another one of those. I hope this one is his. And I hope it works out for him.*

Lloyd stared at me. He wasn't going to get the reaction he wanted because I didn't have one to give. Further indication that I made the right decision. I had enough sense not to take him back. I would be this young lady he just proposed to. Maybe Lloyd wanted to be rescued. Perhaps he thought I would feel some type of jealousy and break up his moment. Nope. I had a moment of my own. A lifetime of my own sitting next to me. I wasn't given that up for anything, especially not Lloyd.

"How are you feeling about that?"

"Nothing over there concerns me. I have what I need and want right here with you."

Chapter 30

The spacious, beautifully decorated bridal suite was not spacious enough to soak up the nervous energy that swirled around me like the latest rumor. I munched on the tray of snacks and downed several bottles of water to create a distraction and to comfort myself. Without self-control, I'd be too bloated to fit into my wedding dress, which was designed to once again hug my curve-a-licious frame.

What was I saying? The wedding jitters created all kinds of what-ifs. It was just that the last time I was doing this . . . *Just be quiet. Foolish talk.*

I watched my dress like I was watching a baby for the first time—closely. The white beaded, laced mermaid gown with the colorful African bridal belt and matching African fabric that was stitched in with my short train hung on a padded hanger waiting to envelop my body. *I cannot believe I'm attempting this again. We should've eloped.* The crunch from the carrot was loud enough to send Tracy waddling my way.

"Hey, you, knock it off and just breathe," Tracy spoke to me like I was delivering a baby and she was the coach.

I tried to bite another carrot, but she snatched it from my hand.

"Look," Tracy said and pointed around the room. "Look at the love and laughter around you. I've never been married before, but I understand what you are going through. You need to calm down." She grabbed both of my shoulders and turned me so that I faced her. "Match my breaths." Tracy slowly inhaled and exhaled. Our breaths eventually synced. She whispered in my ear, "There is so much love and beauty in this room, and nothing will interfere with that love nor prevent the merging of two different cultures."

Peace KO'd the nervous energy. I felt recentered. "Thank you, Tracy."

"That's what I'm here for. Obasi is not Lloyd. Two different calibers of men. Don't make Obasi pay because of the lesser-caliber man. This wedding is happening even if I have to give up my post as your maid of honor and work security."

My head bobbed in agreement like I was bobbing to my favorite up-tempo song. Tracy had always been a pillar during my dark times.

"Besides, the only person around here who will be giving birth is me." Tracy rubbed her pregnant belly. "Your niece is kicking my butt."

"Good girl," I said to Tracy's stomach as I rubbed it. "And what's even more special little lady, the voice you hear is your auntie Avery, who will deliver you."

"I am so happy you finally took your ass back to work. I couldn't see myself allowing anyone else to deliver my baby."

"I know we are besties and all, but I am dreading having to look at your vagina."

Tracy rolled her eyes. "Oh, well. I'm just thrilled that you didn't let some trifling Negro and tramp permanently take you away from something that you worked so hard to earn."

I sat down for the makeup artist to start on my face. "I wish you'd come back to work with me," I told Tracy.

"Maybe one day. Right now, your brother insists that I will be a stay-at-home mom. He claims that as soon as I drop this load, if it's cute, then he is going to get me pregnant again."

I laughed and wondered how my brother made it in life being such an idiot. "So, if the baby is ugly?"

"One and done, he said."

"I hope Amil's ass passes out in the delivery room," I said.

"Me too. I've been lifting five-pound weights, trying to build up enough strength to be able to squeeze his hand and hopefully break it as I'm pushing."

We both laughed.

"Please do."

"Have you heard from your mom?" Tracy asked.

I shrugged. "She sent me a generic congratulatory text."

"You don't think it was sincere?"

"Don't know."

"Still not going to have that sit-down with her that she's been requesting?"

"I don't know. Maybe after the wedding."

"I've tried to convince your brother numerous times to at least hear her out, but he is against it."

"Hell will be covered in ice before Amil agrees. But at least he is still in counseling."

"True. What does Obasi say?"

"Oh, my God. Every day he's like, 'Avery, have you heard from your mother? You need to call her. In my country this and in my country that.' I tell him all the time that this is America. Family is so important to him, and it's important to me, but he did not grow up experiencing what I did. It's easier to accept when you are on the outside looking in. I feel sorry for my mother, and I hope we can move on. I just don't know how."

"Obasi is a good man, Avery. Seeing how he treats you and the way he interacts with his family and your family is priceless."

"Envious is more like it," I added. "The moment Obasi's mom met me, it was nothing but love and affection. She's very complimentary. His whole family is. My dad and brothers love Obasi to death."

Tracy chimed in. "Trust me, I know. Amil speaks very highly of Obasi."

"Everyone does. It's nice to hear the compliments, but it would have been great if I heard them from my own mother." I started to get emotional. "She should be in here with me doing what you are doing, but . . ." There was no need to complete my statement. My voice cracked like a carton of eggs being smashed against a hard surface. I needed to keep my mind focused on my wedding instead of ruining the makeup applied to my face. "I don't want to talk about my mother."

Tracy zipped her lips with her fingers and then unzipped them. "But can I say just one more thing, please?"

"What, Tracy?"

"Mrs. Booker reached out to me to check on the baby and to see what she could buy for us. She asked about you and the wedding. She said she didn't think she was wanted and asked if I would send pictures of her beautiful daughter. She's trying, Avery."

I spun the whole chair around as my eyebrows were being filled in.

"Avery, you need to be still. You have a line up to your hair now," Tracy said.

The makeup artist spun me back around and lightly wiped away the extra line while I tried to contain my composure.

Tracy continued, "I was just going to say that I think it took Mrs. Booker losing her husband and children to realize how much you all mean to her. She's still separated from Mr. Booker, and none of her children talk to her much. She has lost everything she has ever known."

"I don't know. At times I want to give her the benefit of the doubt, but I don't know."

"I think you should. It was a pleasant exchange. Give her a chance. Notice how she sent you a congratulatory text, and it didn't say anything smart. Imagine if Obasi wouldn't have given you the benefit of the doubt. Think about it."

"What are you? Team Florence now?"

"I'm team family and being pregnant worrying what I am going to have to protect my child from. I understand her now. That's all. Plus, you haven't been referring to her as the devil. There's hope."

"Only because Obasi asked me not to, and I want this marriage to last, so I submitted. And since you understand her so well, you can be her daughter," I sneered and gave Tracy two thumbs up for her diligence.

"Okay. Well, think about what I said. It's almost that time, so I am going to get dressed. I will be back to help you get into your dress."

I smiled. "Thank you, Tracy . . . for everything."

She lowered her head against mine. "Wait until you see how beautiful you look. I love you."

"I love you too."

Shortly after the room emptied, the makeup artist spun me around to the mirror. "All done," he said.

"Oh. My. God." Tears filled my eyes. I tilted my head back like I was outside studying the stars. Tracy was right. I looked beautiful. Beyond beautiful. Even better than I did when I was about to marry Lloyd.

"Go ahead and let out those tears. Everything I applied is waterproof."

I laughed, cried, and hugged the makeup artist before he left the room. It was just me and my thoughts—time to reflect. I thought back to my high school yearbook. Lloyd and I were voted most likely to marry, and those predictions almost came true, but God had other plans. I didn't see it then or even understand it. I still didn't understand it. The answer no longer mattered, because I could look up to heaven and smile, knowing I was covered with a peace I had never felt. Over this journey, I'd realized it was okay to declutter by tossing things, people, ideas, and more into the discard pile to make room for what was meant to be in that once-cluttered space.

"All right, chickadee. You ready to get dressed and married?" Tracy asked as she waddled back into the room like a penguin.

First, I squealed, then smiled, showing all my recently whitened teeth. "More than ready."

Tracy pulled down the hanger with my dress on it from the rack. "Well, come on, let's get you into this dress."

"I was hoping I could help."

Tracy and I swung around. My mother stood at the door. Tracy looked at me, her eyes asking for permission. When I nodded, she hung the dress back on the rack and exited the room without saying a word.

"You look beautiful," my mother said. "May I?" She pointed toward my dress.

"I'd like that." Thank God for waterproof makeup, because I was bawling my eyes out.

I watched as she delicately took the dress from the hanger and carefully carried it over to me. I took my robe off and allowed her to help me into my gown. We were both staring at each other through the mirror.

"You look flawless. Any man would be crazy not to do right by you. Just as crazy as I am for not being a good mother to you and your brothers. As I was growing up, my parents never showed me affection, and instead of treating my children how I wanted to be treated, I followed in their footsteps. Then because I lost love and watched the love and relationship the three of you had with your dad, I became bitter, jealous, and judgmental."

I turned around to face her in case I was looking into one of those fake mirrors at a carnival.

"I'm sorry, Avery," she said as her voice cracked the way mine did when I was talking to Tracy. "I was so nervous about coming in here, so thank you for letting me help with your dress."

I squeezed her so tight I was surprised I didn't crack any bones. "No, thank you for this moment. I am almost complete."

My dad tapped on the door and peeked in. "Showtime, sweetheart." He took a few steps closer and put his hand over his heart. "Wow! You look . . . Beautiful cannot even describe the glow in you."

"Thank you, Dad. Mother helped with my dress." I smiled at her, and so did my dad.

"Stop with that silly 'Mother' mess. Call me whatever you want to call me."

I nodded. "Okay. Dad, doesn't Mom look stunning herself?"

"She does." They held a brief embrace.

"Well, let me get to my seat," my mother said.

"Wait!" I yelled like this would be the last moment I would ever have with her. "If it's okay with Dad, I'd like for both of you to walk me down the aisle." I looked over at my dad, hoping my idea didn't hurt his feelings.

My mother gasped and started crying again.

"I am okay with whatever you want, sweetheart." My dad kissed my cheek and interlocked his arm with mine. And my mother did the same after she placed my *gele* atop my head.

The crowd gasped as the three of us made our descent down the makeshift aisle to the smooth instrumental of Stevie Wonder's "Isn't She Lovely," which played from the outdoor piano. Yep! An outdoor spring wedding. No worries. I'd begun regular treatment with an allergist.

I took in the scenery. Scottsdale and his crew did wonders with the decor. Two cultures blended. Some guests opted to wear traditional wedding attire, and some chose to incorporate African fabric to their attire.

No flower pedals this time. Just a candlelit path led me to the man who had restored the light to my spirit. I could see Obasi just ahead standing under the draped wedding arbor. This was the first time I had ever seen him in his cultural garb. He looked sizzling in his *Agbada* and *fila* hat. The bridesmaids wore traditional bridesmaid gowns with a *gele,* and the groomsmen all wore a tunic-pant set. The decor and attire came together better than I could have ever dreamed.

When I made it to the altar, Obasi looked at me like I was the most beautiful girl in the world. The way he stared melted me like an ice cube sitting on a sidewalk during a hot summer day in the South.

The wedding started, and all was well until the minister asked, "If there is anyone here who can show just cause why these two should not be man and wife, speak now or forever hold your peace."

The panic attack ensued. My airway felt obstructed. It was like a firm hand was pressed against my mouth and nose to purposely restrict my breathing. I thought I was suffocating from fear. I wanted to look around in case any surprises were headed down the aisle, but instead, I looked at Obasi's loafers. My eyes remained there. I'd have rather not seen it coming.

Obasi must've sensed my uneasiness, because he gripped my hands tighter. "Look at me," he whispered. I wanted to, but I was scared that he was about to drop a bombshell on me. "Look at me."

I tried, but it felt as if my head were bolted in place. I didn't know what was going to kill me first: waiting for a surprise objector or holding my breath while waiting for a surprise objector.

He gripped my chin and made me look at him. "I am here. There is nothing down there. You have nothing to worry about," he said as he smiled at me.

His reassurance reassured me. *Things are going to be okay. He will be a good husband, I am going to be a good wife, and we will have a good life.*

After what seemed like the most prolonged pause, the minister continued. No surprises. No objections. No issues.

You know how weddings go, only this time we got to exchange our self-written vows, say, "I do," and seal it with a kiss. We danced the night away at the reception. Obasi, Amil, and a few groomsmen entertained us with another BBD "Poison" performance. The extra gyrating had me ready to leave the reception early and sad that Obasi and I didn't fool around on the limo ride over. We consummated our marriage enough times in one night that made me sure I was never letting him go. It's true what they say: men who can dance can certainly put it down in the sack. The following day before we boarded a flight to Nigeria, we opened some of our wedding gifts. Guess what Anthony got us? A fake-ass Buddha, holding a sign that said I TOLD YOU SO. But it was okay. Nothing could ruin this feeling. I was already in love with being Avery Adebayo. That's right. No hyphen. I felt complete.

Epilogue

Three Years Later

"Welcome to the family. Welcome to the family. Welcome LJ. Welcome to the family." My family and I harmonized made-up lyrics, officially welcoming LJ to the family.

"Blow out the candles, li'l man." Obasi tilted LJ over and coached him.

I needed to sit. My feet had started to swell, but I loved being up close and personal, watching Obasi interact with LJ.

"How are you doing, Mommy?" Tracy came up behind me with my niece on her hip.

"Exhausted. Between court, delivering babies, and staring at swatches for hours, I'm beat. My body feels like it's been running full speed on the treadmill with the incline at its highest." I was tired, energetic, and in pain all at once, but I still held my hands out to take Amelia. "I can't believe how much this child looks like Amil."

Tracy laughed. "Scary, ain't it?"

I nodded and kissed Amelia's chubby cheeks. "When are you and my brother popping out another one of these cutie pies?"

"She's a beautiful baby, but one and done. We will wait for you and Obasi to pop out those seventeen babies he said y'all were having."

"Shitting me. We sure as hell won't be doing that. I am on the one and done train with you. We got the best of both worlds, and I only had to get pregnant once. Seventeen kids my ass. Obasi just says shit to say shit."

"Watch your mouth in front of my daughter," Amil said, taking Amelia from my arms.

"Yeah, Avery, ever since you've been pregnant, your mouth is extra foul," Tracy added.

"Probably because I'm miserable. This pregnancy is kicking my butt. I can't wait to push this girl out."

"Exactly why I'm not having any more. Amelia is it."

Amil tapped Tracy on the shoulder to get her attention. "Yes, you are. I'm getting you pregnant tonight."

"Boy, whatever. It's wear and tear on my body. I thought I'd finally get my Georgia peach, but instead, I got a smaller booty than what I had before the pregnancy."

"Sure did." Amil grimaced and looked Tracy up and down. When she drew back to hit him, he laughed and added, "But booty or no booty, I love you and appreciate you for this beautiful baby girl."

I shook my head. "The two of y'all are meant for each other."

"You can at least give me a son, Tracy."

She pointed at LJ. "Be satisfied with your nephew." Tracy sighed. "I still can't believe you and Obasi adopted Oakley's . . . Tamika's . . . whatever her name is. Hell, your sister. I still can't believe you did that after all the hell she put y'all through."

I always wanted a biological sister, but Oakley would never be that outside of the title.

"It wasn't easy. It took a lot of prayers, conversations with Obasi, and letters to God." Those pros and cons lists that I made for my mother and Lloyd, I burned them in the outdoor fireplace.

"Yeah, but I don't know too many men who will support their woman through adopting their crazy estranged sister's child she tried to pin on her soon-to-be brother-in-law. Look how Obasi is with LJ. You can't tell he's not the biological father. And the fact that he fought you on keeping LJ's name as Lloyd, he's amazing."

"I was all for changing his entire name instead of tweaking it." Obasi believed the universe picked your first name. He told me to pick my favorite J name since LJ was familiar with being called LJ, and I said that it was Jordan, so we went with Lloyd Jordan Adebayo. I looked over as Obasi lifted LJ in the air. I smiled at their giggles. "Obasi is great in general. His parents spoil LJ. His whole family does. They all just love him."

"Y'all wanna hear something funny?" Amil asked, interrupting the moment.

We passed, but Amil is Amil, so he told us anyway. "Man, look at Pop's shoes." The three of us looked and burst into laughter. My dad always said he would never be a mall walker, yet he and my mother got up and went every morning. And he also told us he'd never wear socks with sandals, but that was what he had on his feet.

Obasi joined us. "What's going on over here?"

Tracy, Amil, and I pointed at my dad's feet and laughed. When the laughter subsided, we sat back and relished all the love surrounding us.

"Man, Pops is notorious with that camera. The minute Scottsdale and I walked in, he wanted us to pose," Anthony said and pulled up a chair for himself and Scottsdale.

"Right? Always sticking it in people's faces, talking about let's create memories," Amil mocked our dad.

"And what's wrong with his shoes?" Anthony asked.

Scottsdale even chimed in. "That is not fashion."

We all laughed again. "We've already talked about him and his shoes," I said.

"When Pops became a grandfather, he went crazy."

"You need not talk, Amil. That's how you're going to be when you become a grandfather," I teased.

He turned Amelia around to face him. "I ain't never becoming a grandfather, ain't that right?" She smiled, oblivious to the nut she had for a father. He tapped his gun that was holstered to his waist. "Boys are nasty. Hashtag virgin for life." Amelia smiled some more. He put her down, and she ran over to our parents. Specifically, my mother. Amelia loved her grandmother.

"If we live to get old, then old people's behavior is inevitable," I said. "But look at them. They look so happy, and they are so good with the kids."

"Yeah. Never thought I'd see the day," Amil said. "Especially not the three of us having a relationship with Mom, and especially not her babysitting my daughter."

"Ditto," Tracy added.

"I did," Anthony said.

We all turned to him and frowned.

"I have been telling you feeble-minded people for years that you have to look at things with a different lens. Life isn't black and white. There is so much color, and color has meaning if you interpret it accurately."

"Man, bro, things were peaceful before you showed up. Don't start with that freakazoid shit."

"Amil, you're just mad," Scottsdale said. "My baby is smart. That's why I love him."

Anthony came out. I didn't see that coming. None of us did. But then I remembered the conversation we had at breakfast: "Love isn't determined by dating a person of a different gender anymore. Personality is key." Apparently, the night of the Super Bowl was a magical night for all the Bookers. What was more surprising was that my mother hooked Scottsdale and Anthony up. She said, "I may not have been an affectionate mother, but I know my children."

My mother had even tried to learn about her firstborn. We didn't want anything to do with Tamika, but our mother wanted to fix her wrongs. She wrote Tamika once a month at the Georgia Women's Detention Center, where she was serving fifteen years for extortion. Nothing had returned to the post office box yet, but my mother checked it faithfully. Since we moved my mom and dad into the guest house for safety concerns, there was no way Tamika would be getting our address.

It was funny how things had changed. Years ago, I dreaded living with my parents, but now I was stoked to have them living with me. They were safe. They were happy in love. And they were the best grandparents and caretakers to Amelia and LJ and would be to my and Obasi's daughter, Olivia, once she was born.

"You think Oakley Tamika will try to kidnap LJ once she's released?"

I shook my head. "I honestly don't think she will try anything."

"In case that crazy bitch does, LJ will be old enough to understand, and his auntie Tracy will equip him with the tools to kick her ass if she tries anything."

"We are not teaching our child to hit women, Tracy."

"Not women, just Oakley Tamika."

I laughed it off. She didn't want a baby to begin with. She admitted that in court. The boyfriend gave up his rights shortly after her sentencing. LJ was headed to foster care, but my mother stepped in as the biological grandparent and was awarded temporary custody. Everyone was worried about how I would handle LJ being around. I worried too. But I fell in love with him at first glance. We all did. My parents were too old to care for a child with autism twenty-four hours a day, so Obasi and I adopted him. Tamika had an outburst in court, blaming my mother's young pregnancy for his diagnosis.

As I took in my family like I'd never seen them before, past thoughts replayed. I never thought I would be in such a peaceful place after the church bombshell. Pain once flooded my body like a hurricane, and I never thought I would evacuate. I had to sit in it and filter through the remnants of the disaster. Had I been judged by my crumbled outer appearance, I would have been ruled a lost cause. There was not much hope that my life would be rebuilt. There were days when I wanted to go to sleep and not wake up. It wasn't until Anthony told me, "You're in a cocoon. Give it some time, you beautiful butterfly." I just thought he was being Anthony—weird.

I'd be the first to admit I was naive and sometimes shallow. Bitter and mean. Depressed and hopeless, but God helps those in times of trouble, and I came out of my trouble a better person. Even though it hurt like hell, I wouldn't have it any other way.

Change is hard, but unexpected negative change is harder, especially when filled with depression and heartache. What was meant to destroy me gave me a new life. What was meant to destroy us brought us closer together.

"Gather around," my dad said. "Family photo." We all bunched together while my dad set the timer on the camera.

Amil whispered, "I hope the camera doesn't catch Pop's shoes."

"On three, scream, 'Family.'"

We all laughed at Amil and counted in unison. "One, two, three . . . Family!"

The End